WHEN THEY COME CALLING

WHEN THEY COME CALLING

SARAH FLEMING MOUNTFORD

Atthis Arts, LLC

WHEN THEY COME CALLING

Published by Atthis Arts, LLC
Centerville, Ohio
www.atthisarts.com

ISBN (paperback) 978-1-945009-00-6

Library of Congress Control Number: 2016933600

This one is for M.

CHAPTER ONE

THE IMPACT sent me sprawling back onto the sidewalk and a massive weight landed on top of me, pushing the air from my lungs. My head hit the ice-coated pavement with a painful thump. Tiny flickering dots filled my vision as a truck raced by, honking angrily.

How had I not seen that coming? Midtown wasn't always a safe place for a woman to walk alone after dark. I'd been foolish to let myself get so distracted. My thoughts jumbled together. Was I being assaulted or had a malicious ghost played a trick on me? Even distracted, I should have noticed a ghost if it had been nearby. I recognized the beer company's logo on the back of the truck before it hurtled out of sight.

The realization hit me as the form on top of me started to move. A beer truck nearly ran me over. I'd be offended by the cliché as soon as I had time to think about it. My attacker, or perhaps he was my rescuer, lifted his weight off me and I sucked frozen air into my lungs. He was on his feet in an instant, standing over my body, staring at the place the truck had been. I felt defenseless on the ground but my body wouldn't let me do anything else until I could breathe properly. My autonomic system was in control.

"Are you hurt?" His deep voice was full of concern. He scanned the area as if he expected another threat, but maybe he just wanted to make sure no one was around to witness whatever else he had planned. A woman had been attacked in broad daylight two streets over a week ago. I'd called the police and treated her injuries when she'd limped to my clinic afterward.

I gasped in another breath, which caused icicles of pain to shoot through my skull. I still had that panicky feeling from having the breath knocked out of me. Even though I knew I was breathing, it felt like I couldn't.

At least the man wasn't a ghost. I hadn't seen one in a while, but it seemed like they were attracted to me. Sometimes they sought me out, and every now and then one decided that the best way to get my attention was to mess with me. Getting me to step in front of a beer truck was beyond the ghost tricks I'd experienced so far, but I wouldn't put it past them.

"Can you speak?" His voice rumbled low, like distant thunder. He was the size of a grizzly, but it was so dark I couldn't make out anything else. He might have saved me from getting run over by the truck, but that didn't guarantee he wouldn't try to hurt me next. They hadn't caught the guy last week.

My head hurt. *How badly am I damaged?* You didn't have to be a doctor to know that skulls don't fare well against concrete, but I was one. The chunk of pavement I was lying on was less than a block from my free health clinic, where I took care of anyone who walked through the doors. Most of them were homeless or living under the poverty level, just scraping by. The vast majority of them were good people, but I knew a few had questionable pasts and there were a handful who might be wanted by the law. It wasn't my concern. I was charged with their healthcare, not their moral standing in the community.

I noticed that the street was empty. The nights had gotten colder, and no one stayed outside longer than necessary. If I needed help, there wasn't anyone to provide it. My lungs still heaved with the effort of breathing, but I forced myself to scoot back from between the man's legs. The motion ricocheted shots of pain through my head.

"Will you allow me to assist you?" He started to bend towards me.

"No!" It was more of a grunt than actual speech. I didn't feel like I could breathe, much less talk. I might not be able to get up yet, but I could incapacitate him from my current position if I needed to defend myself. As if he sensed that I was calculating the necessary angle to kick him in the groin, the man stepped away and inspected the shadows next to a shrub.

I searched my pocket for my cell phone, but it was gone. My head reeled from the effort, and I felt sick. If I were smart, I'd carry pepper spray, but I never had. I had always felt safe. Enough people in this area knew me and looked out for me. Not now, though, not this late on a cold January night. I had stayed at work too long.

The man loomed over me like a mountain cloaked in the shadow of a lone tree, and I didn't have the wherewithal to move. My heart rate seemed sluggish and I cataloged my symptoms: shock, possible concussion, hip contusion. My side hurt, but not enough to indicate that I'd fractured something. A quick jolt of adrenaline would help get me moving but my hypothalamus might be too banged up to do what it was supposed to. I was dazed and I needed to get over it before something worse happened.

"You dropped this." The man reached out to me and I crawled backward into the pool of light cast by a street lamp. My effort wasn't very effective. He took one step and was over me again. I knew that he might be a threat, but I couldn't make myself move any faster. My brain signals were misfiring. I stared at him, a deer caught in headlights.

He dropped to one knee in front of me. He wasn't the roughest looking individual I'd seen that day, but he was a mess. He had an open wound over one eyebrow in such a straight line I suspected it was from a knife. The flesh around it was an angry red. I'd seen a lot of knife injuries in my line of work, and this cut needed stitches. His jeans were stained and scuffed, and his jacket was covered with dark spots as if he'd been sleeping in mud or under a bridge.

I forced myself to take shallow breaths because he didn't smell very good either. Poor personal hygiene was not an unusual thing in the population I worked with. If you didn't have access to a shower and laundry facilities, it was hard to keep clean.

He was still on his knee in front of me when I came to the conclusion that if he had wanted to hurt me, he could have already. As near as I could tell, he had saved me from being flattened by a truck. I tried to focus on the object in his hand, but the struggle was one that my eyes and brain didn't want to cooperate with. By the time I recognized the slender metallic object as my cell phone, I was nauseous again with the effort.

His head was covered in dark tangled curls. His expression masked by a thick beard. He might have been nice looking without it. I liked large men, but this one was bigger than most. It didn't look like he was fat, more like he had good muscle mass and big bones. I wondered if he was single and then realized that I must have a concussion or I wouldn't be thinking about a homeless man like that.

I took my cell phone and knew that I ought to do something with it, but I wasn't sure what. Call someone to take me home? I laughed because there was no one who lived close enough to call. The harsh cough of my voice sounded sick, even to me.

"Are you injured?" He spoke carefully, as though he had come to the conclusion that I was an idiot. It wasn't an inaccurate assumption. My brain felt too battered to generate the proper signals to my vocal chords so that I could speak. I watched him with caution and found myself mesmerized by how his mouth moved incomprehensibly in a field of beard. I didn't think I'd ever seen so much facial hair.

"Of course you're hurt." He sounded angry as he continued his conversation half turned away from me, so I wasn't sure if he was talking to me or to himself. "You landed on top of her, Jedediah. Crushed her." He turned to me again. "You needed me, and I was late." He paused between each word. "Precise timing is difficult. You were hard to find." I got the impression that he seemed to think he had been looking for me, maybe before the beer truck came along. "We may not be this fortunate again, Anna. You must be more cautious."

My heart skipped a beat. *How does he know my name?* "Are you a patient at the clinic?" I asked, relieved that my brain was able to put together the necessary synapses for speech. He didn't answer my question. It was hard to tell, but from the strange contortions of his beard, it looked like he was smiling. Did that mean yes? I didn't recognize him, but I saw a lot of people every week; it was impossible to remember all of them, although this guy was distinctive. He must have been to the clinic at some point. That knowledge allowed me to relax a little bit. He was just trying to help me.

"I'm sorry, I don't remember your name," I continued. It was high time that I made an effort to pull myself together. It was cold on the sidewalk and I needed to get up. The man offered me a hand, which I ignored because I didn't want to seem weak. I forced myself to my feet.

As soon as I was upright, the equilibrium issues in my brain took over. I crumpled forward onto the sidewalk and vomited the meager contents of my stomach onto the dirty ice. I was relieved that I hadn't eaten supper, or there would have been more mess.

"Slower this time. Let me help you." He sounded exasperated and I noticed an accent so minor that I'd missed it when he spoke earlier. I hesitated, and he grasped me under the arms pulling me to my feet, and then braced me against his body. He was a bear of a man, so tall that my shoulders were against his lower chest. I didn't protest, although some corner of my mind told me that I shouldn't be so close to a stranger.

I abandoned my internal conversation when another wave of nausea swept over me and I leaned against him, trying not to inhale the scent of his jacket. The effort to stand was almost more than my injured brain could cope with. I wanted to get closer to the ground again, except the sidewalk was so very cold. The clinical side of my mind kept track of my symptoms. No loss of consciousness, but I had seen stars. Headache, nausea, vomiting, and vertigo, all of which were consistent with a mild to moderate concussion.

When his arm wrapped around me to hold me up I didn't protest. I didn't think I was capable of standing without assistance. I must have hit my head pretty hard to be having that much difficulty. Part of me knew I should be worried about my state of incapacitation, but I wasn't. I added 'not thinking clearly' to the list of symptoms that supported the concussion diagnosis.

"We need to get you home, Anna. You're not safe here." It was true. Standing on Walnut Street in freezing cold weather wasn't the best place to be. "I will take you home," he informed me.

I considered my options. Since I couldn't stand by myself, I wasn't going to be able to make it solo. Catching a cab this late in the day was about as likely as me being able to walk myself home with a fresh concussion. My best friends lived far enough away that I might freeze to death before they got there. I could go back to the clinic and wait for Ty and Chaz to come rescue me, but I didn't want to bother them. I just wanted to go home.

My house was a few blocks away so it seemed I was down to one option: allow my dubious savior to escort me home. The skull is full of fragile tissue that doesn't take well to being banged against hard surfaces. I couldn't manage the walk in my damaged state without assistance.

I let us both into my condo, a new urban flat that mimicked the loft style with all the comforts of a two-bedroom home. My stranger settled me on the sofa.

"Water?" he asked, as though it was his house.

"Yes, please," I agreed. He returned with a beer from the fridge a moment later. "That's not water."

"It will make you feel better."

Normally I was the one who got to decide what would make someone feel better, but my head hurt too much to argue about it. I took a sip. The nausea dissipated somewhat — perhaps due to the carbonation in the beer — and the tightness in my head lessened a notch. Enough so I could think.

I was sitting in my living room with a homeless man who was twice the size I was, but he had saved my life and then helped me home. He settled down in the chair across from me, brown eyes filled with concern as he watched me through the mane of charcoal hair surrounding his face. The wound on his forehead had oozed and needed care. Blood was matted in the eyebrow beneath it.

I needed to take a painkiller and turn up the heat, then I'd figure out what to do with the man in my house. He had helped me. Maybe I could return the favor.

"Do you need a doctor?" His deep voice startled me as it echoed off of the walls and concrete floor.

"I am a doctor," I reminded him.

"Are you able to heal yourself, then?" I caught a wry smile amidst the facial hair.

Great. My homeless guy had a sense of humor. At least my inner sarcasm was back. Another sign that my brain was recovering.

I touched the back of my head again and verified that it hadn't been bleeding. A small lump had formed, but it didn't seem to be growing. Hemorrhage was doubtful. Since I didn't crack it hard enough to knock myself unconscious, my risk of anything worse than a minor concussion was minimal. My cognitive ability was improving, which was another good sign.

"I think I'm okay." I rose with caution, and he moved as if to help me but I waved him down. "I need you to stay right there for a few minutes." I used my 'I'm in control here' voice and he looked surprised but sank back into the chair. I didn't want to explain that

I needed to clean myself up and that I didn't want him wandering around my house while I was gone.

"I won't move. Unless you need my help." His voice was gentle, as if he was speaking to a skittish horse that he didn't want to startle.

"Thank you." I made it to the kitchen counter and braced myself while I waited for a dizzy spell to pass. When I got to my bedroom, I locked the door behind me. My little door lock wouldn't keep out a man the size of the one in my living room, but having it made me feel better.

I adjusted the heat up a few degrees and sat on the edge of my bed to take off my jacket. My backside felt a little bruised, but the substantial padding of my knee length winter coat had saved me from the worst of it. I managed to strip off the rest of my clothing without falling down, and put on some comfortable sweats emblazoned with my college insignia, UMKC. I wondered where the cat was, but knew she'd be hiding from the stranger in the other room. She had a fierce case of xenophobia.

In the bathroom, I washed my hands, brushed my teeth and evaluated my condition in the mirror. A petite brunette with dark eyes set into a thin face and wavy shoulder length hair looked back at me. Given how much my head hurt, part of me expected to see bruises but my skin was the usual shade of pale. I pulled my hair back in a ponytail and took a good look at my pupils. They were contracted to the same small size, given the bright bathroom lights, which was another good indication that I was going to be fine. Knowing that made me feel a little better.

Bending over to extract my medical kit from the cabinet beneath the sink made me feel nauseous again, but it was essential. The pink arts and crafts box was filled with all of the supplies I needed for home surgeries and minor medical emergencies. The last time I'd needed it I'd cut myself cooking dinner and didn't want to bother with a trip to the emergency room. Not that my best surgical work was done on myself, but it had been known to happen.

When I emerged from the bedroom the bear was still sitting ramrod straight in his chair, which he had turned so he could see the bedroom door. My solid-black cat who was usually afraid of strangers was sprawled across his lap. I could hear the abrasive rumble of her purr even though he wasn't touching her.

"I stayed," he told me.

"Thank you. Luna seems to like you." I couldn't keep the tone of surprise out of my voice. Luna rolled on him like a cat in heat who had just found her tom. I set the medical kit on the table and flicked on the lights over the island counter. The microwave clock said 8:43 p.m., and I was surprised because it felt later than that.

"You call this beast Luna?" He looked appalled at the shameless way she was treating him. I couldn't disagree. She grabbed his arm with both paws and rubbed her face on it. She looked pretty worked up, and I hoped she didn't decide to bite. When I had gotten her at the shelter she was declawed, so at least she couldn't scratch him.

"Yes, her name is Luna. Are you allergic? I can put her in the bedroom if she's bothering you. She doesn't tend to like people this much." Luna had hated my ex, which in hindsight made me suspect that the cat had better taste in men than I did.

"No. I like animals." His expression belied his words, but if he didn't want me to move her, I would let her stay.

"She's declawed, so she won't scratch you." He relaxed a notch and let his fingertips caress the top of her head. She rewarded him by upping the purr volume.

"That's a nasty cut on your forehead," I observed. His hand went to it as if he was surprised to learn it was there.

"It's nothing." He glowered, eyes menacing through the lion's mane. "A man thought to take my valuables while I was resting. He caught me unawares. It will not happen again." I gave him a sympathetic smile. I often heard stories about life on the streets, and none of them were pleasant. It was one of the reasons I kept the clinic open. It was one of the few ways I could make a difference.

"Thank you, by the way." He looked surprised, but it was hard to be certain through the hair. "For getting me out of the way of that truck," I explained. "I think you saved my life."

"If I had been there sooner you wouldn't have been injured."

I noticed the hint of his accent again. I didn't think he was from the Midwest. Maybe people talked like that on the East coast. I'd never been. I wondered how he'd wound up in Kansas City but didn't want to pry.

"My bumped head isn't as bad as what would have happened, so thank you." I still couldn't figure out how I missed seeing the truck.

If I couldn't blame a ghost with a bad sense of humor then I had to assume I'd been preoccupied with something else. After knocking my head against concrete, I couldn't remember what.

"You're most welcome." He gave me a little half-bow from the chair and Luna uttered a brief protest as she got smashed. He straightened up and she sat upright, appraising him with indignation. "I apologize, small beast called Luna." He seemed serious and I suppressed a chuckle. This bear of a man didn't seem like most of the population that I dealt with, and I realized I had relaxed with him. The headache may have had something to do with that.

I threw caution to the wind, downed an anti-inflammatory tablet with the beer he had gotten me, and sat across from him. Luna would normally be in my lap the moment I sat, but she was too enamored with our stranger.

"Where do you stay?" I asked him. He looked confused. Maybe I should have started with easier questions. "The City Mission?" The Mission was the main homeless shelter in town, though we had several. "I could take you back there. I think their doors close at nine." He continued to stare at me. "Do you have an apartment?" Maybe I was mistaken and he wasn't homeless, just disheveled. "Is there someplace else I could take you?"

His mouth curved up as if he was amused. "I don't require transportation."

"Do you have friends you can stay with?" I asked with hope and he responded with a shake of the head. He was homeless, then, as I suspected. He just didn't want to admit it.

Now I felt responsible for him. He saved my life not two hours ago. The temperature was supposed to dip well below zero in the middle of the night making it the coldest night of the year. I couldn't see turning him out into that. I could pay a night in a hotel for him, although, with my concussion, I should give it twenty-four hours before driving, and the chance of getting a taxi to show up in my neighborhood after dark was remote. I sighed.

"I don't want to offend you, but would you like to clean up? Maybe take a shower? I think I can find something for you to wear while we wash your clothes." As the temperature rose in the condo it became apparent that he hadn't showered in a few days.

"I'm sorry. I know I'm not at my best." I interpreted the twitching his beard made as chagrin. "Thank you for your hospitality. I don't think your clothes will fit me." He added the last as an afterthought, once he'd given the idea some consideration.

I laughed, pleased to find that it didn't make my head hurt as much as it had before. My clothes definitely wouldn't fit him. "That's the guest bathroom." I gestured to the doorway at the opposite end of the kitchen. "I can loan you some of my boyfriend's clothes." The things Eric left behind when he moved out wouldn't be big enough for my guest, but I hoped he'd be able to squeeze into them.

He looked around as if he expected me to produce said boyfriend at that very instant. "Where is your man? Why wasn't he protecting you today?"

This was too personal and borderline insulting.

"He'll be home later." The bear stared at me for a long moment and I got the disturbing impression that he knew full well I was lying. I wasn't about to tell a man I didn't know that I lived alone. I preferred for him to believe someone could be home any minute.

If he guessed the truth, he didn't pursue it. "Thank you for your offer. I accept." I took this to mean that he would like to shower, despite the fact that he appeared to be speaking to the cat.

I collected an old set of Eric's scrubs out of the upper reaches of my closet. I also came up with a towel, scissors, a disposable razor, shaving cream (just in case), a new toothbrush and travel toothpaste. The shower was well stocked with soap and shampoo.

When I emerged he was still in the chair, Luna glued to his lap. "Make yourself at home." I indicated the bathroom. When he picked the cat up and deposited her on the chair with gentle hands she sat and glared at him, offended at having been uprooted from her spot.

"My apologies, small beast called Luna." He bowed to her and she lapped it up, acting her queenly cat best. I shook my head and stifled a smile. It's hard to not like someone who treats your pet well.

I heard the sound of water in the guest bath and allowed myself to relax back on the sofa. I ought to figure out what to do with my strange houseguest, but I had a pounding headache and was swept by exhaustion. I told myself that I'd just rest for a few minutes, and closed my eyes.

When I awakened, a very different man sat across from me. He'd shaved the beard, and I was startled by how much it changed his face. "How long have you been watching me?" Sleeping in front of someone was an intimate act, and it made me uncomfortable. I felt as if he'd been able to see too much of me.

"I didn't want to disturb you." It wasn't an answer. The borrowed scrubs must not have fit very well because he was wearing a blue bath towel around his shoulders. It was funny, given how furry his face had been, that he didn't have more hair on his chest and shoulders. He looked like he was in his late thirties, and his body looked like the result of many hours at the gym, which was unusual for a homeless man.

Well-defined muscles made up the bulk of his upper body. He also had several interesting scars on his chest and arms that I could see, healed surgical incisions. If we were close, I would ask about them. I didn't ask.

He had managed to get the pants on. I considered that good news, though given what the top half of him looked like, the rest might be just as nice. His dark hair was pulled back with a ponytail holder. I was surprised that he looked so good, so attractive. The forehead wound was the only defect on him that I could see. The sight of it spurred me to action. I should have taken care of it before he took the shower.

"Do you feel well?" he asked as I started to move.

"I think I have a mild concussion." I pushed myself upright without feeling sick. The sardonic voice in my head was unimpressed. It was a small victory. "I'll be all right. Will you let me take a look at your forehead?"

"This is nothing." His tone was dismissive, but I wasn't going to let it go.

"I don't think you'll die from it, but it is at high risk for infection. I just want to clean it up, maybe put a few stitches in it so that it heals well. Otherwise, you'll have a nasty scar. It's no trouble." I flipped the medical kit open and pulled out a sterile surgical set and a pre-packaged suture kit. "I'll use these. It may hurt a little bit."

"I don't fear pain." He sounded affronted as if I'd challenged his manhood. Whatever. His desire to save face got him out of the chair. He crossed the room, and I found that he moved with a surprising degree of grace for his size. I hadn't noticed that earlier. The scrub pants were too short on him and clung to his thighs. Through the thin material, they appeared to be just as muscled as his torso.

I tried to look clinical and distracted myself by flicking on more overhead lamps. My headache protested the sudden increase in light but I ignored it. Medical school and residency taught you how to keep functioning no matter how ill or exhausted you were.

The bear lowered himself to sit on a bar stool at the kitchen island. I washed my hands and bemoaned the fact that my kit was out of sterile gloves. They wouldn't save me from a contaminated needle but would have protected me against blood-borne illnesses. I had no room for error.

"Do you have any medical history that I need to know about?" I asked, hoping my voice didn't portray my concern as I unrolled the surgical set and laid it out on the counter.

"I have a great deal that I must tell you, but this isn't the time."

Maybe I needed to be more specific. "Any blood pressure problems, drug or alcohol use, illnesses?"

He considered this before answering. "I'm not certain."

"Do you use drugs?"

"No." This one, at least, he knew. This question was the most important one since recreational drug use was one of the biggest risk factors for HIV, which would be contagious if I stabbed myself with the needle. I didn't intend to do that, but accidents happened.

"Do you have problems with your blood pressure?"

"I don't believe so."

"Do you have episodes where you get dizzy, lightheaded, or faint?"

Now he looked amused. Without the facial hair, his expressions were easier to read. "I don't."

"Do you have Hepatitis or HIV?"

"If these are illnesses, then I assure you I am quite well."

I stifled a sigh and decided that my attempt to get a complete medical history on him was futile. Normally I'd ask more questions, whether he'd ever broken any bones, and what his parents and grandparents died from, but those details weren't pertinent to sewing up a forehead laceration.

"Are you allergic to anything?"

He hesitated before answering, "No.".

Not too many people had allergic reactions to chlorhexidine and Lidocaine, so his answer shouldn't matter much anyway. I examined the wound and pulled the edges apart so I could check the depth. It looked pretty angry but I didn't see any overt signs of infection or contamination.

"I'm going to need to freshen up the edges of the cut so I can sew it back together. I'll inject some Lidocaine so it won't hurt, but it stings a bit going in. Like a bee sting." I reached for a syringe and the Lidocaine but he grabbed my wrist, his long fingers folding around it until they overlapped each other. He had big hands but he didn't hurt me, just stopped me from reaching for the drug.

"I don't need this . . . Lidocaine."

"It's going to hurt quite a bit without it," I warned him.

"This small wound is nothing to me."

I paused and considered. He wasn't the first person I'd known who was too macho for Lidocaine and wanted to be sewn up without it. "All right. If you change your mind we can stop and put some in before I finish." I stepped back and fixed my sternest gaze on him. "You have to stay very still while I am working on this. You can't jump or jerk, even when it hurts. Do you understand?"

"I understand," he agreed. His tone was serious, but he flashed me those white, even teeth. It occurred to me that not many of the homeless people I'd run into had had such stellar orthodontia care in their lives. What had happened in his life to make him wind up on the streets?

"Hold still." I leaned back into his personal space. "It looks pretty clean. Did it bleed a lot?" He nodded. "That helped wash it out. I'm going to clean it with anti-bacterial soap. This may sting a little."

I scrubbed the wound with chlorhexidine and then rinsed it out with normal saline. The edges didn't look too bad, but they did look old.

"How long ago did this happen?"

"Tuesday."

My suspicion was correct. I was going to have to cut the dead tissue away so that I could sew the wound back together again. I was a doctor, but I didn't like to cause pain. "I'm sorry, but this will hurt. Don't move, okay?"

"I will be still," he reiterated, and I again got the feeling that he was laughing at me.

He was so immobile that I wondered if I should check to see if he was still breathing. He didn't even wince while I revised the edges of the wound back to fresh tissue and then sewed it together with neat, close set sutures. I was surprised by how impervious he was to pain. I rewashed the surface of the stitches and then stepped back to admire my handiwork. Not bad. He'd still have a scar, but over time, it shouldn't be too noticeable.

"That should do it. Your stitches need to come out in about five days. If you'll drop by the clinic, I'll take them out there."

"Thank you." He sounded appreciative despite his earlier protests.

"It's not a problem." I washed my hands and considered what was next. I was hungry, and my houseguest might be as well. According to the clock, it was after ten o'clock. I admitted to myself that I was going to let him stay the night. "Are you hungry?"

"I am. Let me cook for you. Sit."

"That's very nice of you, but I have some stew in the fridge. I have plenty for both of us if you think that sounds good. If not, I could make some spaghetti . . ."

"The stew would be very good." He smiled, transforming his face. Even with the sutures over his eye, he looked nice. I repressed the urge to reach out and touch his smooth cheek.

Turning away from him was difficult. I set the stewpot on one of the burners of my pride and joy Viking range and turned the flames up to medium heat. "You haven't told me your name." I was embarrassed that I hadn't asked earlier. The head injury had rattled my manners as well as my brain.

"Anna, I'm Jedediah." He sounded alarmed and I glanced over to find him staring at me. "You don't know me?"

"No . . . Jedediah. I'm sorry. If you were a patient at the clinic . . . I just don't recall." I was pretty sure he hadn't been a patient. He was too distinctive for me to have forgotten.

"Anna, you should know me, just as I know you." His stare made me question myself. I was a member of the community, though. I attended the benefit dinners and community potlucks. A year ago I'd been given the Greater Kansas City Building Better Communities award. I'd met more of the cities' glitterati that night than I cared to recall, but I didn't think that my homeless man was one of them.

His stare felt strange, but it was possible that we had met, somewhere along the way. It bothered me that I couldn't remember him, but I had hit my head and there were consequences to that.

"Maybe the concussion is interfering with my memory." I tried to smile but failed. "When did we meet?"

"We haven't, in person." He was quick to reassure me. "I thought you might have heard of me, though. It's not important." I got the impression that he thought it was important, but he didn't want to push the issue while I had a concussion. Maybe by tomorrow, I'd be able to figure out who our mutual connection was.

He'd saved my life and been a model houseguest. For whatever reason, I trusted him. I believed in trusting myself when I got strong feelings about someone, good or bad. The only thing resonating off the bear named Jedediah was honesty. Luna even liked him. In an odd way, I felt better with him there.

I also knew how cold it was outside. Enough homeless people would be struggling to survive overnight in Kansas City. I didn't want this man to be one of them. I set the alarm system for the night and then ladled hot soup into bowls. I pulled a few slices of whole grain bread out of the toaster and slid both bowls across the counter.

"So, Jed." His mouth twitched at the shortening of his name. "Do you mind if I call you that?"

"You may, if you wish."

"Jedediah is a mouthful," I explained.

"At one time, it was a popular name, but in these times it is . . . long," he admitted. "It means, one who is loved by God."

I raised my eyebrows. "An auspicious name." It isn't usually a good time to tell someone you are an atheist after they've just told you their name means that god loves them. I kept it to myself. "What's your last name?" It was a benign question but he paused, fork halfway to his mouth.

"Peters," he said. I got the strange impression that he was lying, but pushed the feeling away. Why would he lie about his last name?

Jedediah wiped up the remains of his stew with toast while I was still working on the first half of mine. I'd forgotten how much food men could eat.

I nodded towards the pot. "We have plenty. Help yourself."

"I shouldn't eat all of your food. How will you eat this week?" His tone resonated with concern.

"I'll figure something out. I can always order pizza. If you're hungry, you're welcome to it."

His second bowl was gone before I finished my first, and the pot was empty. How long had it been since he'd had a proper meal? I felt guilty that I hadn't given him more to eat and promised myself to make him breakfast in the morning. I wasn't due at the clinic until nine, so I'd have time to cook before I pointed him in the direction of the shelter. Right now, I was tired.

"The guest room has clean sheets on the bed." He interpreted my polite dismissal with grace.

"I thank you for your hospitality." He didn't seem surprised, as if he had expected to stay all along.

"Thank you for saving me from that truck." His eyes glittered in the light, and instead of answering, he gave his little bow again. The move should have looked awkward from the barstool, but it didn't. Bowing wasn't a talent most Americans learned. Was he an actor? Shakespearean, perhaps . . . mayhaps . . .

I felt a surge of inappropriate giggles and suppressed them. The dull pounding in my head wasn't up for more laughter. I hoped my headache improved by morning. Jedediah started to clear the dishes.

"Thank you, but leave them. We can get them in the morning." I needed to go to bed but couldn't do so while my houseguest did the dishes. He hesitated, and then acquiesced.

"Very well. Goodnight, Anna."

"Goodnight, Jedediah." Luna stood on the back of the sofa and preened towards him as he walked past her. He ignored her and she jumped down to follow him. Too late, the guestroom door clicked shut in front of her. She turned back to me with a soft meow that I almost couldn't hear.

"Traitorous wench." I walked into my room and she followed me, still complaining. "I know, you like him. You've made that very clear. You'll see him again in the morning," I told her and she jumped onto the bed and blinked at me. Talking to the cat when no one else was around was a habit of mine. I thought she liked it, though with cats, you couldn't always tell.

Given the concussion and my visitor, I decided against my nor-mal nighttime medication. I wouldn't rest as well, but at least I knew I was more likely to awaken if I needed to. I locked my door before I crawled under the covers and succumbed again to sleep.

CHAPTER TWO

"**S**HE IS HERE." The ghost's voice echoed from the dark of sleep and pulled me deeper in.

"Did he bring her?" Another spirit, this one connected to a form that filled with colors until she stood before me, clothed in vibrant blue silks and shimmering bronze hair.

"I do not sense him." The first voice lurked in the shadows and I got the feeling that I'd prefer for it to stay there.

"But she lives." The woman explored the edges of my consciousness as if she expected to find someone standing there. She seemed familiar to me somehow, as if I had seen her somewhere before.

"Then he has fulfilled his task."

"She is here." It confirmed again, and I realized they were talking about me. "Why does she not speak to us?"

"This one is not strong enough."

"No matter. It's too late." She turned towards her companion, her tone ominous and dark. "Far too late. The traitor grows strong."

I shivered with apprehension. Who was the traitor and what was too late?

"She could still serve our needs." The other voice gathered enough light around him for me to see that he was a grotesque skeleton. His flesh fell from his bones like rotten meat, his face was half eroded. He turned towards me and a chunk of flesh dropped off his cheek. I opened my mouth to scream, but no sound emerged.

"Yes, my darling. We will use her." The woman reached up to him and caressed that blackened rotting flesh with fondness. I gagged. I tried to focus my energy, but my power had no effect on these ghosts. I needed to protect myself against these terrible creatures.

The beautiful ghost cackled at my efforts. "We are safe from you here, but you are not safe from us, Anna." Her knowing laughter echoed off the cavern of my thoughts.

I awakened in a startled sweat to the alarming sound of life in the kitchen. There were footsteps, the refrigerator door opened and a glass milk jug clanked onto the counter.

Eric was making me coffee? I rolled over in confusion. No. He didn't live here anymore. Then it came back to me. The beer truck, the large homeless man who resembled a bear. Who was in my kitchen.

I pushed myself into a sitting position and evaluated my condition. The spot on the back of my head was tender to touch, but I felt better overall. The bedside clock informed me it was five forty-five in the morning, and I spared a moment to curse houseguests who awakened early. Luna pawed at the door, eager to see her new favorite person. I pushed away the lingering uneasiness of my dreams. I had bad dreams every time I failed to take my medication.

Dreaming about ghosts wasn't unusual either. Just because I hadn't seen one in a while didn't mean that my subconscious didn't think about them, or think about what I could do to them. Sometimes ghosts were scary, and it made sense that they would factor into my dreams. I ignored the cat's pleas and headed for the shower.

After a long hot shower, I preferred to lounge around in my robe. Because of my houseguest, I decided to reuse the sweats I'd slept in and emerged from the bedroom a few minutes after six with a towel still wrapped around my wet hair. Jedediah wore the same tight scrubs from the night before and I chided myself for admiring the view.

"Good morning." Since he was looking at Luna, who was twined between his ankles, I wasn't sure if he was talking to me or to her. He slid a blue stoneware mug towards me. I breathed in the smell of coffee and decided to assume it was me that he'd been talking to.

"'Good morning, Jedediah. Thank you."

"There is enough, if anyone else is joining us for breakfast."

I gave him a blank look and then remembered the fictitious boyfriend I'd brought up last night. I flushed. "No. There's no one else."

"Ah." Jed turned away from my embarrassment and reached for his coffee.

Mine was dense and black. I sipped and was glad of my caution when I realized the dregs were still settling inside the mug. "It's been a while since I had a traditional Turkish coffee." I reached for the milk and added a bit, along with a healthy spoonful of sugar, stirring with care so that I wouldn't disturb the grinds.

"I hope it pleases you. I . . . was not sure how to operate that machine." He waved towards my espresso maker with a look of vague consternation. I had to admit that it was a complicated contraption.

"The coffee is very good. Not often served this way in the Midwest, though. Are you from Turkey?" Or someplace else that serves their coffee this way? I had had coffee like this at a Turkish restaurant downtown, but maybe other cultures drank their coffee with the dregs.

"Not quite." His reply startled me out of my reverie. "I did, however, first enjoy coffee on the streets of Constantinople. Although that was many years ago, the habit has stayed with me."

I took another sip and filtered the fine sediment through my front teeth. Turkish coffee wasn't my favorite, but it was strong, and my beans were good quality, roasted at the local coffee shop. I felt more alert. "Istanbul?"

He paused for a moment, and then showed me a half smile "Yes. They call it that now, don't they? I haven't been in many years."

I was pretty sure the city of Constantinople had been referred to as Istanbul for longer than I had been alive, but I wasn't certain enough to challenge him on it. My last history class was a long time ago and it wasn't that important.

He turned towards the windows and watched as the first edges of daylight brightened the night sky. He was still shirtless which left me a perfect view of his well-muscled shoulders and back. I let myself enjoy the moment sipping my coffee and wondering if his ass looked as good as the rest of him did. He turned back around and my cheeks flushed. *Get a grip, Anna.* With any luck, he couldn't tell what I was thinking. I forced my thoughts back to more practical concerns.

I felt responsible for him now that he was my guest, but I didn't know what to do with him. He was personable and well spoken. It seemed like he'd be able to hold down a job and function in society if he had a little help getting off the streets. I flitted through a mental list of my contacts in the social work world. Maybe I could take him to the clinic with me, see if I could find someone who could help him. He'd need housing and employment. There were a few agencies that provided those services, but there were waiting lists. Still, I could make a few calls. I brightened now that I'd come to a decision that didn't involve just sending him on his way.

"I'm going to throw your clothes in the dryer. Then we can have some breakfast." He leaned forward, elbows braced on my countertop. His biceps and pectorals flexed and I tried not to stare. I needed to consider dating. Or find a gigolo.

"Do you go to your work today?"

"Yes. I start work at nine. You can go with me. I'd like to get there by eight thirty, though. Make a few phone calls. See if we can find someplace for you to stay until you get more settled."

"I see." His face was impassive, but his tone did not sound pleased.

"We'll just see," I reassured him. "It's good to know what your options are." I gave him my best 'I'm-a-doctor-so-you-should-trust-me' look and then headed for the laundry.

On our walk to the office, Jedediah placed himself between me and traffic. Before my Aunt Ann and Uncle Will died, my uncle used to walk with me like that. I wasn't sure if Jedediah was raised like a gentleman from a former era, or if he was concerned that I might make a habit of stepping in front of trucks. He looked menacing in his dark jeans and black jacket, and appeared to take the role of my protector seriously. Given that he'd saved me from being run down the day before, it didn't seem like a good time to point out that I'd been taking care of myself for many years before he turned up. I tucked the corners of my red wool scarf deeper around my neck and tried to ignore the bitter winter wind. When the weather was nice, it was an easy walk. When it was this cold I had to convince myself every morning that I didn't need to drive.

At the clinic, I escorted him inside through the back door. "Here we are."

He took in the interior and said in a careful tone, "This is where you work?"

It wasn't worth getting defensive over. I was used to the peeling wallpaper, holes in the walls, leaky faucets, and the fact that you had to hold the handle down on the toilet for a full forty-five seconds before it would flush.

"It's a free health clinic," I reminded him. "Our funding comes from government grants and aid from other non-profits. Most of our patients don't have enough money to pay for medical care and don't have any health insurance. Those that have insurance have Medicaid, which doesn't pay very well. It doesn't leave us much money for overhead. This is my office." I flicked on the light and pointed to a chair in the corner, wedged between a bookshelf and the wall. Jedediah took his place. He sat on the edge of the chair as if he was prepared to launch himself out of it at a moment's notice, but it might have been because the corner was too small for him to fit into.

A small-boned man with flawless rich brown skin paused by the door and appraised the man in my chair with overt appreciation. Jedediah sprang to his feet as if he anticipated a threat. He was jumpy today.

"Good morning, Dr. Anna." Ty addressed me, without looking away from Jedediah.

Ty was my best friend, but in the office, he insisted on calling me by my title. He thought it was disrespectful to do anything else. We'd compromised on my first name after the 'Dr.' instead of my last.

Ty was half African-American, half German. His partner, Chaz, was a former prosecutor who now did work for a local pharmaceutical company. He also did pro-bono work for the Latino community on the side, and we'd had the opportunity to work together there. I'd met Ty through Chaz, and hired him to work with me. The three of us spent a lot of time together. To be truthful, they were just about my only friends.

"Morning, Ty." I tried to act as though everything was normal, as if I came to work accompanied by a massive homeless man every day. Jedediah had relaxed a notch but he seemed like a cat, prepared to pounce on its prey at any moment. "This is Jed. Jed, Ty is my nurse, and my friend."

One of Jedediah's eyebrows quirked at hearing his new nickname again, but all he did was hold out his right hand.

Ty leaned into the small space and shook it. "Well, hello Jed." He turned to me and winked, and I knew I'd hear more from him later. "Dr. Anna, you've got three patients ready to go. We have a John Smith," he held up his fingers and made quotes in the air around the name so that I'd know it was an alias, "in room three. He somehow managed to cut his leg opening a beer bottle last night and needs a few stitches. He says he'll pay cash." Ty flashed a grin. Patients with money, no matter how fictitious their names, were a rare thing. "Miss Mary is in four for her checkup, and we have a new patient in two. She's HIV positive and has a cough and a fever."

He moved on, whistling his way down the corridor. I hung my winter coat on the hook inside the door, pulled the stethoscope off the door handle and stuffed it into my back pocket. I didn't like to wear the traditional white coat because I felt like it distanced me from my patients. They needed me to be as non-threatening as possible if I wanted them to open up to me.

Ty reappeared with two mugs of coffee, set one on my desk and handed the other to Jedediah. "Thanks, Ty. Jed, there are magazines in the exam room across the hall. Help yourself. I'll be back in a bit."

I headed for the paying patient first. The wound was a small one, on his upper thigh. It looked like it was from a knife blade, because it was even, not jagged like it would be if it were from the bottle he claimed had caused it. As far as lacerations go, it was less complex than the one I'd dealt with the night before. The patient was in his forties, wearing now-bloody designer jeans and a Faconnable button down. He didn't ask any questions and didn't answer any of mine. He was eager for anonymity, wouldn't want his neighbors to know where he had been. It happened more often than you might think.

I marked his ticket for three times what we'd charge someone from the neighborhood after offering him a variety of anonymous blood tests for STD's. He declined, and the last I saw of him, he was at the front desk pulling one hundred dollar bills off a large bundle of cash as if they were ones. He handed them to the clinic manager. Rita took the money, checked each bill with the little light to make sure they were real, and offered him a receipt. He declined and limped to the door. Flashing cash like that, he might get knifed again before he left the parking lot.

I shook my head and moved on to room four. Mary was fine, twenty-five weeks pregnant and everything seemed to be going well. We reviewed her diet and I encouraged her to stop smoking while she was pregnant so that her baby had a better chance of making it to full term. At least she wasn't into drinking or drugs – her little one would have more opportunities than many children do.

The new patient took a lot of time. It took a while, but I convinced her to go to the local public hospital, which had a pretty decent infectious diseases team that had agreed to take her on. She was too sick to stay outpatient with the underlying HIV infection. By the time I was finished with her, the two vacated rooms had filled, and Ty's exasperated look told me that the waiting room was full as well.

I swung by my office for a swig of cold coffee. Jedediah's jacket was there, but he wasn't. Bathroom, I presumed, and kept moving. It was around one when Ty promised me we'd seen the last of the morning patients and that sandwiches were on the way.

My office was again empty, and I was on the way to look for my mystery man when Rita plowed through the door with a brown paper sack.

"I got enough for your man too. He's earned it."

Perplexed, I followed her into the hallway and saw Ty staring with fascination into the staff bathroom. I joined him and was taken aback at the sight of the bear, flat on his back, staring up at the underside of the sink. There was brackish water in a bucket next to him. He ignored us while he reattached the drainpipe. I wondered where the wrench had come from.

Rita leaned in behind me and hissed, "He's already fixed the leak in six. Dating a man who has skills – good job!"

She clapped me on the shoulder and was gone before I could tell her we weren't dating. Ty took one look at me and followed Rita, his laugh echoing off the narrow walls. Ty happy was a good sound. I turned back to contemplate the massive man tucked up under the sink.

"Lunch is here," I informed him.

Jedediah looked down the length of his body at me and nodded. "I need to finish this first."

"It's in my office." I left him there.

I worked my way through a feta, hummus, and spinach sandwich while I made a few phone calls. Ruthann was the only one I got through to. She'd been working with Kansas City's homeless population for a long time. It's a hard job and I admired her dedication.

"Dr. Roberts, I'm in the middle of one of the longest cold snaps we've had here in ten years. It's not a good week. What do you want?"

To the point, that was Ruthann. I slid my door closed with the toe of my boot. Jedediah must have still been involved with his plumbing project, which was just as well. "I've got a man in my clinic. He needs shelter. I think this one could hold down a job, Ruthann. He seems good at fixing things. Good social skills. Can you help?"

She groaned with what sounded like frustration. "Look, Anna, I've got two thousand other people in the same boat, every one of them on the brink of freezing to death. The mission is full up and so is every other shelter in town.

"What about that project you have that gets people into apartments?"

"It's got an eight-month waiting list."

"There's got to be something."

"I can recommend a nice heating grate. The former resident froze to death last night."

I paused a moment. Her tone was flippant but I didn't doubt that someone had died in the cold. "Was it anyone I knew?"

"I don't think so."

"I'm sorry to hear it."

"Thanks."

"Ruthann . . . I kept this guy on my sofa last night but he needs someplace else to go."

"You should let him stay in the guest room, doc. Your sofa isn't that comfortable." I didn't respond and she sighed. "How crazy is he?"

"Doesn't seem to be at all."

"Look, doc. If you want to help this guy, keep him warm this week. Call me when the cold snap is over and I'll see if I can slip him onto the housing list. I'm not making any promises, though. What's his name?"

"Jedediah Peters. Ruthann?"

"What?"

"Thanks." She hung up without responding.

When Jedediah walked in, I was flipping through the lab results and mail in my inbox while I picked at the remains of my sandwich. He found his lunch on his chair and consumed it without interrupting me. It took another twenty minutes for me to finish the pile, and by then Jed was done eating. I was disconcerted to find that he was watching me.

"You work very hard," he observed.

"Yes," I admitted, feeling self-conscious. "I don't have to take overnight call, though." The ER's and urgent care centers handled anything that occurred while my office was closed.

"You would make more money if you worked someplace else."

"I'm sure I would, but this is the job I have." I wasn't going to get into the details of my finances with him, or why I chose to work with the clinic instead of a big private practice group in the suburbs. I changed the subject. "I spoke with a friend of mine. She might be able to find you a place to live, maybe in a few weeks. But with the cold snap, the shelters are all full." He lowered his gaze to the floor and I sighed.

"Where would you have slept last night, Jedediah, if you hadn't run across me?"

"I told you, you don't need to concern yourself with my safety. It is I who am concerned with yours." His dark eyes were fixated on me again. He looked amused and I didn't understand what I'd done that was funny.

"You saved my life last night. I may be in a position to help you get some assistance."

"There is no need for you to feel indebted. There are so many here that need your help." He gestured to the door, the exam rooms beyond.

"Do you have anyplace else to stay tonight?"

His eyes darkened. "Yes."

"Where?"

His lack of reply told me everything I needed to know. I wasn't going to let him freeze to death on a heating grate. "Then you'll stay with me again." I balled up the paper from my sandwich and tossed it into the trash, dusted the crumbs from the front of my shirt, and left before he could respond.

It was dark outside my window when the last patient of the day left, and I again faced the large stack of charts that needed review. Jed was absent and I surmised from Rita and Ty's conversation that he had continued to be useful through the afternoon. The building was about to fall apart, and we didn't have the budget for many repairs.

Electricians, plumbers, and plaster repair experts often asked for an hourly wage that exceeded mine.

I had just finished my third chart when a familiar voice interrupted me. "Hey, chica!"

I grinned. "Chaz! What are you doing here?" I greeted him with a hug, happy to be distracted from my paperwork.

"Ty's car is in the shop. I drove him this morning – just came by to pick him up."

"Hey, lover boy." Ty snuggled up against Chaz's short frame and leaned his head against his partner's. Chaz's short black hair contrasted with Ty's shaved head. Their skin matched, despite the differences in their heritage. Chaz came from a first-generation Guatemalan family who escaped the violence there before he was born. Ty's mixed heritage left him with the same skin tone. Despite being a little shorter than he'd like, he was one of the most attractive men I'd ever met, though Chaz was plenty cute too.

"You and Jed should join us for dinner, Anna. McCoy's?" Ty offered, listing a nearby brewpub.

"Who's Jed?" Chaz looked from Ty to me in confusion.

"Anna's new man." Ty's whisper carried well enough that I was sure Jed, wherever he was in the office, could hear him too.

"Shut up, Ty. For the thousandth time, I'm not dating him," I hissed.

"Why not, Anna? He's hot." As if I hadn't noticed. Chaz shook his head at his lover's exuberance.

"You guys go on." I shooed them away. "I have too much to do to go out tonight. Maybe tomorrow," I suggested, though I had no idea how to explain to them that I'd taken in a homeless man. It just wasn't something that people did.

"Come on, Ty. Let's go. Anna has lots of work to do and you're distracting her."

Ty sighed. "Don't do the work, do the man! See you tomorrow, Anna." He gave me a quick wave and let Chaz drag him away. Their fingers were linked before they were halfway down the hallway.

"Those two make me so jealous." Rita leaned against my doorframe. She looked tired.

"Me too." I was glad she'd said it first. I was always happy for Ty and Chaz, but I wanted love like that in my own life.

"Anna, I was thinking." Like Ty, Rita was careful to only call me by my first name when no one else was around. Their rules, not mine.

"What can I do for you?"

"I've talked to your man."

"He's not my man, Rita." I corrected her with a sigh and she grinned at me and brushed that little fact aside.

"Whatever. He's good at fixing things, and I've offered him a salary to stay on, at least until the place is fixed up a bit."

I raised my eyebrows and sat back down. "So the money for this is coming from?"

Rita lowered herself into the corner chair and nodded. "Yeah, we'll have to hold off on getting another medical assistant for a while. But this place is a wreck, and your guy wants to fix it up and he's affordable and skilled." She had planned her case well. It's why she and I were a good team – she had a good head for the priorities of the clinic, while I didn't care to get that involved in the details.

"Is Ty okay with that?" He and Rita both worked harder than they should to do the work that a new medical assistant would do. It was a strain on all of us to be short staffed.

"Are you kidding? And miss the opportunity to have that eye candy around here?" I burst out laughing at that. Rita swept her straight dark hair over her shoulder. "Do you need any more coffee?"

"No, I'm fine. Thanks for your help today." She'd translated a patient visit for me. My Spanish was adequate. It might not be the Spanish that they used in the universities in Mexico City, but it was the language spoken in much of the immigrant community in the city. This patient, though, had been a struggle for me. An older woman with influenza. I'd had trouble understanding her accent.

"It's no problem. I was happy to help the Abuela."

"Stay warm. See you mañana."

"Mañana. Buenas noches."

Shortly thereafter, I heard the front door signal her departure. I delved back into my paperwork. Most clinics had electronic medical record systems, or at least a transcriptionist to type out the doctor's dictation. We didn't have the money for it. I scripted a lengthy note about the HIV positive patient, signed my name, added it to the "done" pile and reached for the next chart.

I heard a sound behind me and saw Jed slide into his chair out of the corner of my eye. I appreciated the fact that he didn't disturb me while I finished the last note. When I was done, I swiveled my chair around to face him.

"Are you ready?" I asked him.

"I am at your leisure," he informed me, and I smiled. He had a strange way with words. It was quaint.

"Let's go, then." I grabbed my coat and redressed for the cold night. It was in the teens out there.

The forecast called for snow, but when we stepped into the frigid air we could see faint stars and the full moon overhead. "It will be a cold night without the clouds to keep the warmth in," I observed and was glad that Jed was going to be inside with me.

He ignored my commentary on the weather. "Do you always work this late?"

"This was a normal day for me." I locked the door and checked it to make sure it was secure.

"This is not safe," he said while he surveyed the street. Unlike the previous night, a few pedestrians made their way down the ice and snow covered sidewalks. A cluster of people huddled together at the bus stop.

I ignored the implication that I couldn't take care of myself and decided it was better not to pursue the conversation. "Let's go this way. There's a grocery store a few blocks down. We need something for supper."

Thirty minutes later we had the makings for steaks, mashed potatoes, and a salad, as well as a few extra breakfast provisions. I led Jed down a back alley away from the store and into a narrow semi-residential side street. It was the shortest way home, but it was not a pretty walk. The first lot we passed was empty except for chunks of old concrete and trash. The building on the other side of the street was an old house that appeared to have been turned into apartments. It looked like it might fall down at any moment, and it wasn't uncommon to see drug deals go down. A rusty Monte Carlo sat at the curb, snow and ice piled around the tires. It had been abandoned there for weeks.

"This is my least favorite section of Midtown," I admitted to Jed. "It's so dark. They need to fix the streetlights." Jed didn't point out the obvious. It was going to take more than streetlights to revitalize this neighborhood.

"It's not safe here. We must go." Jed's tone was urgent and I cast about for the cause of his concern. Was there another truck?

The air was so cold that I almost missed the shivering touch of my sixth sense. A palpable malevolence brushed against me and I froze. Most ghosts aren't malicious. Bitter and confused, but not many are mean. I'd seen spirits that emitted no emotional state whatsoever, some that were content and quite a few that seemed happy.

It was rare and frightening to come across one that exuded a hateful persona. I opened up the possibilities of my other sense and then I could see it. The spirit wasn't well formed, but it seemed angry. Fear gripped me as it swirled towards us in icy particles and I dropped my sack of groceries. It was like a self-contained snowstorm that was still gathering its power. Ghosts can cause harm, and plenty of it, if they are determined to. Most aren't, but the ones that are can be difficult to deal with. Jed stepped to me and wrapped his arms around me.

"Banish it," he whispered.

I'd never thought of it that way, but I knew what he meant. I reached out to the spirit, not with my hands but with my senses. It hissed as I touched it, and its fury accelerated. A harsh wind whipped as the spirit's form encased us. It felt like the flesh would rip from my bones and I heard myself cry out from the violence of its anger.

"Stop!" I ordered it as I harnessed my power. My gift. My curse.

It gathered within me, atom upon atom of it layered into a dense ball of energy. I felt I would explode when it left me. "I release you!" I screamed the words, and the miniature sun within me burst out, burning through every cell as it left my body. I cried out from pain while the ghost shrieked and fought.

It solidified in its effort to stay, and I identified a woman's ragged form as she twisted in the air in front of me. The fine glow of my power surrounded her, clung to her like glitter thrown over a spider web. Then the spirit disintegrated, her shrieking sounds dissipated and echoed in my memory. The wind abated into the still cold of a normal winter night. The ghost was gone, no longer bound to the living earth.

I moaned from the pain that burned through me. The aftereffect from releasing ghosts was bad enough that I never wanted to do it again. I would have collapsed onto the ground, but Jedediah held me fast in his arms.

CHAPTER THREE

I CAME TO and again found myself halfway home. Jed held me close to his chest. My head lolled against his left arm while my legs dangled over his right like a child's. I could hear the rustle of the plastic grocery sacks as they bumped against his legs. *How could he carry my 130 pounds as well as three bags of groceries?* Despite his fast pace, he seemed steady on the sidewalks, which I knew were icy. My body still burned with the familiar internal fire that I emitted whenever I released a ghost. I hadn't experienced it in a while but it was as painful as I remembered.

In general, I tried to avoid the spirits of the dead, and it had been a while since I'd released one. *Where had this one come from? Had Jedediah been able to see it too? Had he told me to release the ghost or had I imagined that part?* It was hard to think around the fire that still burned in me. I struggled against the ignominious position I was in, which resulted in the arms around me tightening.

"Damn it, Jed," I gasped out against his strong hold. "Put me down."

He paused long enough to set me on my feet but kept an arm under my shoulder in order to hold me up.

"Keep walking," he ordered and continued his fast pace while I stumbled to keep up.

"Jed, I'm sure that seemed strange . . ." I pushed against him and he lifted me over a snow bank and half-carried me across the street. We were one block from my condo.

"Let go of me," I ordered. He did, and I staggered a few steps before I got my balance. My legs protested. Jed looked menacing.

"We do not have time for you to take a leisurely stroll, Anna. Everything that is evil in this city felt the touch of your power and will be looking for you." He examined the landscape around us — old houses dilapidated with neglect, beat up cars parked on the side street, another abandoned lot two houses down. "I can't protect you like this."

I stared at him, dumbfounded.

"Let us at least get you home. It offers some measure of safety," He insisted. I stayed put while I tried to assimilate what he'd said. "Anna. Let's go home, I beg you. Then we can talk." He took my arm, urging me in the direction he wanted me to walk. I let him lead me.

I thought of a few hundred questions before we reached the door of my condo. My motor skills hadn't recovered and I fumbled the keys several times before unlocking both deadlocks on the door. Jed ushered me in and then relocked them. He went through the living room closing the blinds on the upper windows as well as the lower.

I leaned against the wall, unfastened my jacket, and removed my gloves. I was surprised to see that although my skin felt blistered it looked normal. I was ravenous. The strange man whom I had thought was a random homeless person seemed to know a great deal more about me than anyone could. I had questions but calories were more important.

I moved to the stove, stepping around Luna who was on her way to find Jed. I turned the heat on low and put on a pan of milk. I'd start with hot chocolate. The sugar would give me the energy I needed to survive until I could make something to eat.

I got out two mugs and spooned cocoa into each. I'd be laid out on the floor soon if I didn't get something in me. The milk started steaming and I took it off the stove and filled both mugs, stirring them until the chocolate had dissolved. I carried them to the coffee table and set them down on coasters.

The corner of the sofa was my refuge. My muscles screamed as I crawled into it. It could be days before I recovered from this. I pulled a chenille throw over me and nodded towards the chair Jed had been in the night before. He picked up his mug and sat as directed.

"I think you had better tell me who you are," I demanded. My voice sounded stronger than I felt.

"I am Jedediah. Your guardian, your protector." He leaned forward onto his knees and gave me a fierce look. "You know nothing of this." It was both a statement and a question.

"I have no idea what you are talking about. How is it that you know about ghosts? More to the point, how did you know about me and ghosts?"

"How do you believe it is that you see them, Anna? You have the gift, the sight. From whence did that come?"

"I don't know. I've been able to see them for as long as I can remember." He shrugged as if that were true for him as well. "I've never met anyone else who could see them." My voice dripped with disbelief, but he had known the ghost was there.

"Unlike me, you do not just see spirits, Anna. You have the power to banish them to the places of the dead."

I was fascinated and unsettled. I'd only told one other person what I could do. It had been a long time ago, and his reaction had taught me not to disclose my unusual ability to anyone else. "How do you know that?"

"I was sent to find you. You are the greatest defense this world has against the evils of the dead." I pulled the blanket higher up on my chest as if it would insulate me from his words, but he didn't stop. "They know of you. Already they seek you out. It may be that they followed me to you, and for that I am sorry."

"No." I shook my head, protested. "That's crazy."

He leaned back in his chair and Luna took the opportunity to take custody of his lap. He stroked her while he looked at me, those dark eyes filled with an intensity that frightened me.

"Do you think it is happenstance that we were accosted by this spirit today, Anna?"

"It didn't accost us, Jed. That's ridiculous. It just happened to be there."

"Perhaps." Silence settled between us for a moment, and then he continued. "I find it a strange coincidence that we happened upon a malice ridden spirit so very close to the place that you live and work. Much less, on the way home from the market you purchase your goods at, the day after I found you."

"Why would a ghost be looking for me? That's crazy." I'd been saying that a lot. "They are ghosts, Jed. They are dead. They don't have agendas or make plans. They don't have higher cortical functioning."

"Anna." He leaned forward again and Luna squawked. "You are right that many spirits do not have these things. Most are . . .

unfortunate souls who failed to find escape when they left their mortal bodies behind. There are some, though, that maintain more of their earthly form." He readjusted and allowed Luna to get comfortable before he continued.

"There are many who have higher levels of thought than you appear to realize. You must know that ghosts are capable of inflicting harm."

I nodded. Even though I tried to avoid the spirits of the dead, I'd seen some scary things in my life. That was one of the reasons I lived in a brand new condo in the midst of a neighborhood of restored and in-need-of restoration Victorians built a century before. New construction was less likely to have a restless ghost in residence.

"Some of these higher level souls are very old, and very powerful. Evil. Perhaps they want to take over this world and make it their own underworld. Perhaps they hope to return to life, to find a body weak enough for them to inhabit." He took a sip of his cocoa and made a face as if surprised by the taste. He took another sip and stared at the contents of his cup as if bemused by it.

"A ghost can take over a body?" I interrupted his inspection of his mug.

"Yes, of course they can. Didn't you know that?"

"No. I've never seen that happen. Never heard of it happening."

"Do not discount what I tell you. They are looking for you, Anna, because they know that you are one of the few beings in this world who can stop them." I felt cold despite the heat that still filled me.

"This is ridiculous." He could see ghosts like I could and he believed some of them were evil, and that they were after me. After a lifetime of being the only person in my world who could see ghosts, it seemed more than a bit farfetched.

"What will it take to convince you?" He looked tired and I needed to think. The last hour had been very strange.

"Right now, I need to eat."

"Of course you do. You used a great deal of energy."

I leaned back and drained the rest of my cocoa. The rest of our conversation would have to wait. Steak, mashed potatoes, and the salad that we'd put together from the salad bar was an easy supper to make and wouldn't take very long.

"I'm going to start dinner," I announced, and Jed moved as if he was going to help me. I waved him down. I wasn't used to anyone helping me cook. "You can stay there."

He didn't, and I was begrudgingly grateful for his help. My muscles protested any movement as the burning sensation settled into my bones. I knew from experience that I'd hurt for a few days. Since med school, I'd thought of it as being similar to a lactic acid buildup in my muscles, except it was body wide. I didn't know if that was an accurate description of what happened or not. I'd never found any medical texts that referenced anything like this, and it wasn't something I could deliberate with colleagues.

I put on a pot of water to boil and fished the potatoes out of the plastic bags. "Can you grill steak?" I asked Jed.

He answered with a grin of perfect white teeth. "I believe I can." I handed him a large butcher knife and turned on the grill burner on my stove. The flavor wasn't as good as charcoal, but it was pretty nice in the winter when it was too cold to grill outside. "I will need salt and pepper," he informed me. I pushed the respective grinders towards him.

For a normal dinner, I would cook six medium potatoes for four people. I suspected that between the large man and me, they would serve two. I chopped them into chunks and dropped them into the boiling water and then sat at one of the kitchen stools while I watched Jed trim the fat off two Kansas City strip steaks.

"How are you feeling?" He asked.

"Like hell. Hungry. Achy. Tired."

He nodded as if this was as he had anticipated. I didn't say angry, but I was. While he had the steaks sizzling, I set the small dining room table and opened a bottle of merlot.

"Would you like some wine?" I asked him even as I poured him a glass.

"Thank you."

I took a hefty sip of mine and hoped the anesthetic effect would help diminish the pain I was in. I finished the first glass while I mashed the potatoes.

We sat down to rare steaks, mashed potatoes, and our shared salad. I poured myself another glass of wine and found that the prospect of food had cleared my head. My strange houseguest's story was too fantastic to be believed, but he knew more about ghosts than anyone I'd ever met.

"Jed, if what you said earlier is true . . ." I paused, uncertain of how to word what I wanted to ask. Jed had a mouthful of steak anyway, so I had some time.

"Yesterday, when you pushed me out of the way of that truck you seemed surprised when I didn't know who you were."

He swallowed and I reached for my wine. My fingers were cramping but I forced them into a careful hold on the wineglass.

"Yes. That is what is most disturbing to me, Anna. You should have known me – from dreams, from visions. I have not done this before, but they said you would recognize me from your dreams."

My hand quivered and I set the wine glass down. "Who are they?"

"The Council." He looked at me as if I should know whom he meant. "The Council is . . . a group of ancient souls. They help maintain the balance between this world and the next. Anna, you should know them. Your dreams-"

I pushed my plate away and cut him off. "I don't have dreams." Except the one that I'd had last night that was filled with ghosts who were talking to me. The female spirit who had given me a sense of déjà vu.

"What do you mean?" He demanded. His knife clattered onto the table, but he ignored it.

"When I was a little girl, I had terrible dreams. I couldn't sleep. It's a disorder called night terrors. I take medication to sleep. I have for years. That way, if I have bad dreams, they don't bother me. I never remember them." I was babbling.

"And you always take this medication?" He sounded alarmed.

"Since I was small, in one drug combination or another. Not always, of course. During my training after medical school, for example, there were lots of nights I couldn't take them."

"And then did you dream?"

"Sometimes," I admitted.

"What did you dream of, Anna?"

"Bad things." I shied away from the memory of my last dream, of the skeleton ghost covered in bits of rotting flesh.

"I can imagine you did." He sounded tender as if he felt sympathy for the young girl who had had nightmares about ghosts.

"I always thought it was because of my experiences with ghosts, but I learned not to tell anyone about that." I was babbling again, but I'd never been able to tell anyone about this part of me.

"They wouldn't have believed you."

I laughed at the irony of it. "If I hadn't seen the ghosts myself, I wouldn't believe me either."

"For some reason, the modern world does not embrace the spiritual realm as people once did." He took another generous bite of steak.

"I hadn't thought about it that way," I acknowledged. He was right, though. What little I knew of ancient cultures was that many of them believed there were close ties to their ancestors. In fact, there were a number of modern cultures that maintained those beliefs. It was the modern western world that had chosen science over the spirit world. I had another sip of wine. The alcohol was helping to dull the burning sensation left over from releasing the ghost.

"So, since you can see the ghosts, why don't you just banish them? Why do you need me?"

He smiled. "I can sense them, much as you do, but I can't release them. That power is yours alone."

"You won't be much of a protector then, will you?"

"I may be able to offer some assistance." He sounded almost sheepish, and his dark eyes twinkled for a moment underneath thick eyebrows.

"Explain." I wasn't amused.

"Do you think that your gifts are the only ones that exist?" He countered.

"Yes," I blurted out. He scooted back from the table, eyes never leaving mine. Then he leaned forward, picked up both plates, and carried them to the sink. "You should have been listening to your dreams, Anna. Listen to them tonight."

Any retort I would have made was forestalled by the touch of something on the edge of my senses. I turned in my chair and saw Jed step back from the sink, his eyes on me. He had felt it too.

"It can't be," I whispered.

"It is." Jed's voice was quiet as if he too feared the ghost would hear us.

I hadn't encountered a spirit in months, but the second one today was trolling outside on the street. My sixth sense was already alert, a remnant of the earlier encounter. I could feel ill will emanating from it as it drifted past my house. I'd always been fascinated by how ghosts telegraphed their emotional state, but right now it was just frightening.

"Should I?" I queried, but Jed shook his head.

"Leave it. It seeks you but it has not found you. Banishing it would alert them to your location. You are still tired from the last one. Now is not the time to fight this battle."

"What battle?"

"The coming battle, Anna. The battle between life and death, that which is good, and that which is not." I would have laughed at the melodramatic words if he hadn't looked so damn serious.

The spirit lingered within the range of my perception, and my sense of dread escalated. "Do you know how crazy this all sounds?"

He regarded me for a time as if contemplating my perspective. "I do not." He gestured towards the covered windows, to where the ghost loitered. "If it is so unbelievable, how do you explain this apparition that seeks you?"

"You don't know it's looking for me." It was a weak retort.

"Would you like for me to ask it?"

"No." I took my wine and returned to my corner of the sofa, folding myself into my blanket. Jedediah followed and assumed his place in the chair across from me.

"When was it that you learned you could see spirits, Anna?" He draped one leg over the other, resting his glass of wine on his thigh.

"I suppose earlier than I realized at the time." His inquiring look invited me to expand on this. "I was so young, I thought it was normal. My aunt and uncle thought I had imaginary friends. In hindsight, I know they were ghosts."

"When did you realize?"

"What I can do?" My laugh was more of an ironic bark. I shook my head. "I've never told that to anyone." I wasn't going to start now.

"Perhaps you have not had the opportunity." He looked empathetic and I realized that this was the first person I'd ever met who might understand what I'd been through. "I would be honored, to be the person that you share it with." Sincere. That was the word. He was sincere.

"I can't." The reason I had night terrors wasn't just because I could see ghosts. It was also related to posttraumatic stress from the horrible thing I had done. That was my theory, anyway.

"All right." He took a sip of his wine and waited as if he knew I'd tell him when I was ready to, if he just gave me the space to do it. I liked that about him.

"I've never told this to anyone."

"You don't have to tell me anything that you don't want to." Luna inserted herself between his stomach and his wine glass in a smooth move and he lifted a hand to her throat, which caused her motor to start rumbling. "If you ever want to tell me, though, I am happy to listen."

"It's pretty awful."

He nodded his understanding. "I too have done things and had things happen that were disturbing."

I didn't think that I wanted to share it, but he was easy to talk to. The words fell out of my memory without my conscious control. "I was living with my aunt and uncle. It was just supposed to be for a few months while my mother was out of the country. She came to me while I was sleeping. She said she wanted to talk to me, but . . ." I stalled, taking a sip of wine while I figured out how to find the words. "I guess I sensed that something was different."

"What made you think this?"

I thought of the young girl I had been, awakened in the night, my mother sitting next to me. The lamp wasn't on, but she was radiant. Too radiant. I'd pulled away from her.

"She wasn't supposed to be there at all, was she? She was in Central America. And she looked different." She had reached to touch me. I couldn't feel her fingers, though I saw her hand, on top of my arm. "And she felt different."

"Your mother came to you after she died."

I nodded. There wasn't much else to say.

"This isn't uncommon, Anna. Spirits often go to those they love most when they pass. Sometimes, though, there is a pressing reason. Do you know why she came to you?"

"I don't know." My voice was dispassionate. A psychiatrist,

should I ever tell them this story, would diagnose me with any number of syndromes, which would include terms like 'delusional disorder', 'depersonalization disorder', or just plain old psychosis. Maybe
schizophrenia, if I told them the whole story.

"Tell me what happened."

"I touched her. And I released her." There was a long silence.
Respectful, maybe. It was a fucked up thing.

"You had never before touched your gift?"

"No."

"Did you realize what happened?"

"I was so young; I thought it was a nightmare. Then the news
came a few days later." I took another sip of wine as if we were having
a normal conversation. "I didn't understand what I'd done, though.
Not until later."

"Why did she come to you?" He asked again.

"That's it, you see. I don't know. My mother came to me from
the dead, and I released her to wherever it is they go." Tears burned
my eyes, which surprised me. I hadn't thought about this in a very
long time, hadn't realized that it still had the power to affect me.
"Whatever it was that she wanted to tell me, or wanted from me, she
never had the chance to say."

"Perhaps she wanted you to release her."

My head shot up. "What?"

"She knew about you."

"How could she?"

"Your gift, it often runs in families. I suspect she knew." His
voice was gentle. Had one of my parents had this ability? I absorbed
this information and decided I couldn't puzzle through it. I tucked it
away, for another time.

"They died together? Your mother and your father?" He changed
the subject as if he knew I needed space from his last comment.

"No. I never knew him."

"You bore his name?"

"Yes, but other than that. He wasn't involved." When my mother died, he didn't come for me. I had spent too much time when I
was young dreaming that he'd contact me, but he never had. Now
that I was an adult I had no desire to look for him. As far as I was
concerned, he'd been a sperm donor.

"Where was she?"

"Guatemala."

"Doing what?"

"Relief work during the civil war." He might not know much about civil strife within Guatemala in the 70's. Most people didn't. I didn't offer to explain. If he was interested, he could read a history book.

"Where were you?"

"I grew up near here. My mother left me with her sister when she went away."

"She must have loved you, to have made her way to you from such a distance."

My eyes burned again. The conversation was too personal. I didn't know Jed and I had shared too much. Maybe it was a natural reaction to meeting someone with a skill similar to mine, but I had become a little too comfortable with my strange houseguest.

"Where are you from, Jed?" I diverted the conversation. It was a benign question, one that didn't center on the spirit world.

"I am from many places."

I waved that aside. "I meant, where were you born? Where were you raised?" He let the question linger, as one might if they needed additional time to craft a response.

"I was born near the lands of modern day Turkey, but I have not maintained a residence there for some time." It was a strange answer to a straightforward question.

"I've never been there. I hear it's a beautiful place."

"I suppose. When I was there, it was harsh." He made it sound like a long time ago but he couldn't be too much older than I was. I didn't know much about Turkey, though. My studies and work had taken up most of my life and I hadn't traveled much.

"I imagine it could be."

He lifted one shoulder in a light shrug, and the cat took that as an invitation to reposition. He tolerated her with good nature as she circled several times and settled back into a tight ball against his abdomen.

"How did you happen to come to the States?"

"I did not happen upon it. When the time came, I booked passage."

"How did you know it was time?" He leaned back in the chair, relaxed, and I noted that the spirit outside had moved on and I couldn't sense it anymore. I'd almost forgotten about it, but I had a feeling that Jed had been keeping tabs on it the whole time.

"The Council told me it was time for me to find you."

"And how did this Council know where you would find me?"

"They foresaw your death."

"What?" My breath stuck in my throat.

"The truck, Anna. In one version of the future, it killed you."

"The Council came to you in Turkey and sent you to Kansas City to find me because they thought I was going to be run over by a beer truck." I was pleased with the cynicism anchored into my tone.

"Because you had not contacted them they suspected something was wrong. With no other means to find you, they foresaw your death and sent me to you. To protect you."

"How could they predict that I would die?"

"The dead do not see time as the living do. Not all events are sequential."

"Why did they choose you?"

He paused for a moment too long. "They knew I would help them."

"This sounds absurd, Jed."

"Yet you know it to be true, or you would have already sent me from you."

"I don't know it to be true," I protested, but he was right. If I didn't trust him, I wouldn't let him stay.

"Is it less believable than a girl who grows up in Missouri with the ability to banish ghosts to the realm of the dead?"

"I don't know. I've always known about that."

"There are many things we do not understand, but that doesn't make them less real."

That was true. I often wondered what additional scientific truths we would discover; life on other planets, the true beginning of the universe. My eyes drifted closed and I suppressed a yawn. I was too tired to continue this conversation. I had a lot to think about, and we would have time tomorrow.

"I need to go to bed."

"Goodnight, Anna."

When I closed the door to my bedroom he was still sitting in the same position, Luna curled in his lap. I locked the door.

CHAPTER FOUR

I DIDN'T TAKE my medication, not because Jed had asked me not to, but because there was a strange man in my house, and stranger ghosts in the vicinity. The penalty was that my mind raced for so long that it was a shock to wake up and realize I had been asleep. A moment later I heard what had awakened me. A rasping sound, like cats claws on wood. I must have locked Luna in the living room. I rolled over in bed and found the cat pressed next to me and remembered I'd let her in earlier. She was awake and had her head cocked sideways as she listened to the same noise I heard.

Whatever it was scratched along the outside wall of the house. I scrabbled away from the head of the bed that pressed against the exterior wall. It was a ghost. Its malicious focus radiated through the wall and I half fell off my bed. I pulled myself to my feet and tiptoed towards the door. I didn't know if it could sense me the way I sensed it, but I didn't plan to lie in bed while it figured out how to get into my house. It could if it wanted to. The lock clicked in my door as I unlatched it and the scratching stopped. It was listening for me. I slid the door open and fled.

I crashed into something large and solid, with arms that grabbed ahold of me. A petrified shriek emanated from my throat and I tried to pull away from the threat.

"Quiet," Jed hissed in my ear as his arms tightened against my backward motion and I whimpered with relief. When I stopped my struggles he released me.

"It's outside my room," I whispered as I tried to get a grip on the feeling of panic.

"It's not the only one."

Panic sounded pretty good. "What?" I hissed, and listened with that extra sense of mine. He was right. Another form was above us, perhaps on the roof. It was still outside, but that wouldn't last long. It took more than walls to keep a ghost out.

"How'd they find us?" My voice had an edge to it as fear transitioned into anger. Anger was best right now. I'd function better mad than scared.

"Perhaps something followed me." He circled around me and flicked on the lights over the island.

"What are you doing?" I demanded. He shrugged.

"They know we're here. They can see in the dark, but you can't. I see no reason for us to be at a disadvantage."

I didn't argue with him, but I felt less safe in the light. He was right, though. They could see us, though I didn't know how. Did they sense things the same way the living did? Had they retained the ability of the eyes without the central nervous system or the ocular tissue? How they transferred that information into images, I couldn't imagine.

I shook myself out of my scientific reverie. We were in trouble and the fact that the spirit world defied everything that science had trained me to believe possible was irrelevant. I could work on my theories for Discover magazine another time. For now, I needed to figure out how to stay alive.

"Anna. Are you all right?" I looked at Jed and realized I'd backed into the island counter, as if that offered some protection.

"Is there any way to prevent them from getting in?" Now I hoped that he had been telling the truth, that he did have other talents.

"I don't believe so."

"That's not good."

"Anna, you must face them and banish them. If they get away from us, they will bring reinforcements and return again in numbers that may be beyond your strength. It's better if they do come in. We were forewarned, so we're ready to face them."

"You mean me." I heard the icy tone of my voice but didn't do anything to try to alter it. I could look forbidding, and would have as I stood there with my arms crossed and my dark eyes flashing, were it not for the fact that I was in my pajamas and bare feet, with hair still tangled from sleeping.

"I do not have the power to send the dead to the world beyond. That burden is yours alone. I will do all that I can to assist you, and protect you." He bowed to me, a graceful motion that exuded respect. It felt weird. I turned away and realized that we were about to have company.

"The one overhead is coming through the stove venting," I told him, backing away from it as if I expected some evil gas to start pouring out of the hood.

"The other will not be far behind," Jed warned me. "If they don't come in together then you will have to take them as they come."

"I've never done more than one on the same day, and I did that one earlier," I informed him. "Do you have a backup plan?"

"Do you possess an automobile?" He asked.

I laughed a short barking sound. "That's your backup plan?"

He put a hand on my arm. "Don't use all of your energy on the first one, Anna. You just have to banish it to the next world, not the next universe."

"I don't know that this is something I have any control over." I sensed the presence in my stove venting growing closer. It would be in the kitchen with us in moments.

"You have the ability. You must learn to use it."

"How?"

"I'm not sure how to explain it, Anna. I didn't anticipate that you would be so untrained." He edged away from the stove so that I had a clear path to it.

"Very helpful, Jed."

I moved past him and placed my hands on the metal hood. The ghost was still in there. Maybe it wasn't able to pass through metal, but it could go through the conduit. I forced myself to put aside the metaphysical questions and opened myself to the fire within me, prepared to set it free. I imagined the burst of energy coursing through the metal of the hood, trapping the spirit encased inside. I took a deep breath and braced myself for the pain.

"I release you," I cried as the energy exploded out of me and the burning routed through me. It set fire to every cell in my body. The energy rattled upwards through the stove vent and the cabinetry like a wide-spread net. The metal hood of the stove shook as if I'd hit it with a sledgehammer and the house alarm glass break sensor sounded in response to the noise.

"Well done." Jed grabbed me and hauled me out of the kitchen.

His touch amplified my pain. "Stay with me, Anna. The next one is upon us." I didn't know how it had come in, but I saw it too. Parts of it were just as real as any living being. Its skeletal thin hands clawed forward, reaching from a half-formed body. The faceless head was opaque and blurred as if it hadn't enough energy to solidify its entire form. Legs disappeared into a gray haze below its knees.

I couldn't guess what power moved it forwards. Its bony hand plucked a butcher knife from the wooden block on the counter with the ease of a practiced chef and I realized it meant to kill us.

Jedediah thrust me behind him and propelled us both away from the sharp blade. "Anna, are you ready?"

I still burned from the energy of the first two releases. I'd never tried to do another one so soon. Could I do three in less than a day? I eyed the advancing kitchen knife and wished I hadn't felt compelled to buy the best cutlery I could find. The thought of my Shun carbon-steel blades being used to carve my own flesh made me cringe.

"I'll try."

Jed edged us towards the guestroom, keeping about twenty feet between us and the ghost. I wondered how quick this one was. I'd seen some that could move as fast as a horse can run.

Jedediah reached into the bathroom, pulled a broom out, and brandished it in front of him. The spirit paused as if it had to take a breath, and then leaped for him. Jed pushed us both back until we were at the end of the hallway. I opened myself up, searching for the power to release another soul, and didn't find it at the ready.

Jed swung the handle of the broom like a sword and it caught the spirits hand. The knife clattered to the floor. The ghost hissed and lashed out at him. Jed knocked its hand away with the broom and blocked me from it. I'd never seen a broom handle used for defense, but Jed seemed pretty handy with it.

As if the ghost recognized the futility of fighting Jed and his broom, the hands lost their clear definition. The loss of form didn't stop it from sweeping the knife off the floor, but the one swipe Jed took at it resulted in the handle getting stuck for a moment in the ghost's substance, which had changed into a thick, nebulous mass.

When Jed pulled free of it, the ghost held the blade again, well away from the broom handle that Jed twirled like a character straight out of a martial arts movie.

The knife slashed out and Jed slid backward, just out of range. I pressed hard against the wall, groaning as my skin burned with the contact. We were trapped. How long Jed could hold off a spirit with this determination I didn't know. I wasn't used to being protected. Maybe I'd been alone too long to like it.

I focused on my second sight. It was hard to see through the screaming siren of the alarm. I centered myself and ignored the noise until all I could see was the essence of the spirit as it swirled before me. I could see Jed's too, though not as well. I had never been able to see the living this way, but maybe the frequent use of my sixth sense in the last twelve hours had amplified my abilities. I concentrated on the power within me. I collected it and gathered it into an imaginary ball of fire. I held it in my hands while it scorched my skin. When I had enough of it, I threw it and Jed leaped out of the way.

"By Christ, woman. Be careful who you direct that at!" He picked himself up off the bathroom floor as if I'd knocked him in there. The strands of my power, that glowing net of energy, enshrouded the spirit. My kitchen knife fell again to the floor as the ghost lost form. The spirit screamed as if it burned as much as I did. The grating sound of its cry was audible above the shrieking of the alarm. It was the first noise it had made, and the sound was too human. I shivered as nausea ran through me.

"Are you well?" Jed's voice surfaced somewhere over me and the light darkened. I was in his shadow, slumped on the floor against the wall. I didn't recall sitting down. "Anna." He sounded troubled. "There are sirens approaching. This noise that your house makes. Your neighbors may have contacted the authorities."

Ah. The alarm.

"Anna. I'm not sure what they will think if the police find you sitting here on the floor. Can you get up?" He didn't wait for an answer but hauled me to my feet. He dragged me to a stool at the bar, through the spot where the spirit had been. The golden shreds of my power lingered on the floor, and when he drug me through them they coalesced on my toes, drenching them in yellow. I watched, mesmerized by the golden strands that reabsorbed into my skin, restoring some of my energy to me.

"Anna. The alarm." Jed's voice was filled with urgency.

"There's a panel next to the door." My tone was sluggish and I had to focus to get the words out. "Seven-zero-nine-one." I sank my head onto my arms while he went to the front door. After a brief delay, the shrieking stopped, but the sirens outside continued. They were close.

If the cops found me half unconscious, they'd assume this was a domestic dispute, and Jed would spend the night in jail while I spent the rest of the night alone. I shivered. Alone did not sound good right now. My butcher knife still lay on the floor next to the wall in the hallway. I spared a moment to hope that the blade hadn't been damaged during the broom handle fight and then realized that a large knife on the floor would be difficult to explain.

I slipped off the stool and clutched the one next to it as my legs shook. Jed watched through the windows with apprehension. The police sirens wailed one last time and then stopped. My living room was filled with flashes of red and blue light. They would be at the front door soon.

My legs were not cooperating. I crawled across the floor and reached the knife as Jed unlocked the front door.

"Anna," he warned me.

I skittered back to the kitchen like a crab and hauled myself up on the cabinets, sliding the knife back into the butcher's block as the door clicked open. I needed to be sitting down. I wasn't.

Jed let the police in and murmured apologies and excuses that I couldn't quite hear. There were two of them. I made my way around the corner and braced myself between two chairs. I forced myself to smile.

They were about the same age as I was—mid to late thirties. One was a tall African American man with a lanky gait while the other was a thickset redhead who'd be downright portly in a few more years.

"Is everything all right, ma'am?" The tall one spoke first.

"Officers. I'm so sorry for the disturbance. There must be something wrong with the alarm system." The short one was giving me a good looking over. I was sure that I didn't look my best but I didn't think I had any bruises. "Nothing is wrong. I'm sorry for the disturbance," I said, and then realized that it sounded weird to keep saying that.

"Do you mind if we have a look around, to be sure?" He asked and I forced a smile.

"No, of course not." One of them pointed towards my bedroom and I nodded my permission. The other helped himself to a tour of the guest room. Jedediah joined me and lifted me into the stool in one neat motion while they weren't looking. I figured they'd tag team us when they returned, and I wasn't wrong.

"Sir, would you step outside with me for a moment?" The tall officer was polite, but he and his partner were both standing within a foot of Jedediah, just in case he offered resistance.

He looked surprised and glanced at me, as if for permission. I nodded for him. "Of course he will."

Jed looked down at his bare feet. "May I?"

"Please." The officer told him, but he followed Jed to the guest room and watched him put his shoes on. They weren't going to give him the opportunity to find a weapon. I didn't blame them. Police business could be dangerous and Jed was a formidable looking man.

The tall officer followed Jed outside and the door closed. The chubby man shifted in front of me. "Is everything all right, ma'am?" He sounded concerned and it was easy to smile at him.

"Yes, everything is fine, Officer . . ." I squinted at his badge.

"Johnson," he informed me.

"Officer Johnson. I'm not sure what set the alarm off."

"Your name, ma'am?"

"Dr. Anna Roberts."

"You run the clinic on Main." It was a statement, not a question.

"Yes, I do." That knowledge changed what he thought of me, I could see. I wasn't some suburb girl who'd decided it would be neat to live in the city and would be gone again in a year or two. I was a respected member of the local community.

"And your husband is?"

"He's not my husband, Officer Johnson, he's just a friend."

"Where does your friend live, Dr. Roberts?"

"He's visiting from out of town." An evasive answer.

"Dr. Roberts, were you already up when the alarm activated?" He asked.

"I'm a bit of an insomniac." Another evasive response. I hoped he didn't notice.

"Were you and the gentleman having a disagreement?"

"No, we weren't."

He was silent for a moment, and I could see he didn't believe me. "We can protect you if you need help."

I gave him my 'doctor' look. "I appreciate your assistance, Officer Johnson. I'm sorry that my alarm malfunction caused you to drive over here. As you can see, however, everything is fine. Can I offer you a cup of coffee before you go?"

His partner cracked the front door open and glanced in. Johnson shook his head, an apparent signal that there was no trouble to be had, because the door widened and Jedediah was allowed back in.

"No thank you, ma'am . . . I mean Dr. Roberts. Here's my card. If you need us, just call." He handed me the slip of white paper with a pointed look at Jed. "You have a good night." He moved towards the door with some reluctance.

Jed let them out and slid the deadbolt home as soon as the door closed. I laid my head on my arms, relaxed my upper body weight onto the granite, and started giggling. A husky chuckling joined me and I looked up to see Jed, face transformed by his laughter.

I sucked in a breath to steady myself. "Why are you laughing?"

"Because you are." I liked how his eyes twinkled.

"You have some crazy skills with the broom handle."

He gave me a wry smile before he turned to open the refrigerator door. A moment later a glass of orange juice appeared in front of me. The burning sensation had settled into my bones as if it belonged there and I felt shaky.

"Drink."

"Thank you." I drank the juice with gratitude but I wasn't going to let my need for calories derail my interrogation. "How did you learn how to do that? Did you grow up taking martial arts classes?"

"Martial arts?" He shook his head with a bemused smile. "Sword fighting."

"Sword fighting?" That was a new one. "Like fencing?"

"Fencing is with those long skinny bits of metal." He gestured with his hands and I giggled again. "I grew up using a sword with a much larger blade."

"Is that a common sport where you grew up?" I grasped for control over my inappropriate laughter as Jed's mirth subsided.

"It wasn't sport, it was for protection."

"Wow." That was hardcore. "I didn't know anyone still used swords."

"I was living in a harsher area, at the time." It was a sobering reminder of how lucky I was.

"We have to leave, don't we?" I heard my voice quiver.

Jed leaned back against the counter, arms crossed across his chest, black eyes considered my statement and assessed my condition.

"We do."

"How long will it be before it's safe to come back here?" I asked.

Jed shook his head. "Of that, I'm not sure."

I contemplated the options. I hadn't seen a ghost in ages, yet there had been three now, in the last eight hours. Mean ones. Jed's arrival couldn't be coincidental, but thus far his actions had all been helpful. He'd saved my life last night, and put himself between me and a knife wielding apparition a few minutes ago.

I looked him over, how he leaned one hip against the black stone of my counter. His pose should have made him look relaxed, but to me, he looked taut, alert. Ready for whatever came next. I didn't feel responsible for him. I felt safer with him.

"There's a blue cooler in the garage. Can you bring it in for me?" From Jed's expression, I guessed that it wasn't what he had expected me to say but he turned and headed for the garage door.

CHAPTER FIVE

JED MUSCLED THE COOLER into the back end of my SUV and then started stacking in the bags that I had packed. "We need to make a stop on our way," he informed me.

I rested against the side of the car, still shaking from our latest encounter. Packing the contents of my fridge and then gathering enough clothes for a few days away felt like more than I could take. "Where at?"

"The Intercontinental. Are you familiar with it?"

My eyebrows rose. It was the most expensive hotel in town. "Of course. Why do you want to stop there?"

"I have some things there I would like to pick up."

"You have a room at the Intercontinental." I knew that disbelief showed on my face loud and clear.

He stepped back from the car and met my eyes. "Yes."

"You told me you were homeless."

"I did not." He ran a hand through his thick hair and sighed. "I did allow you to . . . make certain assumptions."

"You lied to me." I was angry without being certain why. It was obvious he was more than just a random homeless stranger, but the deception that he needed my assistance set me off.

"I misled you, I admit." He lifted his hands, palm side up. "I have told you nothing that is not true."

"I took you into my home."

"You are very generous."

"I trusted you." My voice squeaked in indignation.

"I did tell you I would be all right without your assistance." He paused and then bowed his head to me. "I apologize for taking advantage of your kindness."

I felt my eyes narrow into slits as I tried to determine if he was just apologizing to placate me. If so, it was just going to make me angrier. Jed glanced into the shadows of the garage as if he was check-ing to see if danger lurked there. It reminded me that we were trying to escape before anything else found us. When he spoke again, his voice was filled with the conflict he faced.

"You should have recognized me, Anna, from your dreams. But you didn't. If I had told you the truth you would have sent me away. I have to be close to you in order to protect you."

"You aren't doing a very good job," I pointed out. "I've been attacked twice since I met you, and you say that more ghosts are hunting me."

"You still live. I can't protect you here. It's better if we leave."

"You think I'm going to take you with me now that I know you've been lying to me?"

"Anna, please. Let me help you." He sounded tired. I wasn't the only one who hadn't gotten much sleep. "If you try to fight these spirits without me, your chances of success diminish."

I laid my head back against the cold car and closed my eyes. My body still burned and the cold window against my scalp felt good.

"I can help you escape." I didn't respond. "If you want me to leave, after I get you to safety, I will respect your wishes." He turned away from me, eyes straining in the dark to catch sight of danger.

Does his sixth sense feel the same way mine does? Why do the men I trust always wind up lying to me? I banged my head back against the car in frustration, though I knew I'd made my decision.

"Let's get the rest of the stuff."

He breathed out in a rush, as if relieved. I brushed past him, into the house. I wasn't done being mad. It would take me a while to let this go.

I coaxed Luna into her cat carrier while the not-so-homeless man loaded the rest of my bags and the sacks of non-perishable gro-ceries that I'd packed up. Luna's crate got strapped into a seatbelt in the backseat and I set the alarm on the house and stepped back into the garage. I'd never left before without knowing when I would re-turn. It unsettled me.

"Would you like me to drive?" Jed asked and my anger flared again.

He presumed too much and I let the cold tone of my voice let him know what I thought about it. "No, thank you."

"Anna." He sounded as if *I* was trying *his* patience. "You are exhausted. Let me drive. You can sleep for a bit."

Sleep! My body cheered at the suggestion, but I wasn't ready to back down. "I don't need your help."

It looked like he wanted to argue with me more but was afraid of what I might do if he pushed me too far. He nodded and held the driver's door open for me.

The cat complained when the car started moving but quieted by the time we'd driven the two miles to Jed's hotel and pulled into the circle drive.

"I'll just be a few minutes. Thank you, for waiting."

I didn't respond. I wanted him to wonder if I'd still be there when he came back down. He stepped out and the door closed, leaving me alone with my petty silence.

Jed disappeared into the hotel through the revolving door. I hit the automatic door locks, as if locked doors would offer protection from ghosts. I'd seen one dematerialize and come through the cracks around a steel door once. I reminded myself that there were other reasons to lock the doors. The living could be dangerous too.

I could drive away. I pondered this thought. Jed didn't need my help, and he'd misled me, at least about being homeless. The extreme cold and the dangers that befell the homeless were the reasons I'd taken him in. That, and because he saved my life. He had a room at the Intercontinental. I probably couldn't afford a room there if I wanted one.

As it happened, I believed him. At least a little bit. I didn't run into spirits very often, and few of those were malevolent. To have had three encounters in one day added credibility to his strange story. Something was going on.

My thoughts swirled. It was difficult to sift through the myriad of thoughts bombarding me. Jed's arrival seemed too convenient. It was possible that he was the one who had gotten the ghosts to come after me. If he wanted me dead, though, why had he saved me from the truck in the first place? I closed my eyes and dozed while my mind swirled through the possibilities. A tap on the window startled me awake.

Jed stood outside with two large suitcases and a laptop bag slung over his shoulder. Unbelievable. I had been planning to take him shopping for clothes. I hit the button to open the hatch with more force than was necessary. When he'd loaded his bags I opened the driver's door, adjusted the seat all the way back to accommodate his height and scooted over the gearshift into the passenger seat. If I was too tired to stay awake for ten minutes, I shouldn't be driving at all.

Jed climbed into the driver's seat with a wary look as if he expected a poisonous snake to greet him. "Have you given thought to a destination?"

"Yes. I have a plan." I didn't volunteer additional information. He stared at me for a moment and then engaged the gear without asking.

"We should stay off the highway." He pulled out onto the street.

I groaned in protest. "Why?"

"They may be looking for us on the major roadways. It would be easier for them to follow us on the highway."

"How? A ghost can't move as fast as a car." I'd seen them go as fast as a horse could run, but not as fast as a car.

"They could join another vehicle traveling the same direction."

He stopped for a red light while I let that information sink in.

"That would be some pretty sophisticated cognition." My voice was flat.

"Yes," he responded as if that went without saying. "If we are on back roads there is less likelihood that one of these tracking spirits will be able to find a vehicle traveling in the same direction."

"A tracking spirit?"

He glanced at me. "Like a ghost that's part bloodhound."

"It will take a lot longer to get there if we aren't on the highway."

"I am capable of driving for as long as is needed."

I said nothing but admitted to myself that he'd bear the brunt of it. I felt feverish and I was exhausted. I'd released three spirits in the space of about twelve hours, and I felt every one of them.

I used the next red light to adjust my navigation system so that it would avoid highways, and plugged in the destination from my favorites list. The farm. My GPS informed me that it would take three hours and twenty-seven minutes to get there. How helpful.

It started to snow. Thick flakes coated the windshield and created a dizzying blur of white as the headlights reflected off them. Jed slowed his speed as the roads grew slick. I was grateful for all wheel drive. A trip that shouldn't take longer than two hours would be a little lengthier, thanks to the weather and the off-highway route.

"Are you comfortable driving in the snow?" I asked.

"I am. I lived in Switzerland for a time."

"Oh." It seemed strange that he hadn't mentioned that sooner, but we hadn't shared our life stories yet. There wasn't much to tell about mine, but it seemed like Jed had been all over the world.

"Who are you, Jed?" Even though I was tired, I had questions, and we had time.

"I will explain everything to you, Anna. You should have known all of this. Since you don't . . ." He glanced over at me. "It's complex. I'd rather explain it to you when we can sit down together and talk about it." That seemed reasonable. I had more questions, but they could wait. "You should sleep, Anna."

"Maybe I will," I mumbled.

"Your car will tell me where to go?"

"Yeah." I turned the volume up on the navigation system so he could follow it. "If you have any trouble, just wake me up," I ordered. I wrapped my coat over myself and angled my seat back.

When I woke we had gone around ninety miles in two and a half hours. It was four fifteen in the morning and at this rate, it seemed like we'd never make it there. "Do you think we're far enough away from the city to risk the Interstate?" The snow had slowed, but the secondary roads looked like they were in terrible condition. I hoped that the highway was in better shape. It might not be this far from the city.

"It should be safe." His answer came after some contemplation. "I don't believe that they could have guessed we would leave town, or that we would travel this direction."

"Then take the next left." The navigation system squawked at him to turn around and I silenced it. Street lights gleamed near the freeway and the snow turned red when it drifted down in front of a Conoco sign. "Turn in here."

I needed food even more than I needed sleep. This truck stop served breakfast and was open twenty-four hours a day. Their pancakes were pretty good.

"I have to eat," I told Jed while he parked my Forester.

I stepped out of the vehicle and groaned as my legs protested the change in position. Jed was by my side in seconds. "May I help you?"

"I'm fine," I growled at him, even though I knew it wasn't true.

He stepped back and measured the sky while he ignored my bad manners with grace. "I do not sense the presence of anything unusual."

I forced myself to lighten up a notch. "Me either." I'd checked as soon as I woke up and felt nothing. The feeling of being pursued stayed with me, though. I hoped I was just being paranoid.

We settled into a cracked faux leather booth with a view of the car, and a yawning fifty-ish waitress brought us black coffee. It had been sitting in the pot long enough that it was bitter. I wrinkled my nose and added two packets of sugar and a packet of creamer. A Starbucks would have been a welcome sight. I would've even been grateful for a cup of Jedediah's Turkish coffee. There wasn't a decent coffee shop until Des Moines, though, which was a fair bit out of our way.

I dug through my bag until I found a small bottle of anti-inflammatory tablets and downed two with the cup of coffee. Jed watched me but I ignored him. I studied the menu with critical detail and decided on pancakes with bacon and eggs.

"Anna," Jed started and I looked up at him. "I understand why you're angry with me." Our waitress took a step towards our table with a look of unmistakable interest. I wasn't planning on being fodder for her entertainment, or of having this conversation with Jedediah.

I motioned to the waitress. "We're ready to order."

She peered over us, pen clasped between three fingers. "What can I get you, hon?"

I was pretty sure the 'hon' hadn't been directed towards me, and ignored it. "I'll have the Big Breakfast with buttermilk pancakes, scrambled eggs, and bacon."

"Do you want toast with that?" Her smile displayed tobacco stained teeth in need of dental care. A black pin on her apron informed me that her name was Doris.

"No. But I'll have a large orange juice, please."

"Sure thing, hon." I cringed as she turned her full attention on my companion. He ordered the steak and eggs, which I had to admit sounded pretty good, although this wouldn't be the place I'd choose to order it. Jed got a big smile from Doris and she lingered for too long after he ordered, while she double and triple checked to see if he needed anything else. In catty fashion, I critiqued her bright blue eye shadow and shabby fake nails while she fussed over Jedediah. Not that I could blame her. It was with obvious reluctance that she left to turn our order in.

"I owe you an apology, Anna. It was wrong of me to let you think that I-"

"I am way too tired to talk about this right now," I interrupted him. I knew I sounded curt but I couldn't bring myself to be polite. I was still mad.

"Of course," He acquiesced and bowed his head in his odd manner. Doris, who seemed to have a keen sense for when we were beginning an interesting conversation, arrived with my orange juice. It had the bitter aftertaste that characterizes 'from concentrate' juice but that didn't stop me from chugging half of it.

"May I ask where we're going?" From his expression, I didn't think he expected me to tell him. I didn't want to be predictable.

"I have a place in the country. A bit farther North." Given that he'd been stalking me, I was a little surprised he didn't know about it.

"The farm."

"Yes. It was my aunt and uncle's place. They didn't have kids of their own, so the property came to me when they died."

"You spent your childhood at this place?"

This wasn't information I shared with random people, but I'd fought ghosts with this man. "Yes. They adopted me after my mother died."

"Why do you live in the city? Don't they need doctors near your farm as well?"

They did, of course. I'd been asked several times to set up a practice in town. Maybe someday I would, but I didn't think so. There were too many painful memories associated with the farm to live there all the time.

"I find my current practice location very rewarding," I informed him. It was my standard answer. He didn't need to know the truth about why I stayed in the city.

His polite smile didn't quite extend to his dark eyes. They evaluated me with a somber stare that was disconcerting. "I'm sure it is."

Doris placed two large platters in front of me, and Jed's expression switched to one of frank amusement. I'd ordered way more food than I could eat. I gave him a rueful smile as I tried to decide which plate to tackle first. The pancakes won.

Thirty-five minutes later I was back in the driver's seat, both hands on the steering wheel. The snow had abated, but that didn't mean the roads were clear.

The sky was just starting to lighten when I turned down the familiar gravel lane that led to the farmhouse. It had taken a long while to think of it as mine, though it had been years since my aunt and uncle died.

We passed a well-kept farmstead with a large house, a series of barns, and neat sheds.

Jed glanced over at me. "Who lives there?"

"It's the Joules' place. They farm my land as well." I hoped that Jed didn't notice the strain in my voice. I saw the curtains rustle in the front window and knew our arrival hadn't gone unnoticed.

Since I always texted him before I came to stay, Ned Joules would be by later to see why I was here. We'd grown up together and had a complicated history. I didn't know yet what I would tell him.

The Subaru slipped up a steep ice covered hill while I adjusted the vehicle's position to get more traction.

We couldn't see much of it in the pre-dawn light, but after the hill, the land flattened out into a wide valley edged with trees and filled with fertile fields. A creek bed drifted through the middle of it, sprouting cottonwoods and towering oaks. The drive crossed it twice on flat wooden bridges. I'd thought about changing the location of the road because of how often the creek flooded when it rained, but it was picturesque.

The drive ended in a loop in front of an aged brick farmhouse tucked into the edge of the trees. Stone pillars framed the front porch and held up the second story. A quaint sitting area complete with porch swing and planting boxes nestled between the pillars. In the summer, I filled the boxes with pink and red impatiens and drank iced tea on the porch. A large pond filled the space between the house and the hill on the far side. Tucked behind the house, a small wood barn completed the pastoral picture.

I parked in my usual spot in front of the porch, fumbled in my bag for the house keys, and grabbed Luna's carrier from the backseat. The sudden motion caused her to voice a complaint. "It's all right, baby, we're here," I crooned and she quieted.

I jiggled the key in the lock and stepped inside. Jed followed me in with the cooler.

"You can put it in the kitchen." I pointed towards the back of the house. I set Luna's carrier down in the sitting room and opted to leave her in it until we'd unloaded the car. I found the thermostat and turned the heat up. It wouldn't take too long for the radiators to warm the house.

Jed brought in the luggage. I noted that the bags he'd picked up at the Intercontinental were expensive and looked brand new. I'd packed a small duffel bag and a shabby old suitcase that he set on the floor in the entryway with the same care as his own luggage. He shut the door with a firm thud and we stared at one another.

"Well, this is the house," I explained after an awkward silence. I waved to the right, where a tidy sitting room led to a small bookshelf-lined study. "That's the parlor and library. You've seen the kitchen." I didn't point out the dining room as it was self-explanatory. A large formal table would seat twelve in a pinch, and a beautifully built-in china cabinet and buffet lined one wall. The other wall opened onto the sun porch, my favorite room in the house.

"The bedrooms are upstairs," I informed him. I let Luna out of her carrier and slid the bolt home on the front door. When I was growing up we never locked the door, but I'd been living alone in the city long enough that I was more comfortable with the doors locked. Ned had keys, but he wouldn't enter the house uninvited with me there.

Luna led the way up the stairs, her meow a plaintive moan. I grabbed my bags over Jedediah's protestations and followed her. There were four doorways in the small corridor. I paused and made a quick decision about where to put Jed. "This is your room," I informed him as I paused at the first doorway on the right. "The sheets on the bed are clean." Ty and Chaz had come to stay a few days with me over Christmas, and I'd put clean sheets on the bed after they left. It was a simple room with a queen size bed and an old family quilt covering it. An heirloom rocking chair rested in one corner, and a wooden dresser sat in the other. A faded throw rug that had been hand knit by my great grandmother graced the hardwood floor.

"Your bathroom is across the hall," I told him and headed down to my room at the end of the hallway. The master bedroom had of course been my aunt and uncle's. They'd favored striped wallpaper, but after they passed on I'd stripped it down to the plaster and painted it the color of a latte. The creamy brown contrasted with the dark wood and made for a homey bedroom. My pride and joy sleigh bed was tucked into a slight recess in the eaves; the ceiling sloped down over it so that a tall man couldn't stand up straight at the head of the bed. I'd had to buff out the marks that Eric had made where he hit his head on the ceiling. The room beyond the bed housed the master bath.

A soft knock on the door alerted me to Jed's presence. I opened the door. "Yes?"

"Will you be resting for a while?"

I nodded. "Yes, I need more sleep. If you aren't tired, though, make yourself at home downstairs. There's food in the kitchen, coffee . . ."

He shook his head. "No. I too would prefer to rest. If you do not require anything further of me?"

I smiled in spite of myself. "No. I'm fine. Goodnight."

"Goodnight," He reiterated, despite the fact that it was after five-thirty in the morning. I left the door open enough for the cat to get in and sighed. I had a few phone calls to make before I could sleep again.

I crawled under the covers and turned on the heating blanket before I called Rita. I explained that something had come up and that I'd had to leave town. I didn't tell her where I'd gone and didn't give too many specifics despite a bevy of questions from her. We had a long-standing relationship with the local family practice residency program. They would cover the clinic while I was gone.

I slid my sweatpants off and crawled back under the covers. The heating blanket was doing its thing, so even my feet felt warm. The heat might help my aching subside. Now that the burning was over with, I was sore. I pulled a spare pillow over my head so I couldn't see the daylight and let sleep overtake me.

"Silly girl." The woman's voice was full of derision.

"I'm not a girl, and I'm not silly." My protest fell flat as if I was a whining teenager. It didn't matter, she ignored the fact that I had spoken.

"The Master will find you, darling."

"Who is that?"

"You'll know him." Her tone dipped low and ominous.

I shivered in response. "Are you with the Council?" I asked. She laughed.

"Oh, sweet child. It's too late for you." I tried to turn away from her but she grabbed my arm with a bony hand. "The Council is made of fools. They can't help you."

"Let go of me." I tried to shake her loose but she gripped tighter so that her hand felt like an iron shackle that was compressing.

"Shall I tell him where you are?" She leaned close so I could smell the scent of death in her breath.

"Go to hell." I reached for my power but it wouldn't respond.

She forced me to my knees while she laughed at me. "I'm going to enjoy watching him consume you." She released me and disappeared in a swirl of pale blue silk.

CHAPTER SIX

I WOKE IN A RUSH of fear. My sixth sense showed me nothing, and the house was silent. Jed must still be asleep. I threw open a curtain to banish the remains of my nightmare and smiled at the sight of the pond, covered in ice. It had been frozen solid over the holidays, and there hadn't been but two days above freezing since. The thermometer showed that at present it was twenty-three degrees Fahrenheit. The pond didn't appear to have much snow on it, so the ice should be fine.

The sky was gray, but it tended to be overcast January through March. It looked like it might snow again. If I was in town, I'd check the weather on the internet, but I tried to keep my farmhouse technology free. No Wi-fi, no cable, no television. My mobile never worked because we were so far from the nearest cell phone tower. I found it freeing. The landline was the sole bit of modern convenience, though I did have a weather radio that came to life if there was a tornado in the area.

After pulling on long underwear, an old pair of Levis and wool boot socks I tiptoed past Jed's door and made my way down the stairs. I avoided the squeaky spots with the expertise of a teenager sneaking out. In the kitchen, I paused long enough to pour Luna a bowl of food and start the coffee pot. The mudroom, off the back of the kitchen, was well stocked with winter gear. I found a Polartec sweatshirt, my red wind-stopper shell, warm gloves and a black wool cap. I slipped my feet into warm boots that came up to my knees and slung my skates over my shoulder. The snow was up to mid-calf around the house, but the wind had blown the pond bare. It took a minute to dust off a log bench by the shore in order to change my shoes. From there it was two steps and I was on ice.

I skated a few cautious rounds, hugging the shoreline while I tested the ice to see if it was as solid as it had been at Christmas. It seemed sure. The pond had frozen before the holidays in a quick thick freeze and the ice wasn't at all milky, just clear and smooth. There were some winters where I didn't get to skate at all, but this winter had been cold enough.

As I grew more confident, I increased my speed and crisscrossed the pond in a brisk series of figure eights. My muscles began to warm up, and I fell into a smooth tempo as I circled the ice. My outside foot crossed over the inside to maintain speed on the turns, a move that had been tricky to learn. The ice was smooth, and the morning was quiet, still, and glistening with fresh snow. A squirrel leaped into a snow bank as I swept past, digging for the remnants of fall acorns. I giggled at the sight of his bushy gray tail twitching as it jutted out of the pristine powder.

The blade of my right foot caught on the left as I skated around the curve and I went down in an ignominious pile. I grunted and took stock for a moment. Nothing broken, maybe not even bruised. Just damaged pride. I hauled myself back upright and started again, more careful this time as I settled back into the turn. I skated away from the edge, headed the long ways across the ice. A quick twist of my body turned me around so I glided backward. The motion of skating backward relaxed into a hypnotizing rhythm. Sometimes I felt the movement when I was lying in bed, moments before falling asleep.

Brush snapped and alerted me to the approaching animal. I swiveled around so I was skating frontwards again and saw the horse and rider make their way to the edge of the pond. I passed them by and then took a large loop back, slowing to drift into line alongside them. The horse eyed me with the snorting concern of an animal looking for an excuse to cause trouble though he knew well none existed.

"Anna." The rider greeted me, touching his hand to his hat. If it was a cowboy hat he'd have tipped it, but it was a winter cap. Somehow the gesture didn't lose its efficacy despite the lack of brim.

"Good morning, Ned. How are you?" He shifted in the saddle and peered down at me. He looked good, but I always thought Ned looked good.

"I'm well, Anna. Saw you came in early. Thought I'd come by, make sure everything's okay." His voice was a calm baritone, as familiar and comforting to me as the house, the farm.

I drifted ahead of them, crossing my left leg over my right and turned a sharp circle so that I came back to the same spot next to him. I was skating faster than the horse walked through the snow. "Everything's fine." I hoped he wouldn't catch the lie.

"That's good, then," He looked away from me as if there was something on the evergreen covered hillside that interested him. "You've always called first. When you're coming." He paused and glanced at me. I kept my head up, watching the coming turn. I didn't want to go down again, not in front of Ned. "We'd have turned the heat up, plowed the drive, had the place a bit more welcoming for you."

"I know. Sorry for surprising you, but I didn't want you to go to any trouble." I put some pressure into my strokes and scooted away from him, crossing the stretch of ice to where my boots were. We knew each other well enough to know he'd end up there. I didn't want his green broke stud blowing steam down the back of my neck while I changed my shoes. I had the boots on by the time they walked up.

I didn't have a ready excuse for why we'd come in the middle of the night. If I were more creative, I could have come up with some sort of story, but I'd always been bad at lying. Not that it was any of his business, I reminded myself. This was my property, not his. I glanced towards the house and saw the back door open. Jed stood in the doorway.

"You have company," Ned remarked. The surprised tone of voice offended me. It wasn't like I never brought anyone with me. It just wasn't often.

"Yes." I heard the sharp edge to my voice but knew Ned would ignore it. "Would you like a cup of coffee?" I offered in a more welcoming tone. It would be rude not to have him in.

"Don't want to impose," he drawled as he leaned back into the saddle like he'd been born to it. He had. So had I, though I didn't ride that much anymore.

I tied the laces of my skates together, slung them back across my shoulder, and headed for the house. We both knew he would follow. The invitation was an act we followed. His protestation was a formality. "It's not an imposition."

"Then I accept." He wouldn't have dreamed of staying away, and

I knew it. Curiosity was killing him, which gave me some satisfaction. "I'll just put Demon in the barn." I nodded my assent.

The barn had two large stalls that Ned kept in good condition. If I was here for any time at all, I could bring one of his horses up for my use, and he always had a ready spot for his.

Jedediah held the door open for me and I walked through while I tried to not brush against his large frame in the tight space. It didn't work. I looked up as my chest touched his. Damp hair that hung in loose clumps of curls showed that he had showered, and his face was clean-shaven. I breathed in an aromatic blend of clove, citrus, and woods. He smelled good. Very good. His eyes stood out against that olive complexion and they were full of regard. For me? My heart sped up and my breath caught in the back of my throat.

I stepped past him into the mudroom and forced myself to breathe as I turned back towards him. I couldn't help but look down too. His designer jeans looked like they'd been custom made for him and they were paired with a thin black v-neck sweater that looked an awful lot like cashmere. I could see the cleft between his collarbones at the base of his throat and wondered if he tasted as good as he smelled.

"You're very good." His words jolted me back.

"Pardon me?"

He gestured to the pond. "I was watching you. You're a very good skater."

I forced myself to regroup. "No better than any other kid in a cold climate raised on a pond. But it's fun." I shrugged out of my coat and pulled off the hoodie that now seemed to be sticking to me. It wasn't the warm air of the house that had me sweating, nor the exertion of exercise. I hoped that he hadn't seen me fall. "You didn't sleep long."

"Nor did you."

I traded the boots for house shoes and headed for the coffee pot. I needed some space to get over my momentary bought of lust. "I suppose not."

I got down three large mugs and poured one full of coffee as the back door opened and closed again. I set the full mug at the end of the counter and then poured the next one three-fourths full. "Jed, I'll let you fix your own."

Ned stepped into the kitchen, sock-footed and dressed in faded blue jeans and a brown zip neck sweatshirt. Light brown hair was tousled from his cap. He carried a carton of eggs under one arm. I could see he hadn't bothered to shave and the stubble added to his rugged appearance. Ned was handsome enough to be a model for high-end mail order catalogs and too much of a farm boy to have ever thought about another vocation. He snagged the mug off the end of the counter.

"Thanks, Anna." He evaluated Jed for one moment and then held his hand out. "Ned Joules."

Jed stepped forward to shake hands. "Jedediah Peters." It looked like they were taking each other's measure, and I wondered if a pissing contest would follow. I busied myself with milk and sugar in order to keep from laughing out loud at the mental image.

"What happened to your face?"

"A youth thought to rob me. He had a knife."

"Looks like he used it." Ned had his country boy grin on. It made me nervous. He didn't tend to try this hard and I wondered what he was up to.

"Yes. It did not end well for him." Jedediah postured against the counter, acting as if he belonged there.

Ned set the eggs on the counter and sank into his usual chair at the small table, the one across from my place. He asserted his own claim, one earned through familiarity. He'd eaten almost as many meals there as I had when we were growing up. His light brown eyes fixed on me.

"I was concerned when I saw you come in at such an odd hour."

"It was a last minute decision." I tried to sound nonchalant.

"Everything all right?" He took a sip of his coffee but never stopped looking at me. I ignored the wistful longing I felt whenever I saw Ned. Too much of me still wished it had been me that he'd wanted to marry.

"Yeah, fine." I gave him a smile as I stood at the head of the table and clutched my coffee cup as though it had the power to save me.

"We were going to stay in the city, but then Anna told me how beautiful it is on the farm when it snows." Jedediah slid into the chair closest to me and I tried not to flinch.

"So you left in the middle of the night, in a snowstorm, to drive out here?" Ned asked.

"I couldn't sleep," I explained. That was halfway true. Though why I felt the need to explain myself to Ned, I didn't want to examine.

"There wasn't too much snow to drive in." Jed threw down his little challenge.

Ned paused, and I could hear his disbelief as it echoed in the silence. Then he leaned forward and gave me a big grin. "Well, it's always nice to see you. I think the house here gets lonely without you." He took a long drink of his coffee and turned his attention to Jed, like a fox angling in on his prey. "Anna hasn't mentioned you before," Ned informed him, his tone too friendly.

Jed smiled and said nothing. The fact that he didn't reply did more to insinuate that we were a couple, and I wasn't doing anything to dissuade Ned of that notion. I couldn't figure out what was going on, but it was interesting to watch. Was Ned trying to assert some ownership over me? We hadn't been a couple since I was twenty-two, but the only man I'd ever brought here that I'd been dating was Eric. Maybe I should remind Ned that taking my virginity didn't mean he maintained any sort of hold over me. He'd lost that when he'd decided to make Carrie his wife.

"What is it that you do, Jedediah, when you aren't touring the Missouri countryside in the middle of the night with Anna?" Ned got up and refilled his coffee.

"Investment banking," Jedediah told him and I tried to not look surprised. My homeless guy was into investment banking?

Ned grinned. "Not sure I know what that means," he drawled. I cast Jed a warning glance. Ned might be pretending to be a simple farm boy, but he was smart. Why he was playing with Jed I didn't know.

"I'm not sure I know either," Jed said, straight-faced.

Ned considered that for a moment and then burst out laughing. "He's all right," he informed me. I rolled my eyes.

Jed settled in his chair and leaned a little closer to me. "I'm sure that Anna is relieved to have your approval."

I said the only thing I could think of. "Breakfast?" I got beaming smiles from both of them. There was no accounting for men.

Sizzling bacon, frying eggs and the smell of pancakes cooking improved their moods. Jed asked casual questions about the farm, the crops, and what breeds of cattle they raised. Ned enjoyed his new audience and preached about sustainable agriculture in the modern world.

After I had settled a large plate of pancakes and eggs in front of each man and positioned a third plate of crisp bacon between them I took my place with my own plate. The exercise and the lack of sleep had made me hungry as well.

"Anna, where did you meet Jed?" Ned asked, his tone too casual. I'd just been here at Christmas, no significant other in tow, and now showed up with a man at my side. We were friends and he had a right to be curious. Possessive was another matter. Maybe he was just trying to be protective, like a brother. We'd been inseparable since age seven and been in love through high school and college. That was too many years together to retreat to the safety of a sibling-like relationship.

"I ran into her on a street corner. Near Midtown." Jed grinned at Ned and I wondered where the hell this man had come from. He glanced over at me, and if he noticed my frown he ignored it. "We bumped into each other." It was easy to reach for the subtle bruise on the back of my head and fall into the charade.

"You just about knocked me out."

"I did." Jed laughed out loud. "I had to help her home. I wanted to take her to the hospital, but she wouldn't hear of it."

Ned's eyes flicked back and forth between us, twinkling with curiosity. "Sounds like quite the tale," he informed us, inviting more details.

"It's not," I said. There wasn't any part of this story that we could share with him and I didn't have it in me to take the game any further.

"It is," the now loquacious Jedediah informed him. I resigned myself to a long morning as I bent over my pancake.

CHAPTER SEVEN

"**N**ICE TO SEE YOU, Ned." I held the door open and he ducked out. "Carrie's been baking since she heard you come in this morning," He told me as he backed away from the door.

Carrie was a domestic goddess on top of being smart, holistic, and pretty. I couldn't help loving her even when I was so jealous of her that I couldn't stand it. I knew why he'd married her and not me. It had been a good choice.

"She's a great cook," I complimented. He beamed with pride as though it was an accomplishment he contributed to. I allowed myself to entertain fantasies of what she might be concocting. Fresh bread? Apple strudel with goat cheese and rosemary?

"The best. I imagine she'll be down later." He glanced at the door behind me. "I'll have her call first."

I felt my face turn red. "That won't be necessary, Ned." I slammed the door in irritation as he pivoted on his heel and made out for the barn, laughing. He could be a bastard. I hoped Demon threw him into a sticker bush. If he could find one under all the snow.

I walked back into the kitchen and shut the door to the mud room behind me. Luna jumped up onto the counter and I shoved her away from the remnants of the bacon. She growled in protest as she jumped down. Jed shifted in his seat and took another sip of coffee. I could have warmed it up for him, but I didn't feel that charitable. I watched Ned's departure out the kitchen window and how Demon's haunches swayed with the motion of his gait. They made for a picturesque scene as they walked along the dam, past the frozen lake. The mares had wandered down the hillside and leaned over the wood fence to talk to Demon. He put his ears down and offered to bite them. They turned and ran, jumping and bucking as if to prove that he didn't scare them. He pranced, preening his neck as he showed off for them. I shook my head again, bemused. Men.

I retreated from the window, refilled my own coffee cup and sat down across from Jed. There was a lot I wanted to ask, but I wasn't sure how to begin. The silence stretched between us, and each moment it went on made it more difficult for me to start talking. I wanted him to bridge the awkward gap, to volunteer all of the information I needed.

He sat back, legs crossed, coffee mug balanced on his knee. He took in the room, the cream walls decorated with my aunt's hand painted plate collection and the oak cabinets that my grandfather had made, in need of refinishing. He looked relaxed, like he felt comfortable here. He looked too comfortable. It was my house and he didn't belong here. I didn't even know who the hell he was.

My anger over his deception rekindled and I set my coffee mug down with a sudden thump. Luna jumped like she'd been bitten, and Jed turned his attention back to me.

"I think you'd better tell me who you are."

"Very well," he acknowledged. "Would you like to talk in this room or would you like to find a more pleasant place to sit?" He had a point. The hardwood kitchen chairs were not the most comfortable.

I took my coffee and led him to a small glassed-in porch off the dining room that was added onto the house when I was twelve. My aunt had wanted a room for her plants in the wintertime. The sunroom had the same view as the kitchen window, but broader. The lake was picturesque. The pastures, framed by hills and woods, were covered in a layer of perfect snow.

It was a little cool with all the windows. A cast iron wood-burning stove sat in one corner with a full wood box next to it. I pulled the door open and selected a few small hunks of wood and three pinecones. A little wad of newspaper under the pinecones and a match and we'd have a roaring fire in no time. I left the lid cracked open so it would draw.

Jed stood in the middle of the room as if unsure where to sit. His size made the rooms at the farm feel smaller. I settled into one of the oversized armchairs and gestured Jed to another. When I looked out on the pastoral view it was hard to believe that there was such a thing as ghosts. Except I knew there were, had known for a long time.

"This tale is not a simple one to tell." His voice was low so that I almost had to strain to hear it.

"Most aren't." I kept my tone gentle so he wouldn't feel defensive. "Why don't you start by telling me who you are."

"As I have told you, my true name is Jedediah, but were you to look at my passport, you would find a different name on it."

"What name would that be?"

"Tobias Peters."

"Tobias?" I repeated.

"Yes."

"Is Jedediah a middle name? A nickname?" I queried.

"I will get to that. Let me first tell you about Tobias."

It was weird that he was talking about himself in the third person.

"Tobias is from a very old German family. He was raised in Switzerland and became an investment banker. He worked with a firm called CBU and then started his own firm when he was twenty-nine. He was ambitious," Jedediah explained.

"And you stole his identity?" I asked, unable to keep the skepticism out of my voice.

Jed smiled but did not look amused. "I have done nothing illegal, Anna, I assure you. May I continue?" I bit my tongue and nodded my assent.

"As is common for young men who grow up in the Swiss Alps, Tobias was a skier. He was very good, but he had an unfortunate accident." Jedediah looked away from me, out over the snow and the hills of Missouri, as if he saw a different kind of winter scenery.

"He was on a mountain that he had skied many times before, but this time, he fell. Perhaps it was a patch of ice that he slipped on, I am unable to remember." He shook his head and looked back at me. "He ran into a tree. He did not regain consciousness."

"So Tobias is dead?" I couldn't figure out where Jed's story was going.

He gave me an odd smile, as though something pained him. "He is, and he is not. His body was kept alive, on machines," he explained. "He was his mother's only son, and she would not allow them to . . ." He gestured.

I filled in the words, "Discontinue life support." I'd seen it before, in residency. Shell-shocked people who would not allow their loved one to be disconnected. They were certain that some piece of them remained. In rare cases, some regained consciousness years later, but those cases were few and far between. Entire facilities existed whose sole purpose was to care for these unfortunate individuals. I felt sorry for Tobias' family. It was a difficult position to be in.

"How long was he like that?"

"When I found him, he had been that way for several months. Fortunately, he was in very good shape, a very athletic man."

"I don't understand what you are trying to tell me. What happened to Tobias?" Had Jed known him?

"No one has harmed Tobias," Jed reassured me. "Anna, you know that when the spirit leaves the body, it does not always go on to heaven or the underworld. Sometimes it stays among the living." His accent grew thicker, with notable overtones of Germanic influence.

"I am quite aware of that fact."

He ignored my sarcastic response. "My soul is one of those that never left the earth, Anna."

"What do you mean?"

"My time among the living was long ago. When I died, my soul did not go to heaven as I had hoped it would. Perhaps I was not as pious as my name suggested." He had a wry smile on his face. "I wandered the earth for many centuries until the Council found me and gave me a way to serve God again. I have now lived a few lives, in bodies like Tobias' that need only the presence of a strong soul in order to live again. The Council foresaw your death as a means to find you and sent me to prevent it. I found Tobias, and I gave his body the chance to live again. The doctors in Switzerland still speak of the miracle of his awakening."

I was speechless.

"A moment, please," he told me and lifted his large form out of the chair. He disappeared into the dining room and I registered the sound of him going upstairs, then coming back down a moment later. He walked back in and handed me a large folder, similar to the kind we kept x-ray film in before the advent of digital x-rays.

"These are copies of his medical records. I thought you might find this information useful."

I opened the envelope and slid out a thick pile of paperwork, and yes, a couple sheets of x-ray film. There was a cervical spine x-ray. I flicked on the lamp next to my chair and held the film up to the light. The tag read "Peters, Tobias 1962.11.12." The patient had a neck brace on. I couldn't see any obvious fractures, but I wasn't a radiologist.

A skull x-ray was next, and I could see the fractured bones along the side of his head. The damage would not likely have been survivable. I felt strange. You saw fractures like this on the cadavers in anatomy class. Not on someone who was living.

I sifted through a stack of papers. There were medical consultations, and a patient history, much of it in German. I found a consult note from a neurologist in the UK and perused it.

The patient demonstrates a significant parietal lobe fracture. Extensive surgery has been performed to allow for swelling in the brain. EMG and MRI scans demonstrate no neurological function though MRI indicates little significant brain tissue damage. Prognosis is poor. Family has indicated they will not be terminating life support. Recommend patient for transfer to long-term care facility.

A small red booklet was at the bottom of the stack. *Schweizer Pass, Passport suisse, Passaporto svizzero* were printed on the front in gold letters. I flicked it open and saw a picture of Jedediah. The photo was identified as one Tobias Peters.

Jedediah rose and added another piece of wood to the fire. "Shall I close this door?" He indicated the fireplace door. The fireplace was putting out a warm glow but I was still cold.

"Yes, thank you." My voice sounded odd to me, detached. Jed approached me as if he worried I would startle like a deer in the woods. He lowered himself down and knelt, tilting his head so that his hair fell across his face and exposed the left side of his skull.

I reached out, hesitant to look though I now knew what I would find. Thick dark hair parted under my fingers and revealed a five-inch scar that extended diagonally from above his ear back across the top of his head. I put one hand on the side of his face to hold him steady and probed his scar line with the other. The transition from bone tissue to metal in the parietal area was palpable, consistent with the area of damage on the skull film. I felt a little sick.

I released him but he stayed crouched in front of me.

"Titanium?" I asked. He nodded.

"Well, it's stronger than the remaining skull bones." I made the joke with a strong feeling of detachment.

Jed grinned, but he was too close. I shifted and he moved towards the windows in order to give me space. I tried not to think of the way his dark hair felt in my hand, the soft wavy curls. I switched my gaze and found his backside silhouetted against the daylight of my windows.

I forced myself to refocus my attention on the fireplace. If he wasn't crazy, and if I wasn't crazy, then he was dead. None of those options made Tobias/Jed the best choice for a bedmate. Was I that desperate?

"Jed, what happened to Tobias' soul?"

"I believe he must have gone on to that which comes next. I found no trace of him."

"Do you have any of his memories?" Even while I swayed between belief and disbelief, my scientific brain came up with a thousand questions.

"A few. This body's mind did retain some information."

I processed that for a moment, tried to find a way to either refute or believe the strange story he had told me. I thought of a family in Switzerland whose son had awakened after being declared brain dead. Whose son was no longer their son. Insanity would be the easiest explanation, but I'd seen the medical report. EEGs and brain function MRIs didn't lie. Tobias Peters had been brain dead, yet he stood before me and claimed that some old soul had taken over his body.

"What happened to his family?" I asked.

"They were overjoyed when Tobias awakened but have found that I have a different personality than Tobias did before his accident." Jed shrugged. "I told them I was taking a vacation, to find myself again." He continued to speak into the void that my silence created. "I've called his mother a few times so that she knows he is doing well," he explained. Which was all well and good except that it wasn't Tobias that was calling home. "She is a nice woman. I think you would like her, Anna."

Luna walked in and leaped into Jed's chair where she sat, yellow eyes wide as she watched her favorite person. My heart hammered in stark contrast to her serenity. I stood and walked out. Tobias Peters didn't follow me.

I didn't pause at the stairs, didn't consider going up for a hot bath to soothe muscles sore from skating. I walked through the kitchen, put my Ugg boots back on, donned a heavy jacket, and grabbed my wool cap and gloves.

The cold air wasn't much of a shock because of how cool the sunroom had been. I swallowed it in gulps as if I needed to quench a fire inside. I followed Ned's footsteps to the barn, stepping wide so that my feet sank into the holes his had left. Several halters with lead ropes, bridles, and other bits of tack dangled from hooks just inside the door. I snagged a bridle and two handfuls of grain from the tack room before I headed to the pasture.

Both mares swiveled their ears at my arrival but did not remove their heads from the foot of snow through which they were foraging for grass. There was hay for them, but they preferred the fresh frozen kind. I held out my peace offering and called out in a language these girls understood. "Whoop-whoo, whoop-whoo!" Heads raised, ears planted forwards. I had their attention.

Charlotte moved first. She was a gray mottled beast who looked a little dirty, as if covered with soot, against the background of snow. Hattie, always Charlotte's second, followed. Her dark brown head rubbed against Charlotte's flank as she walked. I offered Charlotte a mouthful of grain, with the bridle bit. She ate it and took the bit into her mouth, snagging the cloth of my glove with her thick teeth. I pulled the headstall over her ears and secured the strap under her throat. It took a couple of practice hops to get myself midway onto her back. She took one stiff legged step, in an attempt to dislodge me, but I kicked my legs and propelled my body far enough up to swing my right leg over.

It wasn't my most graceful move, and I hoped Jedediah wasn't watching, then I told myself I didn't care and settled into the small of her back. Bareback riding was made for wintertime. Her body was warm against the length of my legs, her midriff beginning to swell with foal. I settled my feet in front of the bulge and the big mare began to shake all over. She started with her head and worked her way through her midsection to her legs and tail as if I was an irritating fly. I relaxed my legs and rode out the shivering.

"Come on, Charlotte," I coaxed her. "It hasn't been that long." She cocked her gray ears back to listen to me, and then she relaxed. I laid my chest across her neck and reached underneath it to re-distribute the reins. She chewed on the bit like it was the final blade of summer grass and she wanted it to last.

Hattie bumped her head against my leg and I scratched her face between the eyes as well as I could with gloves on. Hattie preferred fingernails, but I wasn't going to take my gloves off in the middle of winter if I didn't have to. I nudged Charlotte forward with my knees and she plowed through the snow into the woods towards the ridge-line of the hill.

The woods were too silent in the wintertime. Without the ca-cophony of leaves rustling in the wind and the starlings clustered in the tree branches, cawing as they looked for insects and grubs, I had only my thoughts to keep me company.

I turned Charlotte to the left, along a line of rough gray rock that jutted from the ground in uneven ridges. When we were much younger, Ned and I had played among those rocks. We'd used the caverns when we played hide and seek. Until Ned startled a rattle-snake. I'd known enough first aid then to suck out some of the venom before I caught a horse and got him on it. His parents had not been pleased when they'd seen me leading the animal out of the woods, their son crying as he clutched the horse's mane, bleeding from the leg. He still bore a nasty scar, and I'd been lucky not to poison myself with the venom.

I shook my head at the memory and contemplated the animals that might be using those small caves today. Foxes. Maybe badgers. Snakes hibernated in the hills through the cold months. Charlotte's gentle motion soothed me and my thoughts drifted. Jedediah and Tobias Peters crowded in, but I forced them away. What I thought of his story I couldn't tell. I needed to let it set so I could filter through it later.

My mind drifted to the practical matter of what I should make for dinner. I hadn't brought that much food with me, but the freezer at the farm was pretty well stocked. There was a small roast, vacuum sealed against freezer burn. It would make a nice feast, and the hot oven would help keep the house warm. But I would need to defrost it for a bit. I had some root vegetables in the cellar, buried in a box of sand. They'd still be good. Sun broke through the cloud cover, filtering through the snow-covered trees and refracting into a million points of light.

Charlotte followed the hidden path over the crest of the hill and started down a steep enough slope that I had to grip her sides with my knees in order to avoid sliding up onto her neck. I sank my seat into her back so that I moved in unison with the jolting gait. Hattie slipped behind us and I swiveled and braced one hand on Charlotte's neck to keep my balance.

"You okay, Hattie?" I called back to her. My voice sounded out of place in the serenity of the forest. She regained her footing and continued without a change in her gait. No injury, then. The ground leveled out underneath Charlotte and she led the way towards the place I'd been heading, without realizing it. The one place that could help me.

The old homestead roof had fallen in and disintegrated years ago, but the stone foundation remained. Four walls, half crumbled but distinct enough that you could tell where the house had been. The stone fireplace had been built to last, and it towered over the sad remains of the one room home. I didn't know who had lived here – they'd been gone long before my family bought the land. All but one.

I left the horses ground tied under a towering hedge tree and stepped with care over the threshold. The snow had fallen inside the structure just as it had without, yet it felt warmer to me inside. It was somehow homey, despite the lack of a roof. Past the initial danger of the doorway, I moved with confidence. Over the years, I'd removed the debris from the center of the room and stacked it into a makeshift seat. I brushed the white fluff from the stones and sat while I ignored the unavoidable wet cold that bled through my jeans.

I relaxed in the sunshine. Without a breeze, it wasn't too cold, and the bright sun felt good on my face. Almost warm. The quiet rustling of the winter woods filtered through. Horses breathed, squirrels searched for nuts, scampering up and down the trees. The occasional bird called. My breathing settled into a deep rhythm as I watched and listened. Smaller critters rustled under the snow. A curious doe crept into the sunshine a few yards from the homestead to watch the horses. The temperature warmed by a few degrees and a breeze stirred inside the walls around me.

I smiled and turned around. "Hello, Marnie."

She was all light. Brighter even than the snow. She glistened as if she'd just come out of water. Her luminescence took my breath away. She smiled and her lips moved but made no sound.

Sister, she mouthed back.

"I know it's been a while. I'm sorry." She rushed towards me in a joyful incandescent glow that swirled the snow up in great flurries.

I hugged her as much as anyone can hug a strong breeze. She slipped through my fingers and I breathed in the scent of sunshine when she passed around me.

She coalesced in a glowing haze on the snow crust. If I hadn't been paying attention, I would have thought she had two feet buried in the white fluff. If Marnie had feet, I'd never seen them. She'd had them once, of course, in her first life. Now she was bound to this tiny plot of land. I assumed she'd homesteaded here with her family and died young.

I'd named her for one of the gravestones in the old plot in the tree line. Time had worn the etchings away from all of the stones but I'd used paper and a pencil on them and gotten one name. Marnie. I didn't know for sure if it was her name, but she'd never objected to me using it. Based on what she looked like now, I thought she might have been twelve years old when she died. Illness or an accident could have taken her when she was young. I didn't think it was anything violent because her spirit was so content. She'd never been able to tell me her story, so all of my assumptions were based on my imagination.

She'd been my playmate since after my mother died. She made no sounds, but her facial expressions were clear enough and I had long since learned to read her lips. What little she said, I understood.

Marnie called me sister. Maybe she believed I was the sister she'd once had. Either way, she'd become my friend. She danced away from me now, sparkling like drops of water in the hearth room. I followed her, my damp jeans sticking to my thighs as I tried to catch a spark of her light. We both laughed, though hers was silent. I felt happy and free. She flung snow into the air in a whirlwind and I lost sight of her.

I found my way back to my rock through the torrent of white and sat while the snow floated back to the ground. Gravity would have its way. Marnie materialized out of the snowstorm and drifted back to me. She settled cross-legged in the snow like a little girl, the skirt of her gray summer dress pulled up around indistinct thighs. Long fair hair drifted around her shoulders and I was filled with love for her. I could love a ghost, and have a friendship with one. This was why I had come to see her.

"How are you, Marnie?" My voice sounded strange against the backdrop of a roofless house filled with snow.

Her smile in response blinded me. *I am well.* She mouthed. *I missed you, Sister.*

I smiled, intoxicated by her joy. No one else was ever as happy to see me as Marnie was. "I missed you, too."

Where were you, Sister?

"I had to work," I explained, not for the first time. "I live in the city now."

She frowned and the furrow between her eyebrows was so distinct it looked like I could feel it, if I just reached out.

The city is no place for us. You should come home.

Marnie was insightful, in her own way. "I'm home now," I told her, and was once again rewarded with her brilliant smile.

I'm tired.

"Are you always tired, Marnie? Or just tired right now?"

Her lips turned down to pout. *From playing. It always makes me tired when we play.*

"Are you happy, Marnie?"

She beamed again, like my own beatific angel. *Of course. But I'm happiest when you are with me, Sister.* The day she answered no to that question would be the day that I freed her from her place on this earth. I hoped that day would never come.

Marnie was not a ghost with an agenda. She had pretty limited intellectual functioning, but I knew my visits pleased her. I had tried to get her to tell me her name, what happened to her family, to talk about her life, but such questions were answered in one of two ways. She either gave me a faint smile, as if confused by the question, or she became distraught and disappeared in an explosion of light. I didn't like to make her unhappy, so I'd stopped asking.

Marnie moved so that she snuggled at my feet and laid her head on my knee. She had no physical presence, so I must have imagined I could feel the sensation of pressure against my leg. Maybe it was the electricity of her aura, some remaining energy that I felt. I'd read that some ghosts put out energy waves that could be registered by the right electrical equipment. I was betting Marnie would register. Then again, the equipment was for people who couldn't see ghosts and wanted to prove their existence. I had never doubted.

Marnie looked up at me. *Goodbye, Sister.* I got one last smile from her before she fizzled from view. I felt the emptiness of the cottage and wondered where it was that she went when she left. She had been my friend for many years. Was Jedediah's story that much more incredible?

Charlotte and Hattie waited for me where I'd left them. They'd found a warm spot of sun and half-dozed in the bright light. I leaned against Hattie's flank and contemplated this bit of heaven I'd grown up in. Steep Missouri hills rose away from me, covered in the skeletons of towering oaks, maple, hedge and locust trees with their sharp spines that could puncture a car tire as easily as the sole of your shoe.

The odd brown leaf clung to a branch, but most lay in a thick curtain on the forest floor, decomposing under the snow. Bright clumps of green pine trees dotted the scene. Under the trees were areas where chunks of rock rose out of the earth in cliff shelves and ledges. It held a serene beauty.

Charlotte stood still for me while I mounted, and I turned her away from the cabin, down the valley floor. We made new tracks through the snow as we circled back towards the house.

I heard the sound of the ax long before I could see the source. Splitting wood makes a distinct sound, a rhythmic cracking that ricochets off the hillsides and echoes into the valley. It was Jedediah, jacket off, swinging the blade of the ax in wide arcs with a pause in between swings, like taking a breath. He'd reduced a stack of larger logs into bits of kindling, fire starter intermingled with the larger hunks that I referred to as all-nighters.

Put the right piece of hardwood into the stove at bedtime and when you woke just before dawn to stoke the fire it would still be a hot bed of coals, bright red and ready for the next piece of wood. It was all seasoned locust and oak, from the woods around us – good hard wood that burned hot, and long. It was clear that Jed knew what he was doing.

I directed the girls to the barn. There was no reason for them to stay out in the cold overnight if I was home. They jostled me for handfuls of grain and settled into a shared stall where they nipped at each other over a pile of hay I'd thrown in. The sound of the ax continued. If Jedediah kept it up I wouldn't have to split wood until next winter. The thought cheered me.

I secured the barn door and paused a moment in the sunlight to watch him. He worked the wood with ease. The weight of the ax and the force of the impact didn't appear to bother him. I gave him a wide berth, careful to avoid the area where wood chips would fly and where the head of the ax might go if it released in mid swing.

Inside I did a quick inventory of provisions and pulled the small roast out of the freezer. A frozen chunk of meat can defrost well enough when it's soaked in a sink full of warm water. Carrots and potatoes got peeled and sliced while the roast took its bath. I quartered two small onions and left four cloves of garlic whole. Sprigs of rosemary and winter thyme were salvaged from the summer garden, green and fresh even under the layer of snow. The valley fell silent as Jedediah carted his pile of wood to the boxes under the eaves. He stacked them with great care as if he were the one who would retrieve them through the long winter months.

I rubbed the roast with dry mustard, black pepper and a touch of salt. My aunt's red stoneware casserole pan was my favorite for roasts – a solid lid kept the steam in and the dish was ample enough for the pile of vegetables that I liked to cook in the juice. I found a bottle of pinot, opened it, and took a gentle sip out of the bottle. It was good. I poured a third of it over the meat and put it in the oven at a nice low temperature. It would cook for hours, filling the house with delicious smells, and be tender by suppertime.

A car horn announced its arrival and I saw Carrie behind the wheel of her Explorer. She pulled close in, next to the front steps and bailed out, flinging open the rear hatch to rummage around. I went out to meet her.

"What on earth have you done?" I asked as she pulled out a large cardboard box and headed towards me.

"Anna!" she exclaimed. She sounded both delighted and surprised as if she hadn't expected to find me home. "I'm so happy you came. It feels like it was forever ago that you were here. How are the boys?" Even behind the box, she bubbled with an infectious happiness. I grinned back at her and gave her a hug around the bulky object in her arms. Carrie was impossible not to love. I had tried not to—and failed.

"I made apple pie," she announced. "And baked bread. Farmhouse special. I hope you like it." She leaned close to me as if she was worried someone would overhear us, here in the middle of nowhere. "Can I meet him?"

I flushed red. "It's nothing," I protested as Jedediah rounded the corner. Carrie's breath caught and then let out again.

"Anna . . ." She breathed with appreciation as he joined us. His bulky chest was visible through the thin sweater he had on. I was pretty sure cashmere was not meant for wood splitting, which didn't appear to bother him. He gave her his disarming smile and bowed his half bow.

"Carrie, yes? I am Jedediah." He stepped forward, took the box from her, and invited her into the house. Which annoyed me a little, since it wasn't his house to invite someone into. Carrie followed him to the kitchen, chattering about what a fine day we'd chosen to visit the farm while she blithely ignored the strange hour of our mid-week arrival.

Jedediah caught sight of the bottle of wine. "A glass of wine, perhaps?" He offered, and I suppressed my scowl.

"Thank you, but not for me." Carrie slid out of her jacket and I glanced at her sideways. The flush in her cheeks might have been due to the cold, but that hadn't made her hair shine. Her breasts were larger than normal, and she seemed fuller around her waist. Instead of her normal jeans, she was wearing yoga pants. In most women it might not mean anything, but I had just seen Carrie six weeks ago. She had added some weight.

"Or some tea?" I offered, and Carrie gave me a sheepish smile that seemed to confirm my suspicion that she was pregnant.

"I can't stay. I don't want to intrude, and I see you are in the middle of cooking." She appraised the selection of discarded vegetable ends on the counter and took a quick look in the oven. "You're in luck, Jedediah. If I'm not mistaken that's an organic, grass fed, free range top round roast. And Anna here makes a very good roast." She nodded in my direction.

"You know meat," he remarked.

"I should. Was this Hank?" She asked me and I nodded. The

butcher paper had been well labeled with Hank's name and his date of slaughter.

"You raised this meat?" Jed asked, impressed.

Carrie smiled with satisfaction. "I bottle fed that one."

"I thought that in America you only ate food purchased from stores." His accent sounded more obvious when it was laced with sarcasm. I ignored him.

"Carrie, please. I don't like to eat food that I know." I'd been raised on the farm but I used to get squeamish every time my uncle went to slaughter one of the chickens that I'd grain fed.

"It's better than the food you don't know," she reminded me. "Antibiotic and hormone free."

"I know, I know." She was right of course, but if I thought about Hank, I'd have trouble eating dinner.

Carrie started to unpack the box. It was clear that there was more than pie and bread.

"I brought milk. It hasn't been pasteurized." A glass carafe filled with thick white fluid landed on the table. She waved a hand at me. "You know the drill." She flashed another smile at Jedediah as she laid a pie dish next to the milk. "Fresh milked this morning," she told him.

Carrie was hard-core mother earth. The dairy cow wasn't hers, though, it lived down the road with friends of hers.

"I had to process the rest of my pears before they went bad, so I brought you a jar of freezer jam." A glass jam jar filled with a honey colored substance settled next to the pie. Carrie's pear jam was so good I started salivating.

"Preservative-free, of course. I have more brussels sprouts than I can use . . ." The light green ovals landed behind the milk, followed by a pile of orange and red globes. Beets. They'd go well with the roast. So would the sprouts.

"Farmhouse multi-grain." A loaf of bread emerged, still wrapped in a tea towel. "I used my starter, of course."

"How is Fred?" I asked and she laughed.

"Fred's good, he's hungry, though. I had to feed him again this morning."

"Who is Fred?" Jedediah asked as he leaned against the kitchen counter.

"It's Carrie's pet mold." I explained and Jed looked a little startled.

"Fred is my bread starter." Carrie sounded as if she was explaining rudimentary math to a young child.

"It's a mold." I corrected her.

Carrie's lips twitched with the urge to laugh, but she suppressed it. "It's fermented yeast."

"Yeast is mold, especially the fermented kind that you keep for years. Trust me."

"All right, never argue with a doctor, I know. He makes great bread, though."

"Fred's been with Carrie for years, Jed. She takes better care of it than some people do their own children." Carrie gave a guilty laugh that agreed there was some truth to what I'd said.

"It's been in my family for generations," she told us as if that explained her devotion to a bowl of mold. "Anyway, I brought butter too . . ."

"I hope it's hand churned," I informed her and she laughed as she added a red ceramic crock to the collection on the table.

"Well, it is, but not by me. A friend of mine has dairy cows," She told Jed. "She makes butter with the cream. She gives us milk and butter in exchange for a side of our beef every year."

"It's great butter," I agreed.

"Yeah, it is. I can't stand that stuff they sell at the grocery store anymore. I'm so spoiled."

Jed opened the crock of butter and grinned at Carrie as if she'd reminded him of the best day of his childhood. "I thought that this was a lost art in this age."

"Not lost, though you don't find it much around here," Carrie admitted with another smile. "Where are you from, Jed?"

"Switzerland," he answered without pause and I jumped in to interrupt. I didn't think he'd go into the whole ghost story now but wasn't sure.

"You've done too much, Carrie. You shouldn't have gone to all this effort."

"No," she protested. "I was glad to do it. I go a little crazy when it snows like this. It was nice to have you to cook for. And I made two pies, so Ned's taken care of too."

"You guys should come have dinner with us," I offered and to my consternation Jed agreed.

"Yes, there is more than enough here for us to share." It seemed he had forgotten that he was a guest here. It wasn't his hospitality to offer.

"No, no, we couldn't," Carrie protested. "I just wanted to give you a few things, I'm sure you didn't bring enough food with you, and with the weather like this . . ." She trailed off and looked out the windows at the sun reflecting off the snow. "There's another storm coming, but I'm sure you knew that." I grimaced because I hadn't checked the weather before we came and I didn't know.

Carrie wiped her hands on my dishtowel. "Well, I should go."

"Are you sure you won't come for dinner?" I asked as I trailed her through the house. She headed for the front door, her jacket over one arm.

"No, thank you. Another time, though. Wonderful to see you." She leaned in for a hug and I reciprocated.

"What is this, about three months?" I whispered into her ear and she froze. "Is everything okay?" I felt her nod, and she gripped me a little tighter. I hugged her back. "Good. If there's anything I can do to help, just let me know."

When she pulled away, she had tears in her eyes. "Thanks. I've just been holding my breath to see if it takes. We lost the first one, you know."

"Oh, Carrie. I'm so sorry." I hadn't known, but miscarriage was more common than most people knew. "When was that?"

"Last summer. I thought Ned would have told you." Her face seemed distant for a moment, and I hoped that she didn't worry about the history between Ned and me. It was in the past and I'd never seen a man more devoted to his wife. She had nothing to worry about.

"We don't talk that much about personal stuff." I tried to reassure her. "I'm sure it's hard, but you're doing all the right stuff. Just remember to put your feet up and relax some. Breathe."

"Doctor's orders?"

"Yes."

She wiped her eyes and flashed me her smile. "You guys have a nice stay. If there's anything you need, you know where we are." She waved down the hall at Jedediah. "Hope we see you again." She disappeared through the front door.

I took a deep breath as I closed the door behind her. I didn't think about having my own family very often, but every now and then it hit me. The childbearing years were limited and I was more than halfway through mine. I wasn't any closer to having someone in my life that I wanted to have a baby with than I was when I'd finished my medical training. Pretty soon I'd have a choice to make. Have a baby by myself, or admit that I wasn't going to. A family wasn't something I was ready to let go of yet.

CHAPTER EIGHT

I WOKE TO A SOUND that was common in the city but dead wrong at the farm. A truck was coming up the road to the house, fast. The only thing that ever meant in the country was that something was wrong. It was five thirteen in the morning. I threw on jeans and a T-shirt and headed down the stairs. It didn't surprise me that Jedediah was right behind me in the stairwell. The vehicle skidded to a halt and I worried it would slam into the front porch given the velocity of the vehicle paired with the snow, but the crash never came. The engine shut off and doors slammed. I unlocked the bolt on the door.

"Don't." Jed leaned over me and held the door closed with the weight of his body. He had me pressed back against the door and I forced myself to stay focused on the problem at hand. I put a reassuring hand on his arm.

"Whatever is following us, Jed, it doesn't arrive like this." He thought about it for a moment and then let me open the door. Carrie and Ned were coming fast, his arm around her, holding her up and propelling her through the doorway. Snow was falling and had been for a while. My Forester was a half-buried lump. I slammed the door behind them and bolted it, as if that would do anything to stop the bad things that were after me.

They looked scared. I crossed to Carrie and took her out of Ned's arms. "Come sit down." I closed my fingers around her bare wrist and felt her pulse: racing, but steady. She was pale, but not clammy. I lowered her into a chair and looked her over. "Are you bleeding? Having any pain?" She didn't answer me, so I leaned her back and palpated her belly as best I could through her clothes. "Does this hurt?"

"No," she answered, her voice soft and shaky. Ned stood behind her. He had something to say but was keeping it to himself until I'd made sure his wife and baby were all right.

"Carrie, I need you to tell me if you are having any pain." I used my assertive voice, the one that commanded people who were half dead to respond to me. I pushed in a new spot on her belly, around the area of her enlarged uterus, but not directly on it. If she was miscarrying, unless we could get through the roads, there was nothing I could do to prevent it. I would be able to keep her alive, though. At least at this stage of pregnancy, the physical risks to the mother were limited if she miscarried. Emotional damage after a second miscarriage was another matter.

"No, that doesn't hurt." Her voice sounded a little stronger. I leaned back on my heels and crouched in front of her knees.

"Were you bleeding?" I asked again.

"No, it wasn't that," Ned answered for her. He sounded calm despite the panicked arrival. He rested a protective hand on Carrie's head. She leaned her cheek onto his thigh.

"What is it that brought you in such haste?" Jedediah interjected.

"There was something in our house. Something we couldn't see." Ned related this as though he had read it in a newspaper article. "Things were breaking. Dishes, mirrors. A dresser fell over onto our bed." Carrie moaned, her face pressed into Ned's Levi's. She'd seen something that had scared her. Or rather hadn't seen, and that was what had her so frightened. He caressed her hair, glaring down at me. "I remember when we were kids, Anna."

Jed disappeared out the front door, and I knew he would check to see what was out there. I needed to do the same. I needed to know what we were facing.

"Yeah, okay. You two stay here. I'm going outside with Jed for a minute." I patted Carrie's knee. "I think your baby's fine, Carrie. Just sit here and rest for a minute." She nodded. I didn't tell her that I couldn't be sure how the baby was without an ultrasound, but a lack of pain and no bleeding were the best signs I had right now. If I was worried about her, I could always offer a more thorough exam later, or we could try to get her to an ultrasound machine. If the highway wasn't closed. With this much snow, it might be.

I went through the kitchen to the back porch and slipped on my boots and my jacket. The snow was deep, over the tops of my boots, so we'd already had another four or five inches. When I looked up I saw the flakes falling through the blaze of the outdoor lights. I was getting tired of winter. Snow melted in my hair and I regretted not having grabbed my hat. I heard a noise behind me and whirled towards it but it was Jed rounding the corner of the house. "Did you find anything?"

He nodded, "Listen."

I opened myself to the world that most people couldn't see. At first, there was nothing, but then I sensed it. Sensed them. They weren't close, but they were out there, surrounding us. Closing in on us. I counted thirteen of them and took an involuntary step back to the house and bumped into Jed's massive form. He reached out to steady me but I forced myself away from him. The urge to lean into him for protection was strong and I didn't like to appear weak.

"Can we leave?" I asked.

"They surround us. How do you leave without them seeing which way you run? Without them challenging you?"

"I don't know." I turned in a quick frantic circle, as though expecting to find something that would help us. "Can we get Carrie and Ned out?"

"They were already attacked. I do not believe they will be safe."

"I don't think they're safe here either."

"Staying with you, they may have a better chance."

"I can't fight that many, Jed. You know I can't." I had a sinking feeling, the kind that you get just as you realize that you can't stop on an icy hill and you're going to slide through the red light at the bottom.

"All of them at one time, perhaps not." He walked a few steps towards the frozen pond and looked up at the snow that fell in clumps out of the trees. The door opened behind us and Ned walked out, letting it clang closed behind him.

"What the hell is going on, Anna?" Ned demanded, the playful banter from the previous morning gone, a growl in its place. The calm he'd shown when they'd arrived had been for Carrie's benefit. His family had been threatened, and he wasn't going to allow it.

Jed returned to my side and stepped a little in front of me, poised to put himself between Ned and me if the situation worsened. My heart cheered that Jed was ready to protect me. It was pretty sweet, even if Ned wasn't a threat. It had been a long time since someone had tried to protect me.

"I don't know, Ned. There's been some strange stuff going on." It made me nervous to talk to Ned about ghosts, and I babbled when I got nervous. "That's why we came here in the first place. I'm sorry. I had no idea that anything would be able to follow me here. I was trying to get away from places where people could get hurt. Instead, I've pulled you into it."

"Strange stuff? What does that mean?" Some people's voices go shrill when they are frightened. Not Ned's. His voice dropped an octave lower, and he sounded mad.

"Let's go back in, check on Carrie, and I'll tell you about it," I suggested.

He didn't answer, just turned and stormed back into the house. I looked back over the pond hoping that I would see the hint of dawn coming, but it was too early. Daylight didn't offer any protection against ghosts, but it made me feel safer. In lieu of the sun, I reached out and touched Jed's arm.

"What do they want, Jed?" I was ready to believe he might have the answers.

"They want you." He looked around. "Not all of the spirits here are hunters. Some of them are just watching for you, helping to keep you penned in." His eyes narrowed. "It's as if they are waiting for something. Or perhaps they wait for someone."

"Someone?" There was something peculiar in Jed's tone. He wouldn't meet my gaze and I knew I was right. "What the hell, Jed? What aren't you telling me?"

He exhaled and in seconds, his breath turned to frost. "I don't know for certain, Anna." He sounded mad, but I didn't think it was me he was frustrated with. "I'm just worried."

If there was something out there that concerned Jedediah, then it frightened the hell out of me. "Worried about what?"

"It's possible that someone I once knew is involved in this."

"Someone you once knew." I breathed in and only the ice in my lungs kept me from saying more.

"My brother."

"Tobias has a brother?"

"No. Long ago, Jedediah did."

"And this brother?" I wished he would be more forthcoming so I didn't have to drag every bit of information out of him.

"He was not an honorable man. I don't believe his demeanor has improved since then."

"Is he involved in this?"

Jed shrugged as if it wasn't important, but he looked concerned. "It is possible."

"You gave me some bullshit line about being here to help me, Jed. Was that just saving me from that truck or do you have something else to offer?"

"I can assist you, but I cannot release them, Anna. You are the only one with that power." He paused and drew himself up. My breath hitched in the back of my throat as his presence commanded my attention. "I was once a warrior and a king, and I am still somewhat like they are. I may yet be of use to you." He turned and walked into the house. There was little for me to do but follow him.

Inside the lights were on in every room. I wasn't the only one who felt scared in the dark. Carrie was in the kitchen. It smelled like fresh coffee and she was slicing potatoes. I noticed that the broiler was on. Ned wasn't in the room.

"Carrie, you're supposed to be resting," I protested as she slid a cup of coffee towards me.

"You know as well as I do that that's hogwash, Dr. Roberts. Women don't need rest when they're pregnant. They need exercise and activity. It keeps everybody healthy."

"You were pretty shocky. It would be best to relax for a bit, be on the safe side, Carrie. I can cook."

"I was just frightened, but I'm all right now." She flashed me a fantastic grin. "Ned told me some story about you and a ghost, once. I didn't believe him." She went back to the potatoes. "I should have known that where the great Anna is concerned, embellishment isn't required." She was taking the news about the spirit world well.

The front door closed and I jumped, but it was Ned. He had a huge duffel bag slung over one shoulder. His shotgun was in his other hand, the one he kept in the back window of his pickup.

"Ned, the stuff we are up against isn't affected by bullets," I warned him.

He gave me a wry smile and gestured with his shotgun. "You never know. I'd rather have it with me."

"Put that thing down, Nathaniel Edward David Joules! We're in the house." Carrie ordered, and I raised my eyebrows. I wasn't brave enough to call Ned by his full name. His mother had been the last person I'd heard use it.

"What's in the bag?" Jed asked, and Ned grinned for real.

"The contents of my gun room." He set it on the floor in the hallway and I could hear metal, lots of it, clacking together.

I groaned and Carrie transferred the potato slices to a bowl and started trimming the excess fat off some steak. "I couldn't stop him," she told me.

"Where'd the steaks come from?" I asked, perplexed.

"I raided the fridge while he was raiding the gun room. I wasn't going to leave my food there for the haunts to have."

Jed laughed, and I couldn't help but join him. The moment of lightheartedness improved my mood and I was glad Carrie was there. "At least let me help," I offered, but she shook me off.

"No. I don't know what's happening here, but it's pretty clear that you're involved. I think we need you to get us out of this, Anna. So why don't you let me do what I do, and I'll let you do what you do." She paused for a second, and then added, "Whatever that may be."

I took my coffee and sat down at the table once again with Ned and Jedediah. The clock on the wall ticked towards six. I laid my head on the table and wondered what it was that I was supposed to do. I'd used my power too many days in a row, with too little sleep. It felt like when I was in training and was on call at the hospital for two consecutive thirty-six-hour shifts. We were supposed to get twelve hours off in between, but in the world of hospital medicine, that didn't always happen.

"You all right, Anna?" Ned drawled. I didn't answer him.

"It's been a hard week for her. I believe she is tired. I had hoped that last night she would get more sleep," Jed told him. I kept my head down, eyes closed. I heard the sound of meat sizzling in the broiler, and eggs cracked into a pan. Potatoes were frying up in an iron skillet. Carrie was going full out on the traditional farmer's breakfast. We wouldn't go hungry with her around, but I was going to gain ten pounds.

Someone refilled my coffee cup and a large dinner plate landed next to my head with a thump. Carrie ordered the men to set the table, and I heard the silverware being passed around. More plates arrived.

Carrie nudged me. "Come on, Anna. Eat." I sat up to face my plate. I had a bone-in KC strip steak, Carrie style hashed browns, and two fried eggs. She handed me a slice of toast, already buttered. The boys weren't waiting for Carrie to take her place across from me.

I stared at the platter of food and realized how hungry I was. "Thank you so much. This looks amazing." She gave me a quick grin before she turned her attention to her own plate. If she'd had any trouble with morning sickness, she was over it.

The fried potatoes, the eggs, and the steak were all incredible. With the coffee, I almost started to feel normal again.

"So what's going on here, Anna?" Ned's tone was more demanding now that he'd been fed. I took a sip of my coffee and studied the mug instead of him.

"I don't know." I picked my fork up and stirred strips of potato into the runny yellow of my egg yolk. I remembered the summer when I'd told him I could see ghosts. He'd laughed at me, teased me for it, even though he knew it was true. I hadn't spoken to him for months over it, but my silence hadn't stopped him from making fun of me. I didn't relish being derided again. But they were here, wrapped up in it with me. There wasn't much to do but tell them what little I knew. We weren't ten years old, anymore.

"The first time happened a few days ago. We were walking to the store from the clinic and we came across a spirit. A ghost." I paused and tried to gauge the level of incredulity in Ned's gaze. "It attacked us."

"Did you make it disappear, Anna?" He asked, and there was more than a trace of scorn.

"Nathaniel Edward." Carrie's voice whipped out and he tucked his head like a chastised dog. She wasn't planning to let him make fun of me.

"Anna banished it." Jedediah stepped into the conversation, his voice so calm and steady I'd have believed him if he'd told me that the moon was indeed, as cliché would have it, made out of cheese. Ned scooted backward with a snort but said nothing.

"What do you mean by banished?" Carrie's attention was focused on the bear-like man next to me.

"Anna has a gift. She can give spirits eternity." He gave them an earnest smile. "She can release them from the bounds of the earth."

The silence from Carrie and Ned spoke volumes. They wouldn't be converted to Jed's kind of religion any time soon, but Carrie was too polite to challenge him on it, and Ned wasn't dumb enough to cross Carrie. I didn't need either of them to be believers, I just wanted to keep them safe.

"So for reasons I don't understand we've been attacked. It's happened three times in the last two days. I don't know what they want. We came here to get away from them and it looks like they followed us somehow." How they'd managed that, I didn't know. They had to have known about the property. "I'm really sorry that you're involved in this." I gave my head a shake as if that would clear the mental confusion that clouded it. I put my knife and fork on my empty plate. "I need to freshen up so I can think." I suspected Carrie might appreciate that option as well. "The room upstairs next to the bath is empty. You're welcome to it," I told her.

When I stood, Jed stood with me in the kind of chivalrous gesture that men of my generation didn't make.

I took a hot shower to wash the sleep out of my eyes and wake me up. Jed's words droned through my skull with the pounding water on my head. 'I was once a warrior and a king.' What the hell was that supposed to mean?

Whether it was the hot shower or the super minty toothpaste I wasn't sure, but after brushing my teeth, I felt human again. By the time I'd dried my hair, the turning of our planet had chased the darkness away. I craved the sun, but the overcast sky hung in a gray snow producing mass as far as I could see. The lack of sunshine didn't appear to affect the wildlife, though.

Birds flitted around the vacant space above the pond while they chattered their nonsense. I stretched my senses past the redheaded woodpecker as he banged the fandango into an old maple tree, past the snow-covered barn, into the woods beyond.

That's where the ghosts were, their still forms lurking like alien guardians of the forest. I was pretty sure they weren't there to guard the trees. If they wanted me dead, why wait? We were outnumbered. There were more of them than I could banish in a week. I didn't know how to get us out of this. I shook my head in frustration and headed to the kitchen to find out if any coffee remained.

It did, though I wasn't allowed any of it. Carrie had taken over my farmhouse kitchen. She insisted on boiling water and brewed me a fresh cup through my uncle's old cone filter. It took a lot longer than pouring the last cup out of the pot from earlier that morning, but it tasted better. I thanked her and scooted out the back door, steaming mug in hand. I wasn't going to win any fights with Carrie over kitchen territory, and as long as she was doing the cooking, I didn't want to.

I was looking for Jed and was surprised to find Ned in the barn trying to groom his stallion.

"How did you get Demon?"

"I found him in the mare's paddock." Ned's tone was short.

"How'd he get there?"

Ned shrugged, "I don't know. I left him in the barn, but he's a smart horse. Lets himself out sometimes." Considering I'd been stalked by ghosts for the last few days, I guessed a horse that could throw the bolt on his own stall wasn't that strange.

"He's safe at least."

Ned didn't reply but he was wrestling with Demon who was busy trying to impress the girls. Charlotte snapped at him, her teeth bared and ears laid flat back against her head. Pregnancy had settled her hormones enough to not be impressed by the young stallion.

Hattie, however, preened in front of him, stretching her neck over the top rail and lifting her tail in a pretty arc. From her behavior, she was pretty close to going into heat. I stepped sideways to avoid Demon's haunches as he twisted away from his handler. Ned was so focused on the stallion's antics that I was surprised when he spoke again.

"Your boyfriend says that those things are still out there." He sounded incredulous, like we'd made this up to somehow corral him.

"They are," I confirmed, unsure of what else to add.

"Then we need a plan," he informed me.

"Yeah." It was a lame reply. I didn't have a plan. I was a doctor, not a strategist.

He yanked on the horse's head a little too hard, but it seemed to get Demon's attention. He stopped prancing and stood still for a moment. "That's not an answer, Anna."

I knew that, but to say so would sound flippant.

"I won't let them hurt Carrie." He sounded resigned, as if he'd always known that he would give his life for hers, but never expected that he might have to.

"Neither will I." It was the one thing we agreed on at the moment. His vibrant wife and her unborn child. I left out the small side door and headed towards the pond.

Jed stood under the weeping willow. Its long leafless branches had sheltered him from view, but once I could see him, he bowed. He played a long flexible stem between his fingers and I realized that all of us were suffering from nerves.

"There are too many of them," he announced as if I hadn't figured that out.

I wasn't sure how to answer without being a complete smart ass. I settled for, "I know." Which was smart enough that, were my aunt still living, she'd have scolded me. I thought of her, standing amidst a cluster of cabbages in the garden, and then blinked the image back, along with a handful of tears. I was always amazed at how the deceased stayed with us even as we tried to continue living.

"You're the warrior." I regrouped by adding an edge to my voice. I was mad. Somehow all of this came back to him. "Don't you have a plan?"

He tossed a bit of willow branch into the clump of snow-encrusted grass next to him as if he was a farm-raised boy. "There are options."

"And they would be?" I took a sip of my coffee and hugged my arms in to protect against the cold and the wet snow.

Jedediah took the hint and began to walk towards the house. "We could attack them."

"I can't take on that many of them," I reminded him.

"No. If, however, your friends prepared to challenge them on one end," he gestured towards the woods to our left, "and at the same time I was over here," he pointed to the right, "we would isolate a few spirits between us."

"Which leaves me?" I asked though I knew the answer.

"In between, using your powers to release any spirit within your sphere."

"My sphere?"

"You are accustomed, I believe, to having only one of the dead to banish at a time."

I stayed silent because I didn't know what he meant. He grabbed my upper arm, gripping tightly through my jacket. My coffee sloshed into the snow, barely missing my pants.

"Your power arcs away from you." He made a huge swoosh through the snow with his willow branch. "If there is one creature in your arc, then it is banished." He picked a few small dead leaves off of the branch and scattered them on the far side of his swoosh. "Should more than one of the dead fall into the sphere of your power, then they will all . . . " He shrugged, and scooped up a handful of snow, sweeping it into the air around us. It swirled from one clump into three and then countless snowflakes drifted to the ground.

I stared at the half circle he'd drawn in the snow. It hit me, what he was saying. The snowflakes, bits of ghosts dissolving into wherever it was souls went when they died. "Oh my god."

"We should return."

I stared at my hands. He believed I could release more than one of them at a time. I had never considered the possibility before. I jumped when Jedediah put his arm around my shoulders. He guided me with him back across the dam. A formula started in my mind, but I didn't know enough of the variables.

I needed to know how much energy was required in order to cover a certain amount of square footage. I had to determine how much force it would take to spread the arc over a larger distance. Would the wind be a factor that I had to worry about? My mind was buzzing with the possibilities. Would I be even more drained if I was releasing more than one spirit? I shuddered; my bones still ached from the last spirit I'd released. My left foot sank into a hole in the snow and I fell partway to the ground, Jed caught me and hauled me back to my feet before I lost my balance.

"Careful," he admonished, and his hold on me tightened. One arm wrapped around my waist, the other gripped my right arm. He wasn't wearing gloves and I wondered how he could stand the cold. It couldn't be more than twenty-five degrees out.

"Thanks," I muttered. I could feel the heat from his arm around me, his hand on my bicep. It felt too intimate, being this close to him. I tried to pull away, but he didn't release me. Ned burst through the barn door and slammed it behind him. He saw us and tempered his pace. He gave a wave as if our meeting were happenstance. A surprise. I tried to shrug away from Jed, but he still didn't let go.

"Hello, Ned," he called out in a jovial tone. Ned looked us over and I schooled my expression, hoping to get across to Ned that we weren't a couple. Then I remembered that I didn't care if Ned thought we were a couple. Because we weren't. I elbowed Jed, but through our mutual jackets, it had little impact. He tightened his grip on my waist.

His head bent down to my ear, and I felt his breath on my cheek. He smelled like coffee and mint. "It's time for us to talk to them, your friends." The motion of our bodies as we walked together brought his lips in contact with my temple. I felt dizzy again. It had been way too long since I'd had a lover, and Jed unsettled me. "We need their help, and they will need ours," he explained while I focused on not falling again.

Jed's pace quickened so that we were on a trajectory to meet Ned right at the door to the house. When we drew up next to him, both men paused, and I came to a stop along with Jed.

Ned opened his mouth to speak, but Jed beat him to it. "I've spilled Anna's coffee. We can talk inside while I make her a fresh cup."

Ned pulled the door open, and Jed released me into the doorway.

CHAPTER NINE

I COULD SENSE THEM. A silent and immobile ring, they formed an invisible perimeter through the woods. We were penned in. Thanks to the forced practice, my abilities had grown stronger. With my second sight stretched wide, I could even see the bright shining star that was Marnie in her ruined cabin in the lower vale. She moved in between the standing walls as if she was restless and could feel me watching her.

We were every bit as captive as she was, and I felt the bond between us like a tether, be it real or imagined. Ned shifted in his chair at the kitchen table, and sipped his coffee, staring at me. I met his gaze and wondered if there was any hope that we would get out of this alive.

"What the hell is going on here, Anna?" It was worded like a question, but he didn't say it like one.

"I'd like to know too." I looked over at Jed. "Care to enlighten us?"

Jed shifted his large frame in the chair and caused it to creak. I wondered if it would collapse under his weight and had to stifle the inappropriate giggle that came with the image. His words were enough to sober my mood. "Some of the dead are after Anna."

They spoke at the same time.

"What's that supposed to mean?" From Ned.

"Why?" Carrie asked. She was cooking again, maybe just as a way to keep herself busy, since it wasn't lunchtime yet.

"Those that do not escape this world when they die take too much interest in the affairs of the living." Even from Jed, it was a cryptic statement.

"So why are they after me?" I was pretty sure I knew the answer, but I wanted to hear him say it.

His dark eyes fixed on me. "You have the ability to stop them."

"Stop them from what?" Carrie asked, and I thought it was interesting that she asked what instead of how.

He took a sip of coffee and spoke as if the answer was obvious. "They hope to make this world their own."

"Why are they here?" Ned asked and I knew that one.

"They never left, Ned. They never left." When we were kids, we'd seen a ghost one summer. Or rather, I had seen it. It was a sad spirit. It keened as it passed through the woods, its cry terrible with desolation. The sound was often mistaken that year for a large tree limb, creaky with age, sure to fall soon. Our parents admonished us to stay away from the old oak for fear that the great branch must be close to falling.

Ned was with me when I banished it, but his logical mind had never been able to accept what had happened. I never talked to him about ghosts again because he'd made fun of me that day, and I'd loved him a little less after that. Years later, I understood that it was his fear talking.

Ned got up and paced the length of the kitchen, then paused to stare out into the dizzying flurries that drifted through the glow of the outdoor lights. Nine in the morning but the sky was so dark that the floodlights had come on. The gray winter weather was depressing. "We can't just sit here and wait for them," he began to argue as if one of us had said something to the contrary a moment before.

"I'm not sure we could go anywhere anyway. Not with the snow this deep." Carrie nudged him out of her way like you might an old dog as she moved between the refrigerator and the kitchen counter and retrieved some of the items she'd brought the day before. Before she'd realized that I'd brought a nightmare with me.

Jed tapped his forefinger on the edge of his coffee cup. It was a contemplative gesture, not the kind of repetitive noise that puts people on edge.

"What would they do, Jed, if they could take over here?" I asked.

The tapping stopped and then started again before he answered. "What would you do, if you could take over another person's body?" There was a long silence.

"Like possession?" Carrie asked.

"Like," I confirmed. Carrie's face morphed into an expression of contemplation, which surprised me because I'd expected disbelief, fear, or some combination of the two.

"What would you do, if you had no morals and you didn't value another being's life?" Jedediah, full of the philosophical questions today. *Tap, tap.* He might have meant it to be rhetorical but the answers started coming.

"I'd take over POTUS, and then I'd rule the free world." Ned, working on world domination.

"The military's nuclear launch codes would be at risk then, right?" Carrie joined in her husband's fascist goals with a disturbing amount of enthusiasm.

I sucked in a deep breath while I processed the short and terrible end our world would endure if these ghosts controlled our nuclear arsenal.

"What if a serial killer came back?" Ned seemed to be enjoying the game of 'what if'.

"What if a dozen of them did?" I asked.

"Hitler," Carrie suggested.

"Is someone we definitely can't allow to return to power." I hoped his soul wasn't still tramping around Earth. Even though I didn't believe in hell, he was one person who belonged in it.

"How many ghosts are we talking about?" Ned's casual tone was downright disturbing. Was he hoping to martial his own army?

"It troubles me that they have attacked Anna. It suggests that they think they are well enough equipped to move forward, or they wouldn't be after her."

"Maybe they just thought they'd get her out of the way ahead of time," Ned suggested and I shivered at his casual reference to the ghosts' attempts to murder me.

Jed's fingers continued their monotonous rhythm on the edge of his glass. "That is possible. We should assume that they have hundreds." He took a breath. "There could be thousands, even tens of thousands." He shrugged. "There could be many more." He looked me in the eyes, and I wondered. *He admitted he's a ghost. Does he think of himself as some higher spirit seeking salvation among the living?* My doubts swirled. *What guarantee do I have that he isn't part of the group of ghosts that has us corralled like a bunch of stupid cattle?*

The metal plate in his head was from an injury he shouldn't have survived. He had gained consciousness in a body that was brain dead. A few days ago I would have said that those things were impossible. He'd lied to me, too. With him sitting in my kitchen, contemplating ways to overcome what faced us, I felt inclined to overlook that part. He'd saved my life and fought spirits with me. I trusted him, even when I wanted to doubt him.

"What are you thinking, Anna?" Ned asked me and I realized I'd been staring at Jedediah a little too long. I looked away as I felt my cheeks coloring.

I shook my head. "I'm just wondering what it would take to get you all out of here."

"Get us out of here? You mean get all of us out of here." Carrie's tone warned of resolve. She had the kind of determination that made arguments futile. You knew you were going to lose, so why bother with the fight?

"It's me they want, Carrie. I think you guys are just hostages." I shrugged, and Jed nodded in agreement. I was on the right track.

"I don't know what you two are talking about," Ned broke in. He sounded mad again. "Nobody's a hostage."

"Aren't you?" Jed asked, his voice low and calm. "Anna cares for you both. It is clear that you are her family. She would do anything to protect you. They think that she loves you enough to die for you. They will not hesitate to use her humanity against her."

"How so?" Ned leaned forward, balancing his elbows on his knees.

"They could have killed us at our house, Ned." Carrie sounded like she was teaching a high school history class. "They were trying to scare us. It was a show. The ghosts used us to make their point."

"What point?" Ned asked.

"That we were vulnerable and Anna couldn't protect us."

How could Carrie stay so calm when she said those words? "Nobody's going to die on my watch," I inserted into the conversation.

Trapped in my farmhouse, amid the hills and snow of my little valley, I couldn't see a way out. Jed was right. If anyone threatened Carrie and Ned, I would give myself up for them in a heartbeat. *Will the ghosts kill me?* It was a surreal thought. As a physician, I faced death every day, but it had never been my own mortality at stake.

"I don't believe this." Ned's hand slammed down on the counter and Carrie and I both jumped. He stormed through the back door, into the darkness beyond. Carrie looked stricken, her left hand paused mid stroke with my farmhouse butcher knife. The onion looked nervous underneath her wavering blade.

"It's okay, Carrie, they aren't close right now. There's nothing that close to us." I reassured her as I followed him out. Someone had to protect him.

I ran out into the snow, into a wall of air so cold it iced my lungs. I hadn't grabbed a jacket or my boots. I shoved my hands into my pockets and whirled in a circle. Ned was gone. I released my sixth sense and felt him in the barn. At least it would be warm in there. Beyond us, in the hills, the spirits kept their ring around us, penning us in as effectively as a circle of fire. "Water douses flames every time," I shouted into the wind. I hoped they could hear me.

I tugged the barn door open and slipped through, sliding it closed behind me. The sky had darkened like it was night out, but I didn't need light to know where Ned was. His soul was like a beacon in Demon's stall. I was stronger. I could see the dead as if they were alive, and the living shone.

"This isn't your battle, Ned." I half whispered into the dark of the barn. His anger was palpable. It wasn't something I felt from him very often.

"You made it mine, didn't you?"

"I didn't know. I didn't know they would come here, and I don't know why they are after me." He stayed silent. "I came here because I thought it would be safe. I'm sorry."

"He isn't just your boyfriend." His tone was accusatory as if I'd tried to pass a bunch of poison ivy off as roses.

"If you are talking about Jed, he isn't my boyfriend at all."

"What is he, then? He sees them too. He's some kind of freak, isn't he?"

I stepped backward against the door. It hurt more than if he'd hit me. They rushed back to me, all the reasons Ned had left me. And Eric, too. I was different. Too different.

"Yes, Ned. He's a freak. Just like me." My voice was devoid of emotion. It was why, at the end of the day, I only had a handful of friends, and always slept alone. I stepped back into the snow, stumbling into the darkness. Just because I could see ghosts didn't mean I could see in the dark.

"Anna!" Ned's voice followed me, but I ignored him. I brushed past Carrie in the doorway of the house. I remembered to kick off my wet house shoes in the mud room and padded, cold and shivering, past Jed who still sat at the kitchen table with his cup of coffee. He watched me but said nothing. It was just as well. I didn't have anything to say to him.

I sulked in my room and watched the ghosts that surrounded us. What kind of lives had they led and why were they following me now? If the spirit world was strong enough to take over the land of the living, there wasn't much that I could do to stop them.

So why mess with me? I was just one person. I had a helpful skill in this situation but not one that could obliterate the souls of all the dead that still walked the earth. Maybe some enterprising spirit had decided to get rid of me because I might be able to interfere with their plans. If that was the case, then I just needed to release the ghosts surrounding us, along with whoever they worked for, and then we could all go on with our lives. I couldn't contemplate the darker scenarios. My scientific self just couldn't accept the possibility that an army of ghosts was trying to take over the world. It was too crazy.

I headed downstairs to share my conclusions with Jed. There were candles lit on my aunt's oak table as if we were preparing for a power outage. Given the heavy snow, it was a realistic possibility. I had a generator but in the meantime, the candles provided a quiet ambiance. They were nice. I should use them more often. I slipped into the kitchen and found Carrie over the stove. A large pot of simmering liquid gave off wonderful steamy smells. I reached over to hug Carrie sideways.

"How are you feeling?"

She gave me a smile, but I could see that the day was wearing on her. "I'm good. Tired. But I feel fine."

"Have you been cooking all morning? You need to rest."

"Yeah." She looked sheepish. "I was kind of freaked out earlier. Hard to sleep like that."

"Maybe you could rest after lunch." My voice was confident. She thought it through and nodded. I didn't tell her my plan to attack the ghosts right away so that we weren't stuck for much longer. We all needed resolution.

"Okay then. After lunch, I'll try to rest."

"Good. Now tell me what I can do to help." I looked around. "Where are the guys?"

"Discussing tactics in the sunroom." She rolled her eyes, and I laughed.

"Is lunch ready?"

"The soup is. If you're ready to eat, I think the bread is done too."

"I am hungry." I felt sheepish about eating so much, but if the rest of my day went the way I thought it would, I'd need the fuel.

When the bread came hot out of the oven the smell called the men to the kitchen as if we'd rung a supper bell. Carrie filled heaping bowls with soup, and Ned carried them to the table.

"I call this one snowstorm stew." Carrie sat across from me at the foot of the table. I took a generous bite and burned my tongue.

"Thank you for the meal," Jed spoke after a few bites. "I have never heard of snowstorm stew. Is it a common meal here?"

Ned answered for her, and I could hear the relaxation in his voice. It appeared some male bonding had occurred while I was upstairs and Carrie cooked.

"She makes snowstorm stew when we get snowed in and have to make soup from whatever we happen to have on hand. No two pots are the same, and it's delicious every time."

He reached over and touched his wife's leg in an intimate gesture that made me jealous. Not jealous of Carrie, just jealous because I didn't have anyone to touch me in such a tender way. With love, friendship, and affection.

It had been a long time since Eric left me, but I still missed him sometimes. We'd met at medical school, dated for a couple of years and then moved in together. He went into Cardiology because it was sexier than Family Practice. Apparently the other cardiologists were also sexier, because within a year of starting his residency program he announced he was dating another cardiology resident and moved out. He married her less than a year later. It still stung. I'd been on a few dates since then but hadn't met anyone interesting. Or maybe I just wasn't willing to trust anyone enough to let them get close to me.

I looked up from the table and met Jed's eyes. He'd cleaned up at some point that morning. He was freshly shaved and dressed in a gray pullover sweater with a zip front. He'd left it partially unzipped, which revealed his lack of undershirt, and plenty of brown skin underneath. I tried not to stare at the hollow of his throat and forced myself to look back up at his face. His laceration looked like it was healing well and I forced myself to focus on it while I did a quick count of the days.

"We need to take your stitches out tomorrow." If we lived that long. It felt weird to be discussing something so normal.

He put a hand up to touch the tough fibers sticking out of his skin and nodded at me. "Very well." His hands were great. Long fingers, too thick to be considered delicate, but not fleshy or fat. They looked strong. From what I remembered of Jed the night I met him, he didn't have much in the way of fat on him. Just that tall frame with big bones and lots of muscles.

Jed noticed I was staring at him again. The smallest bit of a smile touched the edge of his mouth and my face flushed. I turned back to my soup with furious attention.

"So what's the plan, boys?" Carrie asked, though whether she was saving me from my own embarrassment or had just picked an opportune time to speak, I wasn't sure. "Have you figured out a way to save us?"

"We'll leave right after lunch," Ned announced. I had been planning to suggest the same thing.

"I don't think I can get my Subaru out. It's buried." I was exaggerating, we could dig the vehicle out, but I was thinking of the roads. It was a solid two miles to the main road and we were too far from town. The county didn't plow our roads. Chances were that the Interstate was closed too.

"We'll take the horses to our house. Get the tractor and head back this way – dig out the trucks. Then it's just a matter of following the tractor."

"Plowing as we go?" I asked and Jed nodded.

"I'm sure you boys have this all figured out, but how is it that we get from here to there?" Carrie didn't sound as scared as she had earlier. "Aren't those . . . things still out there?"

"Anna and I will take care of them." Carrie's gaze flicked back and forth between the two of us. Her voice was filled with doubt. "How?"

"It's hard to explain." I hoped that someday I'd understand what happened enough to explain it to someone. "I'll tell you everything one of these days, but as long as you stay close to me they won't get near you."

Carrie nodded. She didn't have any idea what it was that I could do, but I was willing to bet that she'd keep her horse glued to mine and that it was my car she'd get in. I just hoped Jed was right, and that I could release a bunch of the things at once. And then do it all over again if I had to.

"Okay, so we get to your house, get the tractor, get back here and dig out the cars, get to the main road and find it's passable. Then what do we do?" I looked back at Jed. It had been my idea to come to the farm, and it hadn't been a good one. I hoped that he had a better plan.

"We will make our way to the airport, Anna. There are others who can help. Provide guidance. But they will not come to you. We must go to them."

"Your Council."

"Yes, they can advise us. Help us."

I gave him a doubtful look. The scary woman I kept dreaming about didn't seem to think that Jed's Council had much to offer. I hadn't told him about my dreams, and he hadn't asked. I wondered if he knew who she was, or why she hated me so much. I was tired of ghosts.

"I have to get back to work, Jed. I can't keep gallivanting around the countryside with you. We have to finish this thing. I have patients."

"Gall-i-vant-ing?" His voice registered confusion and his Germanic accent was thick as he tried to pronounce it. "I am not familiar with this. What does it mean?"

I tossed my napkin on the table next to my empty bowl. "It means I have a life that I need to get back to. This is ridiculous."

"Will you be able to do your work, Anna? Will the spirits of the dead in your office make it more difficult to heal the sick?" His sense of urgency was palpable. "How long will it be before they find a way to kill you?"

I sucked in my breath and then released it with care. "I don't know."

"What about us?" Carrie redirected my attention.

"We'll go to your mom's for a few days, babe. Jed thinks that the spooks are going to follow them." Ah, the joy of being bait. I felt like a rabbit, with a hound fast on its heels.

"How will we know when they're gone? When can we come home again?" She asked.

"I will know. We'll send you a message when it is safe again." Jed's voice of authority was even better than mine.

"Okay. I guess you can text us. Anna has our email addresses, of course, if that's better," Carrie said. He gave me a perplexed glance. Perhaps his sojourn in this body hadn't included a full introduction to the online world.

"When are we leaving?" My mind turned back to practical concerns. My aunt had raised me, and she'd taught me to never leave dirty dishes in her farmhouse sink. I wasn't sure when I'd be back and it didn't matter how many ghosts were out there, I couldn't leave the kitchen messy.

"How much time do you need to be ready?" Jed asked.

I wanted to leave right away, to flee and get to safety, but I couldn't panic. I needed to be realistic. Plus, Carrie needed a nap. "At least an hour."

Carrie stood up and carried a couple of bowls to the kitchen leaving me to follow her with the remaining two. She stacked them in the sink and then turned around, leaning back against the cabinetry. She looked tired.

"You need to go lie down, Carrie. Rest. I'll take care of this." It was just common sense.

"All right." She didn't hesitate to respond.

Ned stood up as if he'd just realized the extent of his wife's exhaustion. "Come on, babe. You can nap while we get everything ready." He glanced at Jed, as if for permission. Something had changed between those two. What had been a rivalry had turned into a general and his sergeant. What had Jed said that made Ned trust him?

"Take her upstairs. I'll stay with Anna." Jed gathered the rest of the dishes from the table and set them on the counter next to me.

There wasn't room for two people at the sink so he sat at the table behind me.

Ned headed to the stairway, Carrie tucked under his arm. "You'll call me?"

"If there is cause for alarm, I will alert you," Jed promised. Their footsteps sounded up the stairwell, followed by the sounds of running water in the bathroom.

Jed's hands, his strong hands, were on the table, folded together as if in prayer. The fact that we were alone together again dawned on me. I resisted the urge to squirm as I met his gaze and tried to not think about how deep his brown eyes were. I wasn't used to not being in control.

"I want out. I can't do this," I blurted the words out, surprising myself. I hadn't meant to say that.

Jed's lack of response said more than words.

"What do I have to do to end this? What do they want?" I heard myself, my voice more shrill than it should have been. Jed still didn't react, other than dropping his eyes to look at his hands just as I had done moments before. I calmed myself. "What do you want?"

He looked up, at that, but didn't answer. I turned the water on and scrubbed at the bowls as if I needed to get the glaze off them while I let him contemplate his response. It took a few minutes, but at least the dishes were partway done.

"I am not certain what their wishes are," he informed me when he deigned again to speak. "I am not party to the treaties they hold."

I felt my eyebrows go up while I tried to translate from his Swiss and whatever background into English. Not that he wasn't speaking English, he was. This English was different, though. Older.

"That is one question answered out of several." I pointed a wet spoon at him. "Do you have any theories?"

"A theory? Yes. Perhaps it is more than a theory. I believe that they plan to kill you."

An unpleasant thought. "Why?"

"Perhaps they realize that you are one of the very few who can interfere with their plans."

"Which are what?" I still didn't understand his world domination model. I washed off the silverware and kitchen knives and lay them in a wet heap on a tea towel next to the bowls.

"I'm not certain." He'd already told me that. I waited to see if he would say more. One big hand went up to rummage through his hair and then he continued.

"I've told you some of the possibilities that come to mind. There are strong spirits that remain in our world. Very strong," he emphasized. "They wish to reclaim a part of life here on this planet for themselves." He paused again and I knew he was listening, watching those ghosts that encircled us. How he could see ghosts I didn't understand any more than I knew how or why I could. Maybe all of the dead could see each other? If we made it through this I'd be asking a lot more questions.

"So how will they go about accomplishing this world domination that they have in mind, and how am I supposed to stop them?"

"That is not information that I have."

"Who does?"

"You must speak to the Council, Anna. Listen to your dreams."

"I don't have time to go to sleep, Jed." I waved my hand around to indicate the circle of ghosts that had us penned like a bunch of Ned's cattle.

He skipped the emphatic shrug in lieu of a simple stare. He took a sip of his coffee without looking away. "When we are free of this place, then you can sleep. Let them come to you."

I didn't want to get into a conversation about his creepy ghost friends who liked to torment my dreams so I asked another question I'd been wondering about. "How did you take over Tobias' body?"

I got a cautious look. "It was not difficult since his soul was no longer here."

"So it's harder when someone's already in there?" My scientific interest kicked in. "Why is that?"

He gave me an odd look. "I'm not certain."

I started to dry the clean stack of dishes that I'd accumulated during our conversation while I speculated. "We don't know much, from an academic standpoint, about the soul. Lots of scientists don't believe in it at all, and those that do tend to take a more religious view." Jed listened, one eyebrow quirked at an odd angle. "I've always wondered what it is that ties souls to their bodies. Are you as cohered to Tobias' body as my soul is to mine?"

"This body lives because of me, Anna. Without my soul, or without the machines, it would die."

"Well, how did you do it?" I wanted to reach for a pad of paper and start taking notes. This would make for a great editorial in JAMA, if they didn't have me committed for insanity first. "And what happens when we die?" It occurred to me that Jed was the one person alive who could answer that great question.

"What shall we do with the rest of the soup?"

Now he wanted to help with the dishes? "That's not fair," I argued. My curiosity was piqued and I didn't want to put the soup away, I wanted to find out everything about the world that I didn't already know.

He gave me the indulgent smile that adults give exhausted children who have had an exciting day. "We will have time to discuss this and more. Let us get through this day first."

"Will this work?"

"We are trapped here at your farmhouse by snow and by these ghosts. Yet they make no move on us." He let me think about that for a moment. "I think they wait for someone. Or for something. I do not wish for you to still be here when they put their plan into place."

"Can I release that many of them?" It was the thing that worried me most about our crazy plan.

"You can do that and more."

"I can't get on an airplane with you."

"If you go back to your office, you give them a new supply of hostages, Anna."

"I can't just abandon my patients. It's my job. I do have bills to pay." I had enough saved to make it quite a while without working if I had to, but Jed didn't need to know that.

"You will not have a clinic to return to if you don't draw this danger away from it."

"I'm not comfortable being bait."

"You are not some fish to be hooked." Jed's voice was low as he leaned forward to set his coffee cup back on the table. "You are the shark."

His dark eyes locked with mine and I mentally stumbled from his intensity. I looked away. "I need to finish the dishes."

"I will do this. Go get ready. We need to leave." He herded me

towards the stairs by walking towards me. I feared what would happen if I touched him, if he touched me. Not because I thought he
would do something bad to me, but because I was certain I would
want more. I escaped up the stairs to my room.

CHAPTER TEN

THROWING ON CLOTHES for an early afternoon horseback ride through bitter cold and snow was easy. Packing my bag for unknown travel after that horseback ride was more challenging. I hadn't bothered to unpack the suitcase I'd brought with me from my house, so I knelt on the floor next to it and rummaged. It was easy to add some underwear to it, as well as another pair of jeans and some pajamas. I wanted to take my soft robe but I didn't have room for it. I added a couple of hoodies, and a nice sweater. I stuffed my Ugg slippers in sideways and threw some basic toiletries in a plastic bag, just in case I did fly. Done. I scooped Luna up in one arm and threw the duffle over my other.

Ned and Carrie fell in behind me on the stairs. Luna mewled in protest when I shoved her, butt first, into her carrier, but I couldn't leave her. Carrie would take her to her mom's house with them because taking her on a plane wasn't an option. If I was going to fly anywhere. I hadn't made up my mind.

I set Luna's crate next to my duffle and went into the kitchen to snag a cup of coffee. I scooted past Ned to get into the mudroom. We were all quiet, as if too afraid of the coming hour to talk at all. After a quick moment of debating between riding boots and my cozy knee high boots, I chose the riding boots. Being able to ride well was going to be more important than having toasty toes. I just hoped I didn't end up having to walk through the snow in the dark. Even though it was the middle of the day, the thick cloud cover wasn't letting much light through.

Ned joined me on the back porch. "Help me get everybody saddled?" He spoke in a hushed tone and I replied in a whisper.

"Sure. What about the luggage?"

"Your man is loading it in the cars now. He says no lights in the barn."

I rolled my eyes but didn't waste my breath on 'he's not my man.' "Maybe we can use a flashlight without attracting too much attention?"

"Yeah," Ned agreed. "We'll use that old lantern you have out there." We both pulled on our jackets. "Ready?" he asked and I nodded in confirmation.

It was still snowing and my breath caught in the cold wind. The horses nickered their welcome as we slipped through the barn door and brushed the snow from our jeans. We might be fooling the ghosts, but the horses knew when their people were on the move.

I found the lantern on its shelf in the tack room with an old box of matches next to it. When the wick was lit I turned the flame down low enough that no light would show through the cracks in the wood. Ned grabbed his saddle off the rack and moved towards Demon's stall while I hefted my own and headed for Charlotte. She stood still for me, nuzzling the back of my jeans and nibbling on my arm while I tightened the girth enough to keep the saddle on but not bother her babe. It seemed impolite to saddle a pregnant mare, but it wouldn't hurt her.

Ned left Demon in his stall tacked up and ready to go while he fetched Uncle Will's western saddle and got to work on Hattie. Since she was taller than Charlotte, I was glad he was going to do it. Lifting a fifteen-pound saddle overhead and placing it on the back of a tall horse was a challenge for anyone who was short.

"Are you done?" he whispered.

"Yes. You?"

"Ready."

I extinguished the little bit of light and set the lamp back on the shelf so I'd be able to find it again next time. Whenever that would be.

"Anna?"

"What?"

"Sorry about earlier." He handed me Hattie's reins.

"It's okay." I tried not to show my surprise. Carrie had probably told him to apologize, but that was okay with me. It was nice that he'd said it. He didn't have to. I gave him a smile that he wouldn't be able to see in the darkness and led Charlotte and Hattie through the doorway into the snow beyond the barn.

Ned left me standing with all three horses while he went in to let

Carrie and Jed know we were ready. I leaned back against Charlotte's warm side – a safe distance from Demon's teeth – and opened myself up so I could see the ghosts. They seemed restless, shifting their positions like young children who needed to go to the bathroom. What that meant for us, I didn't know.

We would, at a minimum, come into contact with the ones that stood between us and Ned's place, so I would be releasing ghosts. Banishing them, as Jedediah called it. I felt the warm glow inside me, the internal fire that was waiting to be released, and felt a little queasy. I knew it would hurt.

The back door clicked open, then closed again. Jed was the first one to sidle into the circle of horses. "I am on the bay mare, I believe?" He asked, his voice low.

"Can you ride, Jed?" I whispered. The thought had just occurred to me.

"I have not done so in this body, but I assure you, I am well trained in the arts of the horse."

I arched my eyebrows and handed him the reins. He ran his hands over the unfamiliar mount and tack, felt the tightness of the girth and ran his hands down Hattie's legs. It looked like he knew what he was doing. When he moved to the other side I stepped in and set to work lengthening the stirrups. I was pretty sure that the last person who'd ridden this saddle was Ty, and Jed was a foot taller. I was glad that Ned's mares were big boned horses. Handling Jed's weight wouldn't be a problem for either of them. When he came back around to my side I handed him Charlotte's reins and ducked under Hattie's neck to fix the stirrup on the other side. They might still be a little short for him, but I hoped he'd be able to manage.

Ned took Demon from me and led the stallion a few steps away where he mounted and then pulled his boot from the stirrup so that Carrie could get up behind him. I would have helped, but she grabbed his arm, got her foot in the stirrup and swung up behind him. It was clear that riding double on Demon was nothing new for them.

I took Charlotte's reins back from Jed and mounted with ease thanks to the presence of the stirrup. The leather creaked underneath my weight, the loudest sound we had made. I couldn't tell if the ghosts could hear us or not. Jed hoisted his huge frame onto Hattie and reined her around to fall in behind me as if he'd spent most of his life on horseback. I stopped worrying about whether he was going to be able to handle his horse or not.

Demon moved into the shadows and I urged Charlotte to fall in behind him with the pressure of my knees. Snow stung my cheeks and I pulled my scarf up so it protected my face. I tucked my gloves into Charlotte's thick gray mane and prepared for a cold ride to the bigger farmhouse. It wasn't very far – a little over a mile on the road, and less than that through the woods. It would be a nice ride if it weren't for the three ghosts in between.

It was easy to concentrate on the spirits while we road. The stillness was broken only by clumps of falling snow and the rustle of an owl's feathers as he swooped from one branch to the next to monitor the equine invasion of his forest. Although the sky was brighter overhead, the woods were still pitch black. There was little to do but follow Demon and let Charlotte choose her path. I kept my body alert, in tune with her movements so that if she stumbled or shied, I'd be able to stay on.

Jed's theory had been that the ghosts wouldn't be able to sense us as well if we were on horseback. Something about the larger mass of the horse and its energy would cloud the ghosts' perceptions. Make them unable to distinguish the smaller human form attached to the horses' backs. It seemed like it was working. The ghosts had settled some. At least they weren't moving like a hive of bees anymore.

We were less than a quarter mile from the nearest spirit when they decided the horses were worth looking at. Two of the ghosts moved to tighten the gap between them. A third ghost took notice and moved towards the first two. I nudged Charlotte forwards, hoping she knew the path between the two houses well enough to not run us into a tree.

We passed Demon on the right and Ned pulled up so that he fell into line behind Jed. *I get to be first, lucky me.* Charlotte flicked her gray ears back as though she could read my mind. I didn't think she could see the ghosts, but her muscles tensed up underneath me. She either sensed them, or she had picked up on my anxiety. I tried to relax my legs but my heart still raced. I'd never tried to banish three ghosts at one time before and didn't know if it would work. I wondered if the others were as scared as I was.

I leaned into Charlotte's neck as she started up the hill onto the ridgeline, plowing through the snow as she went. It wasn't as deep in the woods as it was in the open thanks to the shelter the trees offered. The ghosts were just above us at the top of the hill and I urged Charlotte a little to the northwest of them. I wanted to get a little higher on the ridge so that they would be below me. They looked like a cluster of colorless energy. Watchers, Jed called them. He directed his horse towards the ghosts while Ned and Carrie lagged behind.

We all stopped and the three ghosts glided into the net of our trap. None of the other watchers appeared to take notice of us at all. Charlotte took a few hesitant steps forward as I urged her closer with my legs. I gripped a handful of her mane in my right hand and felt down to that thermal core inside me. The power stirred when I reached for it, and the energy pushed upwards when I willed it to. Jed had said I didn't need to use everything that I had, but I didn't want to risk not getting them all. I didn't know how to temper it anyway. They rushed towards me as if they knew what was about to happen and thought they could stop me.

I lifted my left hand and poured my energy out on them. Fire and water. My inner voice had a moment to celebrate and then Charlotte tried to jump out from under me. I clung to her and fought the fire that burned through my veins. The ghosts dissolved, all three caught in the net of my energy, and then were gone in a burst of light. The mare leaped sideways and dropped me into a pile of snow at the base of a tree as every other ghost on the ridge started towards us.

"Go!" Jed's voice broke out of the darkness and I heard horses grunt as they labored up the hillside, with their heavy cargo. Charlotte raced after her comrades while I tried to figure out if my bones hurt because of the scorching inferno that burned through them or because I'd injured something in the fall. I was too tired to yell for help. My internal fire burned into my lungs, and I peeled the scarf off, hoping that the cold air would dissipate the flames within.

"Are you all right?" Jed and Hattie swept out of the darkness next to me and he was gathering me into his arms before I registered that he'd dismounted. "Your horse passed me. We need to go get her. Can you mount?"

I stared at him in confusion. Mount a horse when my blood had turned to molten lava? Not likely.

He gave me a shake. "Anna, they're coming." Panic made him enunciate every word. "Get on the horse." He half lifted, half pushed me onto the saddle and then jumped up behind me. He pulled me back against him so that he had a tight hold on me and urged Hattie up the hillside.

She couldn't flat-out run with our joint weight but she moved faster than I thought possible given the uncertain terrain and the fact that she was loaded with well over 300 pounds. I held on as well as I could and tried to ignore the fact that my pelvis was getting crushed between Jed and the saddle horn.

We slowed at the top of the ridge and let Hattie pick her own pace downhill. She was spooked, so she slid down the slope faster than she should have, but we arrived at the bottom relatively unscathed.

We heard voices and then saw two horses with riders coming towards the edge of the woods. I felt a rush of relief that they'd caught Charlotte and that she was okay. Carrie wouldn't have been on the mare if she'd been injured.

"I've got Anna," Jed bellowed, "keep going." The riders whirled their horses around and spurred them forwards like they were barrel racing. Hattie caught sight of the farmhouse and followed them. It would have been a thrilling ride if I'd been on my own horse and didn't hurt so much.

"Anna, are you all right?" Jed shouted over the wind. Fire still burned in my throat, so I didn't answer, just held on as best I could.

Demon and Charlotte skidded to a halt in front of the modern metal equipment barn, and Jed slowed our horse to a stop just short of them. We didn't need a mare in heat too close to the stallion while he was wound up from a good run. Ned launched himself off Demon and then held the stallion and Charlotte still while Carrie jumped off.

"Are you okay?" She asked me as she moved over to Demon.

"Yeah," was all the reply I could manage.

Carrie's legs were almost as long as Ned's so she didn't bother changing the stirrup lengths. She pulled Demon around and came back towards us, unconcerned about her ability to control the randy animal. He pranced along underneath her but otherwise did as he was told.

Jed dismounted and then helped me down. He tossed me up

onto Charlotte with a little more care than he had in the woods, but it still hurt. I leaned over her neck and tried to breathe through the pain. Her head flagged and flanks heaved from exertion. I hoped the foal was all right.

"I want you, someday, to explain to me what just happened." Carrie's voice was stern and I nodded.

"When we have time, I'll tell you everything," I agreed.

"Okay then." She pulled a packet out of her pocket and handed it to me. "Jed said you might need some food after this. I can see he was right. Eat."

I peeled back wax paper and found a sandwich – Carrie's bread from lunchtime, leftover roast and a slice of hard cheese. I moaned with sudden hunger and took a huge bite, mumbling my thanks through a mouthful of food.

"You're welcome," she told me before turning her practical attention to Jed. "Are we being pursued?"

"Yes." He remounted and turned back towards the ridgeline. "They're gathering at the top of the hill. They won't let as many of them get caught next time."

The roar of the tractor engine startled the horses into motion and it took us a moment to bring them together again.

"So what's our plan now? How do we get back to the cars?" Carrie asked.

"We three are going to try to wrangle some more ghosts," I told her before I took another big bite of sandwich.

"Can you do that again? Whatever it was? I mean, you look terrible." Carried sounded apologetic, as if she'd told me I looked ugly when I'd just spent hours getting ready for an important date. I laughed around my sandwich.

"She is able to release many of them," Jed answered the question for me.

I raised an eyebrow to express my doubt, but I could tell that the burning sensation was dissipating faster than it had a few days ago. Maybe I was getting used to it since I'd had so much opportunity to practice. The nuclear core inside me felt depleted, though. I needed time to rebuild my reserves.

Ned's John Deere chugged through the doorway of the barn, a huge yellow blade affixed to the front of it. It wasn't the tractor he used for farming, the one with the air-conditioned cab. This was just the utility tractor, for mowing fields and plowing the drives. He idled the engine and jumped down again, slogging through knee-deep snow to close the barn doors.

The spirits must have come to a decision because they started downhill towards us in one large mass. I hoped that they weren't as smart as Jed gave them credit for. I'd rather be able to take them out in one group than attempt to go through the pain of releasing them multiple times. If I could even do that. It was taking all of my focus to stay in the saddle.

Ned hauled himself back onto the tractor and lowered the blade to the ground, scraping snow out of the way as he rolled down the driveway. We stayed where we were and watched him. When he reached the road that connected our houses and turned left onto it the ghosts split. Half continued on towards us while the rest of them changed course to intercept Ned.

Jed and I eyed each other and came to a silent agreement. "We all go with the tractor, then," Jed said. He tapped Hattie with the reins to encourage her down the plowed path.

"What's happened?" Carrie's voice was anxious. She had Demon glued to Charlotte's left flank. She remembered what I'd said earlier.

"The ghosts are smart enough to figure out what we're doing. They've split. Some of them are coming this way and some are headed towards Ned."

She moaned with worry. "What are we going to do?"

I gave her a flat smile. "I'm going to have to release all of them. Come on, let's catch up with Ned." I shoveled in the last bite of sandwich and kneed Charlotte into motion.

When Ned saw us fall in behind him he waved and kept the blade down. We weren't even halfway back to my house before they caught us. Because they'd split, they came in two waves. The first had six ghosts, and they rushed us in a cluster that lowered the temperature another twenty degrees. The need to protect Carrie and her unborn child drove me, and thanks to the sandwich, I almost felt normal again. Charlotte trotted up to meet the ghosts as if she now knew what to expect. I hoped she was right. When they rushed me I forced the remaining energy out of myself.

Fire seared through me, and their souls went on into nothingness, or hell, or the next world, wherever it is that the dead go. Right then, with the flames riding through my body, I didn't care. Charlotte stood her ground and then the next group of them was on us. They didn't stay together.

A swirl of snow exploded under Charlotte's nose and she reared, dumping me onto the plowed surface behind her. The breath went out of me as I landed on my back. My head hit the gravel with a thwack, and my left elbow started hurting. I couldn't remember hitting it, but a fast fall off of a horse can be like that. You land first and then have to do inventory of yourself to figure out if anything has been injured.

I lay there, breathless. Sharp pain radiated across my back, and I wished I'd landed in a pile of snow. I looked up just in time to see the tractor stall and Ned go flying off it. I wondered why he'd bought a tractor that could dump him as easily as my horse could. Demon and Carrie planted themselves between the tractor and Ned, Demon bared his teeth and bit at the air in front of him as if he could see the spirit. Maybe he could.

Jed drew a sword out of his oilskin coat, a massive length of steel that he used to cut through the spirit nearest him. It dissipated as though I had blasted it with my energy. He guided his horse left handed while he used his right to slice through a second ghost. Who the hell did he think he was? King Arthur? I wondered how he'd managed to hide the sword under his coat, but that thought was overtaken by the throbbing in my head. I was going to have to stop hitting it. I lay back against the pavement and watched with mild interest as two ghosts descended over me.

You mussst come with usss.

I looked up at the sick forms of nothing that floated over me. I was more frightened by their hissing speech than anything else that had happened. The fact that they were speaking to me indicated a higher level of consciousness than most of the souls I'd encountered in my life.

"I don't think I will." I waved a dismissive arm at them. They pulled back as if I was dangerous. I contemplated that as they came closer again and remembered that to them, I was dangerous. Jed fought his way towards me, sword swinging like he was trying out for a role in the next movie featuring middle earth and hobbits.

Come with ussss.

Remnants of a face flickered in and out of focus on the one nearest to me and I gagged at the sudden smell of decaying flesh and rotten earth. I tried to scramble backward.

"I said no," I shouted at it. "Go away." I brandished my arm at it and for the third time that morning ghosts dissolved under my power. The burning in my veins grew almost unbearable. I could hear someone crying and then realized that it was me. Someone was screaming. That was probably me too. Through the haze of my pain, I saw something large and green spinning towards me. The tractor.

"Move, Anna," Jed bellowed. Big arms seized me from behind and yanked me back along the pavement, lifting me to my feet as we went. The tractor slid over the spot I'd been lying and drifted into a ditch. Ned's curses were clear and quite creative, which comforted me – at least it meant he was okay.

"There's one more, Anna." Jed clutched me to him, my back pressed against his front, one bear arm wrapped around me, holding me up.

I shook my head back and forth as I slumped against him, tears frozen in rivulets of ice on my cheeks. I couldn't walk, much less banish another ghost. "I can't do it. It hurts too much."

His voice was a fierce whisper against my ear. "You can, Anna. I ask nothing of you that is not possible. You must, now." He spun us both in a half circle, and the road opened up before me. There was one spirit left and it loomed over Carrie and Ned. Their arms were around each other, Carrie half supported Ned as they tried to back away from the threat that they must be able to feel, but couldn't see. They didn't have far to go before they would hit the edge of the road and tumble down the embankment into the creek. Jed had called them hostages, said the spirits would use those that I loved to get me to do their bidding.

"I'm right here," I sobbed into the wind. It turned towards me in a rush of energy and the tractor groaned and shifted in the ditch before it began to levitate and move towards Jed and me. I knew some ghosts could manipulate physical objects, slam doors, tap on walls, turn on your water faucet, but a tractor? It had to weigh three thousand pounds. Jed gave me a little shake.

"Anna?" His voice growled with worry as the tractor made it

back onto the road, hanging a couple of inches off the ground. It was gaining speed. Any remaining adrenaline that my pituitary was holding on to released in a rush.

I'd lost track of how many times I'd released spirits since we'd left the house that morning. Was it three times? Four? I'd never done anything like that. I didn't have anything left to give. If I was right, and I couldn't do it, we would die before I realized that I'd failed.

Jed said I could do it. With a flying tractor bearing down on me, I didn't have much choice. The spirit backed away from us. If I didn't hurry, it might be too far away for me to reach. I screamed as I dredged up a few morsels of energy. I forced it out of me in a rush of heat and threw it as far as I could. Jedediah tossed me away from him, out of the tractor's path. I crashed to the ground and rolled into a drift of white powder. I could feel the snow beginning to melt beneath me and wondered at it. There was clearly a measurable heat to what I did.

Jed stood over me. His lips moved, but I heard nothing. I tried to tell him that the blood boiling in my ears was too loud, but couldn't make my tongue move. He loomed down and pulled my body out of the snowdrift. The movement hurt and I whimpered, but I didn't have the strength left to fight him.

Ned and Carrie rode up on Demon, having once again retrieved Charlotte. Jed pushed me into the saddle for the third time and mounted behind me. He held me against him with both arms, as if he knew my bones had melted. I could tell from Ned's lips that he spoke, knew from the rumble of Jed's chest against me that he responded, but I couldn't hear any of it. The blood pulsed through my veins. The scorch of my energy, too often used, was all I could sense. It hurt so much that I felt dizzy. I closed my eyes. When I felt Jed's arm tighten around me I let consciousness slide.

CHAPTER ELEVEN

THERE WAS A RUSH of voices around me, a cacophony of sound that hurt my still sensitive ears. Which at least meant they registered sound again. Heat seared my muscles, hot coals singed through my blood stream. I drifted in a half conscious haze because I didn't want to face the pain I would feel when I woke up.

"The road is plowed, and both cars are ready. Can we move her yet?" Ned's voice sounded drained.

"I would prefer to give her more time. She will need sustenance as well." Jedediah must have been very close to me. I was still too out of it to flinch away from his voice. Everything seemed too loud. I tried to retreat into the darkness of my mind.

"Jed, here's some coffee for you. I've got a bowl ready for her as soon as she's able to try it. It just needs to be warmed up." Carrie, of course. Food sounded good. Carrie's food was always good. It was almost enough to make me come back.

"I thank you, Carrie. You are very kind."

"I've made sandwiches for the rest of us. They're on the table in the kitchen. Or I can bring you one if you need."

"I will wait. Anna has never exerted herself so much before." He sounded worried. I wondered if I should be concerned. I was okay, though. I hurt, but I thought that I would be okay. In a few weeks. Putting my body back into the snow might help.

"What . . . how did she get rid of them?" Carrie's voice was tremulous.

"Anna has the gift," Jed spoke with patience as if explaining simple addition to a young child. "She can send the souls of those who have lingered too long on this earth to their eternal rest."

I coughed with laughter at Jed's poetic description of the horrible pain I felt every time I used this so-called gift. The half laugh, half gasp bubbled up, incongruous and strange in the stillness of the room. Luna leaped off me. I wondered why she was out of her carrier.

"Anna, are you okay?" Carrie was near me, but I couldn't see her. I swiped at my face and brushed a cold washcloth off my head. The daylight flooded in and I squinted against the sudden rush of light. I wondered when the clouds had dissipated enough to let this much light through. Perhaps the ghosts had caused the overcast day.

"You make it sound very romantic, Jedediah." My voice sounded harsh to me as if the fire inside me had burned up the tissue in my esophagus. He sat next to me in my grandmother's needlepoint chair which he had pulled up to the couch. It was not the sturdiest of chairs, and I wondered that its antique grace had held up under his weight.

He regarded me with his typical calm, his face not reflecting the worry I'd heard in his voice. "It is a noble calling, Anna. Much like how you spend your days giving relief to the living. You offer rest to those who have not transitioned to another plane. It was never intended that your gift be used to protect mankind." The mirth choked out of me. I'd never thought of it that way.

"That was incredible, Anna," Carrie interjected. Only she could be enthusiastic about this. "How does it work? How can you see them? I couldn't see anything out there except for a flying tractor and snow. I knew though, when that last one was in front of us." Her voice shook a little.

"I don't know, Carrie. It feels like energy. Like I have some sort of thermonuclear core." It felt strange, saying this in front of Ned. He'd never asked, just teased me about it. I still cared about him, cared about what he thought of me. In my opinion, we'd known each other too long to have not had this conversation before now. I shouldn't have had to worry that he might laugh at me, and he should have believed me. He looked tense. He didn't say anything in response, but he wasn't laughing.

"How are you feeling, Anna?" Jedediah's voice interjected. Were we boring him? Luna jumped into his lap, and when he didn't boot her to the floor, she began to lick her right front paw with meticulous care.

I tried to glare at him, but he looked so serious that I caved. "I hurt. I'm hungry. I've used this power more times in the last week than I have in my entire life. I'm exhausted." He nodded with empathy, and Carrie burst into motion.

"I can fix the food part," she called from the general direction of the kitchen.

When Jed spoke, he sounded as intense as he looked. Did the man never laugh? "We must change locations, Anna." Ned leaned forward, interested now that the conversation had turned strategic.

"What's your plan now?" I pushed myself into a sitting position on the couch. I had no intention of letting him run my life, but I was willing to find out what he was thinking. It had been a pretty intense day but I had patients to get back to. I had a life.

"They have tracked you well. The best option is to fly. It will be more difficult for them to follow us."

What would my energy burst do to a plane if I had to banish a ghost at thirty thousand feet? It was a scary thought, but in reality, Jed and I would be able to tell if there was one in the area before we took off.

"It would be safer to put some distance between you and this activity." He was getting pushy and I didn't like to feel pressured.

In true physician form, my voice betrayed none of the hysteria I felt. They spend a lot of time in medical school training you to hide your emotions. "Activity? They tossed a tractor at me, Jed. Drove me out of my home. That's a bit more than activity."

As I thought about the end of the fight it made me remember more questions and I tossed them out faster than anyone could answer. "Are the horses okay? What about the tractor? Can we still plow the road? Jed, what's with the sword?" Carrie shut me up when she put a bowl of leftover soup in front of me that looked like it had been supplemented with the remains of my roast. I took the spoon she handed me and started to eat while Ned talked.

"The horses were spooked but they're fine. I've put them out to pasture. The tractor's a bit banged up. It runs, though. The drive's cleared." It usually took about an hour for him to clear the road, and I wondered how long I'd been out. It was brighter outside, and we'd started this madness a bit after noon. That suggested it had only been a few hours, but I was too busy eating to ask. Carrie brought a platter of thick sandwiches out and set them on the coffee table. They looked good. I was hungry enough that I might have one after I finished the bowl in front of me. We were all quiet for a minute while we worked on the food.

"What time is it?" I had to force myself to pause between bites long enough to ask.

"Around four," Carrie answered since the men were both occupied with their bread and meat. My bowl was empty, and I eyed the sandwiches but decided it had to wait. I set my dishes on the table and settled back onto the sofa, warm and full. The pain had just about finished working its way through me. It was happening faster. At this rate, I might not even be very sore tomorrow. A tiny ball of energy lurked deep inside me and I tried to nurture it, in case I needed it again.

"Jed. The sword?" From his expression, it was clear that he had been hoping I'd forget to ask. He put his plate aside and contemplated the tips of his fingers.

"It is very old. It has power in its own right, though it is not as strong as your own."

"If you can banish the ghosts yourself, what do you need me for?"

"The sword does not have that power."

"I saw them disappear, Jed."

"They are not gone. Merely weakened. Your gift serves to release the spirits of the dead. I can but delay them."

"Does that mean they could come back?" Carrie asked hesitantly.

"Yes. It should take them some time to regain enough strength to be a threat to us, but I would prefer to not take the risk."

"How much time?" Ned asked. He sat on the edge of his chair, coiled like a spring.

"I cannot say. Hours. Maybe days. It depends on their natural strength." Jed turned back to me, concern etched on his face. "Are you well enough to travel?"

I nodded, though I still didn't know where we were going. Carrie gathered up some of the dishes from lunch and headed towards the kitchen. When I made as if to get up and help her, she glared at me.

"You stay put," she instructed, her firm voice brooking no resistance. I sank back into the couch. "I might not ever understand what you did out there, but it wore you out. Rest."

Jedediah scooped Luna off his lap and tucked her into the cat carrier next to the door. She didn't even protest. Ned joined Carrie in the kitchen, taking the last of the dishes with him. It was too easy to lie back against the sofa and close my eyes. I heard the murmured conversation drifting from the kitchen as Carrie and Ned washed up.

Even with my eyes shut I could sense Jed's massive form standing over me. His fingertips brushed my cheek with tender care. He opened his hand, and it was big enough that it cupped most of my head, his fingers stroking through my hair. He smelled like sunlight and fresh snow. I wanted to lean into him, breathe in that scent of life as if it would banish the stench of the dead. When I opened my eyes, the look of warmth in his was unmistakable. It had been a long time since I had let someone get close enough to me to have him want me, care for me. It had been a long time, period. My body reminded me in a rush of heat that it hadn't forgotten what desire was, and I flushed. I pulled away from the look in Jed's eyes. He retracted his hand and backed away from me.

"We should depart." His voice was rough. Had he been caught off guard, just as I was?

"Fine." I struggled to my feet in order to put distance between us, and I folded my arms in front of me. I put on my best clinical expression and tried to pretend that my body wasn't whining like a dog in heat. "Where do you want to go?"

"The airport."

"I don't know if we can make it. The roads will be pretty bad."

His eyes were shuttered now, dark and unreadable. I wondered if I'd been mistaken in thinking he cared about me. Then I remembered the feel of his fingers as they caressed my cheek. It didn't seem possible to touch someone like that if you didn't care for them.

"I would get you to safety and then determine what danger it is that we face."

"I thought you knew?" He had that theory, about ghosts wanting to take over the world of the living.

"The end goal and the skirmish today may or may not be related. They wanted to keep you here. Why, I can only guess. I would like for us to leave."

I couldn't argue with that. If something worse was coming I didn't want to be here for it. "Carrie, Ned," I hollered, louder than my little house warranted. "It's time to go."

We had just loaded Luna into Ned's truck when we heard the noise. It was incongruous, on a day with this much snow, this far out into the country.

"What the hell . . ." Ned breathed. A vehicle was coming up the drive, faster than the weather allowed for.

When the black SUV crested the hill the hair on the back of my neck stood up. I didn't recognize the vehicle, and no one ever came the two miles down this drive without a good reason.

"Get back in the house, Carrie," Ned ordered.

"No," I countermanded. "Get in your truck, both of you. Whatever this is, you drive around it when they get here. Get out." Ned's truck was already facing out, ready to go.

"Yes," Jedediah agreed. "There is no reason for you to face further danger. I don't believe this vehicle can block you if you move now." Ned appeared to be caught between the desire to protect his pregnant wife and that stupid need to run headlong into peril, whatever it might be. As if confronting danger kept him from being weak.

When had I learned that weakness came from a thousand flaws and that it took more than facing danger to make you brave? Had Ned missed that lesson?

The SUV was closer. We could see it slip back and forth on the slick road. I didn't know who was in it, but part of me was certain this was some new threat, and I hoped they would skid off the drive before they got to us. "Go," I yelled, and Carrie moved.

"Ned. Let's go," she ordered and jumped into the front seat.

"Damn it, Anna," Ned cursed, but he headed in the right direction. The driver's door slammed and the big diesel engine fired up. The black SUV slid to a stop in front of us, spraying snow behind it. It looked brand new, though under the slushy spray of ice it was difficult to be sure. Dark tinted windows prevented us from seeing inside. It wasn't legal, in Missouri, to have that much tint on your windshield.

Ned's truck rolled forwards. He had enough room to get past the other vehicles in the drive. I ignored his departure as the passenger door on the new car popped open. Ty jumped out and ran through the thick snow to me.

"Ty, what are you doing here?" I looked him over. He looked worried, not his usual self. "Is everything okay?"

"What do you mean? What's wrong with you? Chaz said you needed us out here right away." He looked me over. "You look like hell, Anna." Ty stepped between me and Jed, as though he was protecting me from the big man. Ty was almost as small as me, and I now knew that Jed kept a sword under his long coat. "Did you hurt her?"

"No." Jed's attention was on the SUV. Now that it was parked in my front yard, I could tell it was a Nissan Armada, one of the biggest SUVs on the road.

"Did you guys get a new car, Ty?" I was surprised, because they'd been talking about buying a Prius, not a gas guzzler.

He snorted in disgust. "I don't know what's wrong with Chaz. He came home with it yesterday. Then this morning he said we had to come out here. I guess it's a good thing he traded in the Maxima because it never would have made it here in this weather." He gave me a quick shake. "What's wrong? Was that Carrie and Ned leaving? Why didn't you call me back? I've been leaving you messages all morning."

I rummaged around in my coat pocket and found my cell phone. It was set on 'quiet' and I had missed eight calls that morning. I turned the sound on as the driver door opened. Jed was on full alert. Ned's truck made its way across the bridge, then faltered and came to a standstill as yet another vehicle crested the hill. Jed and I stepped closer together, the instinctive response of two people who have faced danger together and know that they can trust each other in battle.

It was another SUV, black like Chaz's. It pulled up in front of Ned's truck and parked sideways so that it blocked the road. Ned had only plowed one lane through the snow, and the drive was narrow enough that getting two cars by could be tricky even when there wasn't a foot of snow on the ground. Judging where the ravine began was a challenge when you couldn't see it.

"I'm fine, Ty. Why are you here?" Something was going on, I just couldn't figure out how all the pieces fit together.

"Don't lie to me; I'm your best friend. It won't work." Ty nudged me in the arm and indicated the SUV that was blocking Ned's way. "Who's that?"

"I don't know. Why aren't you at the clinic?"

"Because you called Chaz and said you needed us to come up here." Ty was looking at me like I'd lost my mind. I felt like I had.

Jedediah alternated between Chaz's car and the one farther down the driveway. "Anna, did you contact Ty and Chaz and request that they join us here?" His voice was so quiet, I could barely hear him.

"I did not."

"Anna, Chaz says you called him," Ty insisted.

"We must not assume that your friend is himself right now," Jed informed Ty. I sucked in my breath at his implication.

"No. You can't think . . ." I stopped talking because of course that was what he thought. Jed suspected Chaz was possessed by something, just like his spirit had taken over Tobias Peters' body. Tobias hadn't still been in there though, based on the brain scans that I'd seen. "Oh my God."

"Ty, we will explain later, but I would request that you stay here beside us." Ty stepped away from both of us and regarded Jed with suspicion.

"Anna, who is this guy?" It was a reasonable question that didn't have a reasonable answer.

The driver side door on the SUV blocking Ned and Carrie opened and someone got out. It looked like a man, but from this distance I couldn't be sure.

I heard Chaz's familiar voice. He was still sitting in the front seat. "Come back to the car, Ty." Ty started to move towards him but I grabbed onto his jacket sleeve.

"Stay here, Ty. Something's wrong." Events were moving too quickly, unfolding in the clarity of the light that glinted off fresh snow faster than I could process them.

When Ty didn't return to the car, Chaz got out. He wore jeans and a V-neck sweater, and dark sunglasses. Short black hair framed the dark skin of his face. "Ty," he shouted across the distance between us. The hair on the back of my neck prickled again. He looked just like my friend Chaz. He sounded like my friend Chaz. Why was I scared?

The phone in my pocket started to ring. I kept my right hand on Ty and pulled the phone out with my left. It was Ned.

"What's going on out there?" I asked and turned my attention to the two cars almost a quarter mile away.

"You expecting a visit from your old boyfriend?" Ned's voice was cautious.

"What are you talking about?"

"Eric. I never liked him; don't know why he's here now."

"Eric?" Shock resonated through me. Ty stopped trying to pull away from me.

"What does that jerk want? Anna, you aren't talking to him again, are you?" he demanded as his small frame bristled with indignation.

"Anna," Jed's voice commanded attention. "Is this visitor unanticipated? Who is he to you?"

"I haven't seen him in years," I told Jed, feeling testy. It was none of his business what our relationship had been.

Ned's voice continued in my ear. "I don't trust him, Anna."

I thought about Eric, how much I'd loved him and how he'd treated me. Like he loved me at first, but then with condescension. In our final six months together, when he was cheating on me, he had alternated between disdain and outright mean. I'd been convinced I deserved it. It had taken a long time to get over that, and given that I hadn't dated anyone since, maybe I still hadn't. When it came down to it, there was no reason for Eric to be here. It had to be connected to the ghosts.

"No, I'm not expecting Eric." I spoke into the phone in concise syllables to make sure he understood me. "You shouldn't trust him." Jed nodded with approval. "Something is definitely wrong here," I continued. "Chaz told Ty I asked them to come up here this morning, and I didn't." I hoped that I spoke quietly enough that Chaz couldn't overhear me.

"What's going on, Anna? What do you mean you didn't call Chaz?" Ty shook free of my hand.

"We're coming back," Ned informed me, and his diesel started in reverse, retreating back down the drive towards us. I snapped my phone shut and dropped it into my pocket.

Eric, if that's who it really was, got back in his SUV and followed, coming to a stop fifty meters down the drive. He parked right in the middle of the bridge closest to the house, at a bit of an angle. It was an effective means to block everyone in, and I wished that Ned had kept his truck on the other side of the bridge. The car door opened and he again got out, this time close enough that I could see him. It had been a long time, and my heart ached a little bit at the sight of his handsome face and tousled blond hair. I had no idea what he was doing here, but the timing was suspicious.

Ned left his truck running while he and Carrie jumped out and joined our little cluster. "What's happening?"

I was glad Jed answered because I didn't have a clue what was going on. "I believe that this is what the watchers were holding us for. They may have taken over these friends of Anna's. Taken them as hostages so that they can get close to her. That may be what the ghosts in your house were attempting with you."

"Ghosts? Anna, this is crazy. Who's a hostage?" Ty asked, his voice a little shrill.

"They can do that?" Carrie asked. She didn't sound freaked out anymore, just practical.

"It is possible," Jed confirmed. He should know.

"Ty, I don't think I have time to explain right now," I interjected. "Just stay with us here a minute. Things might get strange and I don't want anyone to get hurt." If their plan was to get close to me by threatening the people I loved, it was working. How the hell did they know about Eric, though? That was ancient history.

"Jed, how can we tell if they are . . ." I wasn't sure how to say it. "If they've been taken?"

"It is difficult to see a spirit when it has joined with a body again." That made sense because I couldn't see him like I could see a ghost. I realized that somewhere along the way I'd accepted his story.

"So how do we know?"

"If their behavior has changed, then we should assume something is wrong." It didn't seem like a very foolproof method, and the scientist in me objected.

"Can I release it?"

"Yes, but you run the risk of releasing both spirits in the body."

"What?" I was horrified.

"The power you hold is greater than you realize, Anna. I have told you this."

"You didn't tell me that I could kill someone by accident." The physician's oath resonated in my mind. The most important part of which was 'do no harm.'

"It would not damage their body, but without the soul . . . " He nodded and his voice trailed off.

"This is information you should have shared with me sooner." I was angry, and it showed. "What else have you failed to mention, Jedediah?"

"I don't believe that this is the right time, Anna. As soon as we have the opportunity, I will tell you everything I know."

Chaz strolled out to meet Eric, and they stood there in the cold air, chatting as if they were good friends. They'd known each other, of course, but as far as I knew they hadn't maintained a connection after Eric and I split up.

"What is he doing?" Ty whispered under his breath and started towards Chaz. I stopped him again.

"Please stay here, Ty," I said. "There may be something wrong with Chaz. I didn't call him this morning. I didn't ask you guys to come out here."

He folded his arms and gave me a look that brooked no argument. "Tell me what's going on, Anna."

I kept an eye on the pair of men, but they weren't moving. "You know how I can see ghosts?" I'd told him, once, when we'd had too much to drink. At the time, I knew he didn't quite believe me, who would?

Bless Ty, he didn't raise an eyebrow. "Yes?" was all he said.

"Well, there's a little more to that story than I told you." I hesitated, and Carrie jumped in.

"Let me, Anna. I just learned about this too, so I might be able to explain it the way I understand it."

I quirked an eyebrow at her and she shrugged. "You get a little too far into the science sometimes. It makes you hard to understand." While I pondered that she turned back to Ty. "So, Anna doesn't just see ghosts, she can free their trapped spirits so that they can move on to heaven." Carrie described herself as a 'recovering' Catholic. She hadn't left her God behind when she left the church. "Apparently there are some bad ghosts, though," she continued, "and they're trying to get rid of Anna before she can send them on. They've been wreaking all kinds of havoc here. You should see my kitchen." She paused for a breath. "Jed hasn't admitted it, but he's some sort of guardian angel that's been sent to protect Anna. We're a little concerned that some of these bad ghosts might have taken over your Chaz and Eric and sent them here to hurt Anna. But if she banishes them, she could hurt them for real, so we aren't sure what to do."

Ty stared at Carrie and then looked back at me. There was a long tense moment before he finally spoke.

"That might explain why Chaz was such an ass last night." He paused, thinking it over. "What do I have to do to get my boyfriend back?" This was why I loved Ty so much.

"Ty, there's no way that I'm going to let anything hurt Chaz." I hoped I wasn't making a promise I couldn't keep. "Eric is another matter." Ty's laughter came in a short hard burst.

"No one cares about Eric." Ty informed me. I was joking, but it was pretty clear from Ty's tone and the expression on Ned's face that there was little love lost for my ex-boyfriend. I felt bad about that. He might have been a jerk at the end, but I wouldn't have stayed with him if it had all been bad. He was capable of being sweet too, just not as often as I deserved. Either way, I wasn't going to let the ghosts have him. I was pretty sure that he wouldn't be in this mess if it weren't for me, so it was up to me to fix it.

"So what do we do now?" Ty brought me back to the task at hand.

"I have no idea." It wasn't something that I allowed myself to say often. They train you in medical school to never, ever say anything that might make you sound uncertain of yourself. If you don't at least act like you are speaking God's truth, how are the patients supposed to believe it? There was no way that I was going to pull some doctor bullshit on Ty, though. He'd see through it.

"Jed?" Asking him for advice was becoming too easy. I'd started to rely on him. It scared me, but I didn't have anyone else to turn to. Who else could see the ghosts and fight them with me?

"We need to consult with the Council, Anna. We need to leave here."

I ignored the uneasy feeling I got when he mentioned his council. "We can't just leave Chaz and Eric like this. If they've been possessed, or whatever you call it, then we have to help them." I wasn't going to abandon anyone.

Eric and Chaz started towards us and Jed stepped in front of me. He freed his sword from under his jacket and held it in one hand.

It looked heavy, but he hefted its weight as if it was an extension of his own arm. Ned pulled Carrie next to him and slung his shotgun over his shoulder. With this much weaponry, someone was going to get hurt.

"Stand down, boys," I warned them. "Chaz and Eric aren't our enemies. I don't want anything to happen to them."

"Anna, baby. You look good. How are you?" I shivered at the words. It was Eric's voice, a voice I knew so well. He'd never called me baby, though. It sounded wrong.

"Why are you here, Eric?" I had to shout over Jed's shoulder because he was so determined to protect me. I couldn't see Chaz at all.

"It's been too long, Anna. I've missed you." Eric's voice resonated low and I shifted past Jed enough to see the sardonic smile on his too-pretty face.

"I'm not buying it, Eric. You need to go home to your girlfriend." I was pretty sure they'd gotten married, but I didn't have to acknowledge it.

"She's not in the way anymore, Anna." His voice was chilly and the hair on the back of my neck stood up.

"What's that supposed to mean, Eric?" I felt a sharp pang of concern for the physical safety of the pretty, cardiologist that Eric had left me for. Eric had never been violent. Even when he wasn't being nice, his behavior tended towards emotional abuse rather than physical.

"You don't need to worry about her, Anna. Why don't you come with me, baby, and we can talk about it?"

"I'm not your baby."

"Damn straight, you're not," Ty muttered under his breath and I squeezed his hand.

"Chaz, what's going on?" I hollered over Jed's other shoulder, trying to peek around him to see my friend.

"Anna." He sounded strange too. "Anna, come here. We just want to talk to you." He said my name like it was seductive, like he wanted to flirt with me. Ty tensed beside me, and the only thing that kept him quiet was me squeezing his hand until he winced from the pain. Chaz, by his own admission, hadn't thought about a woman that way in any of his forty years.

Jed straightened which emphasized his intimidating stature.

"Anna is not going to be joining you." It seemed like his deep voice resonated off the hills. "If you want to talk to her, we welcome you." His sword gestured to the space in the snow in front of us. My feet were numb and even in my parka, I started to shiver. If we didn't go inside, all of us were going to die from hypothermia.

"Jedediah. It has been a long time, old friend." It looked like Chaz was trying to smile, but it came out like a pained grimace. I shivered again.

"You presume too much." Jed's voice had a warning tone.

"I find the passage of time never dulls my remembrances of the days I spent living. Is it so with you, Jedediah? Do you think often of Makeda?"

"What is he talking about?" Ty's voice hissed in my ear. I shook my head, unable to answer. I didn't know what was going on any more than Ty did.

"Thousands of years have passed since the Queen of Sheba ruled," Jed replied, but I caught the wary tone in his voice. "Why do such things concern you?"

"Sheba's sons and daughters still rule in her place, Jedediah. Do you not interest yourself in your own descendants?" Chaz's voice was passionate, like a politician giving his most persuasive stump speech.

"My interests are not your concern." Jed was stiff in front of me and his sword never wavered.

"No, I don't suppose you would care about them. After all, when you were living you didn't concern yourself overly much with your family, did you, brother-killer?"

Jed's breath hissed out. "Adonijah."

Chaz flashed his teeth like a rabid dog. "Solomon. Beloved of God." His voice dripped with venom. It didn't sound like Chaz at all. "Finally, you recognize your dearest brother."

"Jed, what is he talking about?"

Jed didn't take his eyes off Chaz. "This is ancient history, Anna. The story is irrelevant."

Chaz's smile curled. "She is beautiful, brother. I look forward to taking her from you, as you took Makeda from me."

"I'm tired of these secrets, Jed." I slapped his arm, which had as much effect as a flea on a mammoth. "I swear to God, you tell me what's going on or I'll go over to Chaz and ask him myself."

"I'm with Anna." Carrie's tone wasn't one I would argue with, but he didn't seem affected by it. "You need to tell us what this is all about."

Jed glanced back at me without dropping the tip of his sword. "It would appear, Anna, that my time as a human has caught up with me. I will explain this 'ancient history' to you when time permits. Now, though, we do not have time. We must go."

"We can't leave Chaz like this," Ty countered.

"No one is leaving Chaz. Or Eric," I added.

"We have no choice, Anna," Jed spoke as if warning a young child of some obvious danger.

"This is not optional." I gritted my teeth in preparation for an argument.

"Listen." His stance didn't change. "They come."

I opened myself to that sixth sense and saw what Jed saw. The horizon to the west hummed and buzzed with the energy of spirits. There were too many to count and adrenaline sang through my veins. My fight or flight reaction had been activated, and these were numbers that we couldn't fight. We barely made it through the last encounter.

"We have to go." My voice was firm. "Jed, we're taking these two with us."

"There's no time, Anna. I can't protect you like this."

"Those ghosts are a ways off. There are only two of them here. We take them with us."

"Jed, if you and Ty can get Chaz into your car, then maybe I can convince Eric to get into mine." Ned shifted his shotgun suggestively.

"Nobody gets hurt here," I reminded him.

I didn't trust Ned's innocent smile. "I'm not planning on shooting him." Carrie elbowed him and he grunted in pain.

"Anna. Time is up. You need to come with us," Chaz called across to me. The spirits looked like a far off ocean wave that rolled towards shore. Ty still held my hand and I could see the crystals of ice that glittered in the air when I breathed. It felt like time itself slowed down.

"Jed, what do they want with me?"

"Anna, with them your life is in danger. I will not turn you over to them."

"We may not have a choice," I pointed out. The odds had shifted. They were not in our favor.

"Not an option, Anna-banana." Ned hadn't rolled the old childhood nickname out in years.

"We must get Anna and Carrie to safety, Ned. More danger approaches." Jed rallied his new second in command.

"Everybody in the car," Ned ordered. Motion erupted around me as Ty released me into Jed's hold. He propelled me towards the Subaru.

"We'll be behind you, Ned," Jed called.

Ned paused. "Carrie – go with Jed. You'll be safer."

"What?" She protested and Ned hugged her to him, he whispered into her ear. Her eyes widened and she pulled away from him. She reached into the truck, grabbed Luna's carrier, ran to the back door of the Subaru and climbed in. Jed tucked me into the passenger seat as Ty got in behind me.

"Put your seat belts on. This may be rough," Carrie ordered. I fastened mine while she hooked the middle belt around the cat carrier. Luna didn't make much noise. I hoped she wasn't as scared as I was.

The diesel roared as it moved forwards and Jed started the Subaru and put it into gear.

"We can't leave Chaz!" Ty yelled over the noise of the engine as Jed pulled out behind the truck. I didn't have an answer for him.

Jed pulled up to Chaz and rolled his window down. "Do you have a mobile number, Adoni?"

Chaz's dark eyes were flat, devoid of their normal light. He jerked his head towards me. "She knows it."

"We will contact you." Jed's voice darkened. "That body is not yours. You will give it back."

"I will trade it now for the girl," said the man that had been Chaz. Ty's breath hissed in shock. Was Chaz still in there? I was frightened for him.

"I will never give her up." Jed's tone had turned to ice.

"Loyalty to one woman is not your way, Jedediah." The Chaz who was not Chaz grinned, but there was no laughter behind it. "But it will not be your choice, brother. She will come to me of her own will."

"Chaz." Ty leaned forward, his fingers stretching towards his lover. "Why are you doing this?"

The flat eyes never glanced at him. "If you want your mate back, you will deliver the woman to me." Chaz/Adoni stepped back against his SUV.

"This can't be happening," Ty whispered.

Carrie grabbed his hand. "Anna can get him back, Ty. I know she can."

"I am so sorry." I shook in the front seat as Jed pulled past Chaz's new car. "I don't know why this is happening, but I never wanted you involved. That's why I came out here. I thought it would be safe."

"I am to blame." Jedediah's tone was matter of fact. "In my haste to find Anna and protect her, I fear I have led the danger to her. To all of you."

"Jed, who is Adoni?" I asked.

"Long ago, he was my brother."

"Why does he hate you so much?" Carrie asked the question that was next on my lips.

"I killed him." Jed turned to me. "It was long ago."

He'd mentioned that. It had gotten old. He interpreted the look of irritation on my face and continued, his tone thick with arrogance.

"Thousands of your years have passed since I lived as a man on this earth. Do not judge me by your world. It was a different time. Had I not had him killed, he would have murdered me."

"I'll kill him if I get the chance," Ty muttered.

"Me too," I added. "I don't think you did the job well enough, Jed." He didn't reply.

The diesel moved again in a quick burst at the bridge and I saw Eric scramble out of its way.

"Ned's going to shove Eric's SUV out of the way if he won't move it," Carrie explained. "That's why he wanted me with you."

"Yes, let's keep you out of any vehicle that's going to be in a collision." Babies and sudden traumatic impact didn't go well together. Carrie shouldn't be here at all. She should be in her kitchen, baking bread and knitting baby sweaters. I fell silent and gripped the door handle as the diesel again shifted forward, a spray of snow shooting out from the rear tires.

"Chaz ... I can't call him that. Adoni is getting in his car." Carrie informed us.

Jed accelerated and swung as wide as he could in the narrow confines of the driveway, but Chaz's SUV was moving, and it wasn't moving out of our way. He was on a collision course. Jed stopped and Chaz did too. It was like a game of chicken, but Chaz's Armada had a serious weight advantage over my Subaru. If the ghost that was controlling Chaz was stupid enough to hit us, my Subaru would crumple like a tin can.

It was my fault. I had put my friends in danger, and I was the one who had the power to put an end to it. Chaz, Ty, Carrie and Ned. Their baby. The danger stopped for them if I wasn't around. Thou shalt do no harm. I unhooked my seatbelt, opened the door, and slid out of the stopped car before Jed could reach for me. I ran towards Chaz as best I could, stumbling on the icy gravel road beneath me. I heard a door on the Subaru open.

"Anna!" It was Jed. He'd be close behind me. He was a big man and I doubted that I could outrun him.

Adoni/Chaz had started moving again, straight towards me. Cold seared my lungs as I pushed myself to run faster. I needed to get to him before Jed could stop me.

The SUV stopped moving. I was close enough that I could see Chaz's inscrutable face through the darkened windshield. I had to remind myself that this wasn't Chaz. Footsteps fell hard on the drive behind me as Jed tried to catch me, but I reached the front end of the black SUV first, my momentum carrying me into it with a thump.

"Adoni." I ran around the passenger side and tried the door. It was locked. The tinted window rolled down as Jed arrived, bristling with anger like a porcupine ready to fire his quills. I grabbed onto the window ledge and reached inside. I gripped the inside of the door handle as hard as I could, as if that could prevent the big man from picking me up and carrying me away if he so chose.

"Give me back Chaz and Eric, Adoni, and you can have me." I remembered to suck air into my lungs. "Leave my friends out of it, though."

"No," Jed bellowed. He leaned around me and grasped the door on either side of me. He still believed he could protect me.

"We will have you either way. I don't have to give up this body." Adoni/Chaz seemed pretty sure of himself.

"It isn't yours," I reminded him and he shrugged.

"No matter."

I leaned my forehead against the doorframe and tried to calculate equations for an energy source that no one but me had ever heard of, with variables I couldn't quantify. "What do you want with me?"

"There are others that wish to meet you. Your skills are unique."

"You're a delivery boy." His arrogant expression faltered for a moment. I had struck a nerve. "You've heard my terms," I insisted. "You give Chaz back. Now. I'll go where you tell me to." Jed's arms tightened in protest, but he stayed quiet.

"It has been some time since I had form. I find that it pleases me."

"It's not yours to keep."

"Banish me and you kill your friend as well."

"You think that I don't know that?" I stomped down on the bridge of Jed's foot with as much force as I could muster. He didn't make a sound but let go of the car for a moment.

There was risk, and it wasn't my risk to choose, but I didn't know any other way. I clung to the car and released a tiny burst of the fire within me. My skin scalded as the energy licked into the car metal, which conducted it as if it were electricity.

It sizzled through the frame and came up through the faux leather seats, through the wood steering wheel. I wasn't surprised by Adoni's choice. He was just a cockroach, fleeing rising water.

I hit the door locks and was halfway into the car when Chaz slumped over onto the steering wheel. Unconscious or dead, I didn't know. His foot came off the brake and the car drifted forwards. I squeaked in alarm.

"Anna," Jed yelled my name and tried to climb in with me. I tried to push Chaz back off the steering wheel and the car turned towards the ditch. I had to see if he was breathing, but I needed the car to stop moving. There wasn't room between Chaz's body and the steering wheel for me to climb onto him and get my foot on the brake.

I dove face first between his knees and pressed my hand to the brake pedal just as the car started to slide. It was too late. For a moment, my body felt suspended in the air. Then we hit. The impact smashed my face into the floorboards and my back into the steering wheel and I lost my hold on the brake pedal. It didn't matter, though, we weren't moving anymore. I laid my hand down on the emergency brake as hard as I could, gratified when it moved several notches. Other than that, I couldn't move. Panic bloomed in my chest as I realized that I was trapped. I took deep breaths to calm myself. Jed would come for me. I heard a commotion of doors opening and the vehicle shifted.

"Anna? Are you hurt?" Jed's hands gripped my thighs. Chaz's legs against my chest were inert. I needed to see if he was okay. My stomach clenched at the thought that I might have sent his soul away.

"Help me up," I shouted, and the noise of my own voice in the tiny space of the floorboard hurt my ears.

He hesitated. "Are you hurt?"

"Get me out," I yelled again.

Big hands gripped my waist and pulled. I scrabbled with my hands to push off of the floorboard. It was only a moment and then Jed had me in his lap. We weren't exactly in the seat because of the angle of the vehicle. My ass was half on his leg, half on the dashboard. His hands pushed my long hair back and he searched my face. Fingers touched my cheek.

"You're bleeding. Are you well?"

"Your hands feel good." It wasn't what I'd meant to say. Jed pulled me against him. I touched my face and felt the sore spot on my cheek. My fingers came away with a smear of blood, but there wasn't much of it.

"Why is it so difficult to keep you safe?" He said it in a murmur as if it was a rhetorical question. I didn't try to respond.

I reached out to Chaz and breathed a cautious sigh of relief because he was alive. His seatbelt was on, but he'd managed to hit his head on something. The skin on his forehead was punctured and oozing blood. A hematoma was already forming. How he'd managed to damage the flat space right above his nose without hitting that prominent feature I didn't know. Based on palpation, though, his nasal bones were intact.

The car had gone down the embankment, but it was still upright, and the airbags hadn't deployed. At least we hadn't rolled.

Chaz's pulse was steady, his breathing untroubled. It seemed like he was just sleeping. I didn't have that sense of the soul being gone like I got with someone who was brain dead, but I couldn't be certain without having the results from a scan.

Ty's face appeared in the window and then Chaz's door popped open with a flurry of snow and cold. He looked at Chaz and hesitated.

"Adoni is gone but he's got a hefty bump on his head. His seat belt is on so there shouldn't be spinal damage, but we can't be sure."

Ty's hand wavered. "Chaz? Baby, are you there?" He reached out and touched Chaz's cheek with his fingers.

"Give me a handful of snow, Ty, would you? I want to get some ice on this." I shifted in Jed's grasp and plucked off my glove. It would do. Ty dumped a few handfuls of snow into it and I laid it against the wound between Chaz's eyes.

I was trying to figure out the best way to extricate Chaz from the vehicle given that we didn't have a backboard to tie him to when the blank expression on his face shifted into discomfort.

"Hey, Chaz. How are you feeling? Any neck pain?" I asked.

"No." He turned his neck and started moving all of his appendages in frantic motions, which was a good sign.

"I feel sick," he announced in a panicked voice.

I unhooked his seatbelt and Ty pulled him out of the car. I could hear the retching and didn't feel compelled to follow. Ty was an RN, he could take care of the bumped head and the vomit. If he saw some indication of trouble, he would ask for help.

"That was a dangerous thing to do." Jed still held me on his lap.

"I hoped the car would absorb some of the impact. I didn't release Adoni. He's still out there."

Jed's answer was silence.

"Now that he's found you, he won't stop, will he?"

"The spirits have dissipated," Jed spoke with a near clinical detachment. "When Adoni fled Chaz, he lost control of them."

"They'll come back." I knew they would.

"They still want you." He agreed.

I leaned my head against Jed's shoulder. He tilted his head towards mine and pressed his lips against my hair. His breath mingled with mine. It was such a tender, intimate feeling. It scared me and I pulled away.

It took a moment to untangle myself and then I jumped out. I landed on my feet with a painful thump.

"Anna," Jed called after me. I stepped out of his reach and then began to scramble up the hillside after Ty and Chaz.

Ned's truck was parked at the bridge. He and Carrie stood with Ty and Chaz, looking down at the Armada. Eric and his SUV were gone. Chaz looked like himself again, something inherent in how he held his body. He leaned against Ty with the weariness of someone who's just finished his first triathlon.

"What happened?" I asked, hoping that my face didn't betray the intimate moment that Jed and I had just shared. The one I had run from.

Ned answered me, his arm tucked around Carrie. "Eric took off right after you guys went down the hillside. Good job getting Chaz back. How much time do we have?"

"They've gone for now, but I'm afraid they'll be back." I looked up the hill as if I could tell where Eric had gone. There was nothing I could do about it right this minute but I would have to find him at some point and make sure he didn't still have a ghost in him.

"They can't have you." Chaz's voice surprised me. He still leaned against Ty, but looked decent for someone who'd been possessed for the last twenty-four hours and then been in a car crash, bashed his head, and vomited up his lunch. Which was to say, he looked like hell, but it could have been worse.

"How are you feeling?" I asked.

"Been better. Don't let them get you, Anna." I rubbed his arm in reassurance.

Jed crested the ledge and made his way towards us. "You must all go. Somewhere where there are no ties to Anna."

"I'm not leaving." Carrie always surprised me.

"The hell you aren't." Ned turned on Carrie. "You'll go to your mother's, like we planned."

"Don't make the mistake of thinking you can order me around, Ned."

"He's right." I jumped into their argument. "I don't want any of you getting hurt. This isn't about you. It's about me."

"You're like my sister. We can help you." The fact that Carrie thought of me as a sister was really sweet.

"You are nothing but hostages to these spirits. They will use you to hurt Anna." Jed's words were harsh, but he spoke with a gentle tone. "In this, Ned is correct. It is best if you go."

"Chaz needs to sit down." Ty called us back from our argument.

"Let's go back to the house for a few minutes. We can get warm, and I can fix a snack for anyone who's hungry. Then we can figure out what to do." Carrie's suggestion was well made. It was cold and we'd been outside far too long. I had touched the core of my power again and craved more calories. I followed her, another moth to the flame. Jed stalked beside me and muttered about the importance of leaving.

Ned moved his truck to the far side of the bridge and parked it in the middle of the drive.

When he walked back past me, he explained. "We won't get hemmed in, this way, and no one can get past us." His shotgun was over his arm again. He nodded at the SUV in the ditch and said, "I'll get the tractor." As he walked away, his shoulders were rigid with anger. Carrie stormed towards the farmhouse with Ty and Chaz in her wake. I scooped up a handful of snow and laid it against my cheek. That much direct cold wasn't good for skin but I needed to get ice on it or I'd have a hell of a bruise.

Jed touched his fingers to my face. "Are you well?"

"It stings." Tears came to my eyes and I had the overwhelming desire to sit down and cry. It had nothing to do with my bruised cheek. It was the culmination of a thousand shocks and never-ending fright.

His hand cupped my face for an instant, and then he turned. "We go with your friends now, but then we will leave. I would have you to safety."

"Why did Adoni mention the Queen of Sheba?" I asked.

Jed stopped. "Happenings of three thousand years ago do not matter today." His face closed over with resolve.

"You've said that already, but I think that I have a right to know," I argued. Whatever was happening between us, it wouldn't happen if I couldn't trust him. He had to tell me who he was.

"I told you that I was once a King."

"Does that mean you had a thing with the Queen of Sheba?" After all we'd been through, I still found these little revelations difficult to grasp.

He stared at me with impassive eyes, which told me more than if he'd just said yes.

"Did you love her?" Why did the thought of that fill me with jealousy?

"She was loved by all." It was, and wasn't an answer to my question.

"Did you have children?" I called, but Jed was already walking away.

CHAPTER TWELVE

CHAZ AND TY SPOKE to each other in hushed tones, a river of Spanish too fast for me to follow, as if they feared we would overhear their words. Chaz looked drawn and tired. He didn't protest as I checked his pulse and felt his face for fever. The hematoma had stopped swelling under ongoing ice. There was only one way to know if he had bleeding or swelling in his brain, but we didn't have access to a CT machine. We could try to get him to a medical center if we needed to, but the nearest one was a solid thirty-minute drive on good roads.

With the snow we'd had, I didn't know if we could get my Subaru out or not. If the situation was critical we could call for the medevac helicopter, but I hoped that wouldn't be necessary.

I was confident that Ty and I could monitor Chaz for any problems related to the head injury. Although the medical training I'd had didn't cover what to do if your patient was possessed by a ghost and then had that spirit driven out. I didn't know how that might affect him. Maybe I should call Father Davies. He was the priest at Our Lady of Perpetual Sorrow just a few blocks from my clinic. He might have access to resources on recovering from possession after all the exorcisms the Catholic Church claimed to have performed.

"It's okay, Anna." Chaz tried to reassure us. "I'm just cold and tired. My head hurts, but nothing terrible. I need to tell you-"

"Later." I interrupted him. "Rest for a bit first. I'll turn the heat back up." I didn't need to tell Ty to let me know if Chaz's condition changed. We had worked together long enough to be able to handle a patient without wasting many words.

Ty grabbed the throw off the back of the couch and pulled it up over his partner's legs. My makeshift glove icepack had been exchanged for a package of freezer peas that I kept around for this purpose with a tea towel tucked between it and Chaz's forehead in order to keep his skin from getting too cold. I followed the sounds of coffee being made and found Carrie and Jed in the kitchen.

"He can be so frustrating." She slammed the coffee grounds canister onto my countertop and I raised my eyebrows. I didn't think I'd ever seen Carrie mad before.

"He would keep you from harm." You could rely on Jed to be rational, even in the face of Carrie's fury.

"I can take care of myself," She spat the words out as if it was a point she was tired of making.

"How will you protect yourself, and your child, from this threat?"

"Ned can't do any better. He acts like I'm helpless."

"It strokes his male ego when you need his help, Carrie," I interjected. "Basic psychology. If he thinks you can manage without him, then he doesn't feel like he brings anything of value to the relationship."

A look of amusement crossed Jed's face and then was gone again. "Indeed," He agreed.

The tractor chugged out of my barn and headed around the corner of the farmhouse towards the black car that was nose down in the edge of my cornfield.

"He does have his uses," Carrie admitted.

"Is your friend well?" Jed inquired.

I sat down next to him. "I think his head is all right, but I can't tell for sure without a brain scan. We'll monitor him, make sure he doesn't worsen. In terms of his soul, I don't have much experience in cases like this. You would know more than I do about it. Is he going to be okay?" Jed leveled dark eyes on me and I shrugged. "Sorry, but I think they already know that you're up to your neck in this. The whole sword thing may have blown your cover."

Carrie whirled around. "I knew you didn't tell us everything. Spill the beans."

I felt bad about disclosing Jed's secret, but then, he hadn't asked me to not tell anyone. Maybe I was the only one who felt weird about it.

"I think I deserve to know, too. Whatever this is involves all of us now." Ty slumped into the chair across from me and accepted the first cup of coffee that Carrie poured with a grateful nod. "Chaz is asleep. We should let him rest for a while. His pulse is pretty rapid and he's a bit shocky." That was Ty's jargon for a stress reaction that was causing dazed symptoms in a patient, not to be confused with the life-threatening condition of shock.

"Very well." Jed sounded resigned to another delay in our departure. I didn't sense any ghosts in the area, so it felt safe to let Chaz rest.

Jed took a sip of coffee and waited for Carrie to stop handing out cups and join us at the table. "You have realized today, if you were not aware already, that there are some spirits that linger on the earth." He paused, took a sip of coffee and let this sink in over his audience. "I am one such spirit. I did not take over another soul's form, as happened to your Chaz." He nodded at Ty. "This body had no spirit, so I was able to fill it."

Carrie leaned forward, fascinated. "I knew you were an old soul. How many lifetimes have you lived?"

"I will tell you much that you wish to know. Have patience."

I noticed that he said much, not all.

"As in all things," Jed slipped into the style of speech that betrayed his age, "there are spirits that are good, and those that are evil. There are some that have not yet been forced to choose. In my brief time as a man, I did not draw a line between light and dark. To me, life was about war and wealth. I was a king of Judah and like many who have power, I did not use it well." Jed took a sip of coffee and continued. "The world was young then. Egypt's power had crested and the Assyrians were the leaders of the world. I tell you this so you know that this time that I speak of was long ago."

The kitchen door opened, a burst of cold air flowed in from the porch. Ned stomped in and shook flakes of snow from his hair. It was too soon for him to be done. He took in the room and gave us a sheepish grin. "Tractor's out of gas."

"There should be some in the canister in the barn," I reminded him.

"I know there is. It's cold out. Thought I'd warm up first." He grabbed the old kitchen stool out of the corner. Brushing the hair off his forehead, he asked, "What'd I miss?"

"Jed is telling us his story. In a former life, he was a king in . . . Where was it, Jed?" Carrie poured a cup of coffee and plunked the chipped coffee mug in front of her husband before she turned her full attention back to the storyteller.

"Judah," Jed reminded her. I wondered if I could find a map. If we were at the condo I'd look it up online, but the farmhouse was off the internet grid.

"There is not time for me to tell you everything. It is enough, I think, that you know where I came from. Even though you may not believe." I looked at Ned and saw the doubt in his eyes. It did sound crazy, especially to someone like me who had devoted the last fifteen years to science. I'd learned to trust Jed in the last four days. If he said he lived in Judah, wherever that was, then I had to believe it, no matter how fantastic it sounded.

"I am not proud of my time as a man. They called me king, but it was an inherited title, not one that I earned. My father chose me as his heir, not because I was most suited, but because he wanted to keep my brother from the throne. Much happened in those times, and someday, perhaps, I will tell you more. For now, you should know that my brother was named Adonijah. He tried to take the throne from me, and I killed him. He may hold a grudge."

"What was your name, when you were king?" My voice sounded off. I thought that I might know the answer, but I needed him to say.

"Solomon. I was King Solomon. My given name is Jedediah."

Carrie's voice ticked up towards the soprano range. "King Solomon, like, in the Bible, King Solomon?"

Jed nodded. "I believe that the man I was is mentioned in that book." He looked embarrassed. "You should not believe all that it says about me."

Carrie and I were going to be reading the Bible looking for references to Solomon as soon as we had the chance. I was pretty sure that my aunt's copy was still on the bookshelf in the parlor, but I wasn't rude enough to read it in front of Jed.

"And the Queen of Sheba?" I asked, hoping I didn't sound petty.

An odd look crossed Jed's face. "Her name was Makeda. She was the greatest ruler of our time. I met her, once. My brother wanted her, but she chose me. Losing the throne wasn't the only thing that made him hate me."

"Do her children still rule?" I was thinking of what Adoni had said.

"It is rumored that her bloodline lives in the rulers of several African nations."

"Is it your bloodline as well? Solomon's, I mean?"

Jed paused long enough for me to wonder why it mattered to me. So what if King Solomon's descendants ruled a few countries in Africa?

"It is possible," he admitted. I tried to suppress the string of jealousy that plucked deep inside me again.

"This history lesson is interesting, but what does any of it have to do with us?" Ned's words sounded harsh, but his tone expressed bewilderment.

"When I died, my soul remained among the living. I was a ghost, as you say. I wandered for many years before I found purpose." Jed took a sip of coffee. "We all must choose our way. Good, or evil."

"Is the distinction always that clear to you?" Carrie asked.

"When I first joined the Council, perhaps not. In the last thousand years, it has become more so."

"What is this Council?" I was exasperated. I couldn't figure out what their purpose was, other than tormenting me when I slept.

"There are a few souls that are more powerful than the rest. Their chosen purpose is to keep the balance between the living and the dead."

"What does that mean?" Ty leaned forwards on the table, the side of his head cradled in his hand. I interrupted Jed's attempt at a reply.

"Who are they?" I shot an apologetic glance at Ty, but the conversation was too esoteric. I needed details.

"They are the Zophasemin." He paused, registered the lack of comprehension on our faces, and clarified. "The Watchers." We must have still looked confused. "Perhaps you are familiar with the term fallen angel?"

"Aren't they evil?" Carrie asked.

"Are they real?" I couldn't keep the disbelief out of my voice. Jed being a historical king was one thing, but angels were too close to organized religion for me to accept.

"You should not believe everything that you read in your Christian Bible. There are many versions of history. Not everything you have been taught is accurate."

"Are you also a fallen angel?" Ned was as much of a skeptic as I was.

"I am not. You should understand, though, the beings that your Bible calls fallen angels are not angels at all," Jed said this as if he knew that there were angels and he was alarmed that the fallen angels would be associated with the real ones.

"So what are they?" Ned asked and Jed gave an exasperated sigh.

"I'm trying to tell you. They are spirits who left this earth when they died and went to heaven. They are said to have angered the Lord in some way. So much so that he sent them back to your world, for eternity."

"If they pissed off God so much, how good can they be?" I thought it was a fair question since Jed wanted me to work with them.

"They hope to atone for their sins and be accepted back into heaven." He said it with a straight face.

"Is that what you are trying to do?" I asked without thinking. An expression of discomfort flitted across Jed's face as if I'd hurt him. When he spoke it was almost a whisper and his dark eyes bored into mine.

"My sole purpose at the present time is to keep you safe, Anna."

Tears pricked the edge of my vision and I looked away to mask my rush of emotions. Ned cleared his throat.

"Jed, I don't quite understand what the Council's purpose is. Can you clarify that?" Carrie jumped into the conversation.

He turned his attention back to her and I took a deep breath to calm myself down. "Of course. The Council tries to maintain the balance between the world of the living, and the realm of the dead. As you now know, some spirits never ascend. A number of those are disturbed beings. The accumulation of these dangerous spirits can be a hazard for the living."

"What does that mean?" Ty looked bewildered.

"There are evil spirits who want to reclaim your world, Ty. They want to return to life. They would wreak havoc upon you and the hell that they would build here would be far worse than the damage humankind has wrought alone."

I shivered. "Where does your brother fit into this story?"

"I did not realize until today the extent of Adonijah's involvement. I knew that he still roamed this world, but it has been many centuries since I last encountered him." Jed took a sip of coffee, and

I thought he had timed it to give himself a moment to think. When he spoke again his words chilled me. "Adoni came here to find Anna. I do not doubt that he would relish the chance to cause me harm, but he has thrown his lot in with the souls aligned against us. Taking Anna, or destroying her, will be his primary goal."

I flung my hands up in the air. "What the hell does this have to do with me?"

"There are only ever a few born with your gift. The ability to release the souls that are trapped here is rare. You are one of the few tools the Council has that can shift the balance of power."

"What do you mean, 'shift'?" Ned appeared to have forgotten about the tractor. "You make it sound like these spooks are stronger than we are, that they already have the upper hand."

"The number of souls compared to the living is not sustainable. The dead could make a stand if they become much stronger. I believe they may try to take over the living world. It is this that we hope to prevent."

"How?" Ned was poised, coiled for action like a great cat watching lesser creatures at the watering hole. Jed wasn't some flighty antelope, though.

"The same way that Adonijah took Chaz. For a strong enough spirit, it is possible to take over the body of a living man, to suppress the rightful soul."

"Jedediah's, uh, donor, was brain dead. He was kept alive on life support. I've seen the medical records. Jed didn't steal someone, like what happened to Chaz." For some reason, it was important to me that they know this about him.

"If Anna is so important, why not get in touch with her earlier? Why wait until now?" Ty had to be thinking that we could have avoided getting anyone else involved in all of this.

"We couldn't find her. The ways that we traditionally would use were . . . closed to us." I was glad he wasn't going to tell them about the fact that I had night terrors and had to take a serious drug cocktail in order to sleep at night. Although I was beginning to believe that this Council caused it. If that was true, I was going to be pissed, because it's a damned inconvenient problem to have.

"If you couldn't find her, then why are all of you here now?" Ned was skeptical again.

"The Council foresaw her death." He held up a hand, an attempt to forestall the inevitable barrage of questions. "They can see the currents of life and death in a way that you cannot imagine. It is possible to watch the future death of someone, yet not know when it will occur. One who knows how to read these waters can see the ripples, follow the impact of such an event."

I knew I was about to get ahead of his narrative, but I was impatient. "Why didn't you just look me up in the phone book, if you knew so much about me?"

"Your name. Anna Roberts. We sought you under your given name. Walker."

"Oh." I guess the Council didn't read legal notifications from the state court. "Walker was my father's name," I explained. "I took my aunt and uncle's last name when they adopted me." I'd never known my father and I'd never been able to ask my mother why she'd given me his name when she'd never married him. Regardless, I'd had no allegiance to it.

"I was given the timeframe of Anna's death, and the location. I spent days watching for her, but did not know her until death was upon her."

"Anna!" Carrie wrapped her arm around me. "What happened? You didn't tell us any of this."

"It was lucky for me that you were there," I admitted to Jed. "I don't think I realized how close a call it was."

"Tell me what happened," she ordered.

"I was walking home from the office. A truck ran a red light and nearly hit me. I suppose it would have if Jed hadn't pushed me out of the way."

"Didn't your auntie teach you to look both ways before crossing the street?" Ned admonished, bringing a welcome moment of levity to the conversation.

I wrinkled my nose at him and played along, dipping my voice into a country drawl. "Not much traffic, out here in the boonies." We all smiled for a moment and then Ned's tone turned more serious.

"So let me see if I have this straight. You and your fellow ghost cronies, some of whom were cast out of heaven," Ned's voice betrayed a hint of skepticism, "need Anna and her super ghost blasting power in order the save the world from some sort of apocalyptic battle where ghosts are going to try to take over the bodies of everyone alive."

"I'd say that's about it." We all started at Chaz's voice.

"You're supposed to be resting." Ty was quick to admonish him, already at his side. Chaz used the wall for support and he still looked ashy pale.

"Hard to sleep when the world's about to end." Chaz clung to Ty and slumped into his boyfriend's freshly vacated chair. "They want you, Anna. They want you bad." He turned to Jed. "I don't know what you did to piss your brother off, but he really hates you."

"Jed got the girl and the throne, and then killed him," Carrie explained.

Chaz nodded in understanding. "That would do it."

"Are there others out there? That can do what I can?" I asked.

Jed looked cautious. "A few."

"Then you don't need me. You can get one of them to fight your little ghost battle." I was looking for a way out.

"I think you know that it is not that simple, Anna. They have brought this to you. They threaten your friends, they threaten you."

Irritation flared inside me. "Tell me, Jed. How did they find me?"

Jed had the grace to look chagrined. "It is possible that I was followed."

"Possible? You think?" I took a deep breath to calm myself, but it didn't work. "I hadn't seen a ghost in ages, Jed. Not until the day after I met you. There's a significant correlation there." I didn't raise my voice often. I had to be very angry.

"I would not have you in danger."

"Even so."

"I cannot change what is done."

"Thanks for the help." I scooted my chair back and left the table for the cold of the back porch. Ned followed me.

"Where you goin'?" he drawled while I pulled on my boots and reached for a heavy coat.

"I don't know." I stomped through the doorway into a knee-deep snowdrift and he followed me, shutting the door behind him. I was just trying to get away from Jed and he knew it. "We could get the truck out of the ditch," I suggested.

"Yeah, we should." Ned leaned up against the door like he wasn't going anyplace soon. "You're kinda hard on him."

"What do you mean?"

"I mean, it can be hard, being your guy."

"Jedediah is not my guy."

"He's the closest thing we've seen around here in some time."

I let that slide. "What do you mean, 'it can be hard'?"

Ned shrugged, a boyishly cute gesture that I used to find irresistible. "It was tough, Anna. You expect a lot, and you're so smart and successful that you're more than a little intimidating. And you're pretty. That's a lot for the average guy to deal with."

"You know, Ned, I've just about had it with the male ego."

"So date women."

I snorted out a laugh. "I might need to consider that." Heavy thick flakes of fresh snow drifted around us. That didn't bode well. "Is that why you broke it off with me? I was too difficult to deal with?"

"That's ancient history, Anna. But no. I knew I was going to be a farmer. We all knew that. You were bigger than this." His look indicated the farmhouse, the countryside. "You needed to go to the city and be a doctor there. You never wanted to be the country bumpkin small town doc."

Tears stung my eyes, not because I still wanted to be with Ned, but for the girl that I'd once been, the one who'd been brokenhearted. "I would have done it."

"I wasn't going to ask you to be something you aren't." He shrugged into his jacket. "Take it easy on Jed. He's an all right guy. I like him."

Great. I was getting advice on my love life from my ex-boyfriend. "There's nothing between Jed and I," I reminded him.

"Lie to yourself if you want to, Anna. It's none of my business, other than I'm your friend and I'd like for you to be happy."

"Isn't it a little strange to be talking about my hypothetical love life when we're all in danger here?"

"I don't know that there's ever a good time. There's always something else going on that you can use as an excuse to keep yourself away from someone good."

"He's a ghost, Ned. He's been dead for three thousand years, and the only reason he can walk around and talk to us is that he took possession of a brain dead man's body. I'm not sure he's great relationship material."

"There you go, setting up all those rules that prevent you from being happy." Ned paused a moment and brushed some of the snow out of his hair. "It warmed up a bit, so the snow's falling heavier again." He stated the obvious, just to change the conversation. "And the wind's blowing. That'll be a problem for us."

"It's been a bad winter." I embraced the chance to talk about the weather instead of my love life. "Let's go get the gas. I'll help with Chaz's car. We don't have much time before it'll be dark out."

He gave me a quick grin. "Sounds good."

The wind picked up falling snow and blew it across the drive in a dizzying swirl. The green of the tractor above me turned gray in the haze of white. I leaned back against Chaz's SUV and tried to keep track of my bearings.

Ned slid down the embankment and joined me. "It's nearing white out conditions. We've got to get this done and get back to the house while we can still find it."

I didn't bother with a reply. I aimed the torch against the undercarriage of the truck, shoveling snow out of the way with my arms so Ned could reach the towing hooks. He checked the chains and then we struggled up the snowy slope.

The massive man stepped out of the swirls next to the tractor and I jumped. "Christ, Jed. You scared me."

"The weather is worsening," he informed me.

"We noticed." Sarcasm appeared to be lost on him as he nodded agreement.

"Good. Should we not leave this until after the storm?"

"Ned checked radar." He'd been fortunate to get reception for long enough to access his weather app. "There's a big band of moisture and we're under a blizzard warning. If we don't get this truck out of the field we won't be able to find it until spring." That might be an exaggeration, but with how hard the winter had been, and how fast the snow was falling I might be right.

The engine on the tractor gave a roar as Ned started forwards. The chains tightened and there was a moment when I wondered if it wouldn't work, as the tractor stopped moving and the truck in the ditch stayed put. Physics won out. The force the tractor exerted was stronger than the inert weight of the SUV. The snow-covered vehicle jostled, resisted, and then began to slide back uphill.

Ned silenced the tractor in front of my house. My little SUV was covered in a fresh blanket of thick wet snow. It would have been perfect for a snowball fight if we weren't worried about how we were going to survive the next few days. In light of the circumstances, I resisted the urge to gather up a nice firm ball of it and fling it at Jed's head. I'd always had good aim and it was a pity to not put that skill to use.

Ned jumped down and helped Jed unhook the tow chains while I tried to see how much damage there was to the front end of Chaz's new truck. I didn't see anything obvious but the light was too bad to be sure. We'd need a nice sunny day in order to see it well.

"I could plow the drive again so that we can get the trucks down it." I heard Ned holler.

I knew where he was going with that. "Don't bother. You can do it when the snow stops."

"We cannot wait, Anna. We must go." Jed looked back and forth between us while the snow whipped dark curls of hair around his face. I made a mental note to give him a handful of my ponytail holders when we were back in the house.

"The highways will have closed by now," I explained. "They won't have plowed the road up to the drive or any of the roads in between here and the Interstate. It's snowed too much. We're stuck until the weather clears, and even then it could be a couple of days before they get out this far." The additional inches we'd gotten since Ty and Chaz arrived had pushed the accumulations over the top. We weren't going anywhere. "There's just been too much snow," I reiterated.

"There must be some way," he argued.

"It's not worth the risk. If we were to get stuck out on the road somewhere we'd be in serious trouble."

Ned agreed, "Hard as it is to believe, we're safer here."

Jed looked baffled. "In Switzerland, this snow would not stop transportation."

I shrugged, but it was Ned who answered. "Well, this ain't Switzerland. It's Missouri. Anna, help me get the horses back in?"

The pasture where the mares were wasn't very far from the house, but it felt like a long walk when I had to slog through snow that was above my knees. By the time we made it back through the wet snow to the barn, I was soaked through. Charlotte and Hattie, who were as wet as I was, were happy to be back in the relative warmth of the barn. I rubbed them dry with chamois and gave each of them a nice scoop of grain while Ned dropped a bale of hay down from the loft. Jed pulled two flakes off the bale and tossed them over the railing to Demon who kicked the back of the barn wall in response.

"Damn fool horse." Ned jumped down and examined the wall to make sure there wasn't any damage while Jed fed the mares. All three were so engrossed in their meals that they didn't look up when Ned drove the tractor in and we closed the sliding door for the night.

Outside the barn, it was twilight. The combination of storm clouds obscuring the sky and the wintertime hour of the setting sun made for an early evening. "I'm tired of snow," I grumbled for the benefit of anyone who might care. No one did.

We trudged inside and disrobed as far as was decent in the close quarters of the mud room. "Wet clothes in the washer," I ordered as I flipped open the front loader door. Having the washer and dryer right there was convenient.

The kitchen was so warm it was shocking after being outside for so long. It was empty of life but filled with incredible smells of vegetables and meat. A look in the large soup pot on the stove revealed another hearty stew. I gave silent thanks to Carrie for being amazing in the kitchen and went in search of Ty and Chaz.

I found them in the living room. Ned headed up the stairs behind me. Ty roused from a light slumber and extracted himself from the sofa he shared with Chaz. I needed to find them a bed, but the house was full.

"How is he?" I whispered.

Ty pulled me across the hall into the dining room, he looked tired. "I'm not sure. He's been kind of in and out, but he rouses enough to have an intelligible conversation if I push him to. He's a bit confused and I think he's had some tachycardia."

"I'll take a look at him."

"I think we should try to get him to a hospital."

"That would be best, I agree, but I don't think we're going to be able to get out of here anytime soon. It's snowing again."

"We barely made it up here. Do you think they'll close the Interstate?"

"I'm sure they have."

Ty leaned back against the doorjamb and sighed. I gave him a quick hug. "You and I can monitor him. If we think he's decompensating then we'll have medevac come out. There's plenty of room to land in the drive." If we cleared more of the snow off of it, there would be room.

Ty nodded in agreement, but still looked worried. I followed him back into the living room and leaned over Chaz.

He was either asleep or unconscious. Sometimes it was hard to tell. His skin was dry and too warm. I laid my head on his chest and heard the too-rapid heartbeat. "He is tachycardic," I agreed.

I pinched the skin on his hand and it stuck together for a second too long after I released it. "Dehydration," I murmured.

"Chaz." I rubbed his arm for a moment to wake him up.

Bleary eyes opened, he lifted his head. "Estoy enferma."

"You feel sick, Chaz?" I spoke in my loud voice, the one that I used to try to keep someone's attention when they weren't focusing well. The fact that I had to use it with Chaz was not a good sign.

"Eh," he grunted and closed his eyes again, though I didn't think he was sleeping. I snagged a little flashlight out of the kitchen drawer and came back.

"Chaz, I need you to talk to me. Can you do that?" I leaned over him and opened one eye, then the other, shining the light in the edges of them. His pupils were a little sluggish. He objected to me messing with him, one arm swung out but I avoided it.

"Chaz, it's just me. Do you know who I am?"

"Anna." He came to and half sat up. "Anna, there's danger. Ty, you have to tell her about them." His words were a fevered rush.

"I know there is, Chaz. Ty and I have talked about it. We're going to take care of everything." I patted his shoulder as he heaved himself into a sitting position. "You're a little dehydrated, my friend. I need to get some fluids in you. Do you think you could drink some water for us, and then eat some soup?" Extra salt should help him too.

"I can try." He nodded, but looked doubtful. Now that he was awake, it seemed like he was a little better.

Ty sat down next to him. "How are you feeling, baby?"

I went back to the kitchen and fetched a glass of cold water and filled a mug with broth from the stove. I added a generous pinch of salt to the broth and stirred it in. Knowing Carrie, there wouldn't be any in the soup, and Chaz needed the sodium. I carried both out and set them on the coffee table in front of the sofa.

"See if you can get these down him and let's do it again in a half hour. If we can rehydrate him he might stabilize for us." Ty nodded and turned back to his partner. "I'll be back in a few."

"Jed." I tapped my knuckles on the guest room door and it opened as if he had been standing there, waiting for me. "I'm very sorry, but can I ask you to give up your room for Ty and Chaz?"

He opened the door wider and I saw that the bed was made, and cases sat against the wall. I wondered when he'd unpacked the cars and hauled everything back in. "It was my intention to see if they would be more comfortable here."

"Thank you, yes. They would be. I offered them my room, but Ty refused it."

"As he should."

"I don't know where I'll put you. I don't usually have this many people here."

"Do not concern yourself with my comfort. I require little."

"I'll figure something out. In the meantime, just put your bags in my room. If you'll just let me know when you need to change, I can give you privacy."

He looked amused, and I wasn't sure why. "I thank you." I got the little bow and then he gathered his things and followed me to my room.

Ty and I got Chaz upstairs and tucked into bed, with Jed's help. He was still in and out of consciousness and I was worried that I'd damaged his soul when I used my power to get Adoni out of him. I wondered if there was anyone out there with a gift that was the opposite of mine. I'd ask Jed when we had a moment of privacy and weren't in the middle of another crisis.

CHAPTER THIRTEEN

IT WAS FULL DARK when the power went out. There were groans from the three of us at the dining room table who were used to the difficulties of farm life in the wintertime.

"Everybody stay put. I can get to the candles, just give me a minute." My chair was the only one that scuffed so I assumed that they were doing as they were told. I made my way around the table by keeping one hand on the chair backs next to me and the other outstretched in case I got to the wall faster than I anticipated. There were three unscented pillars that I managed to light after a few moments of fumbling with the matches. The soft glow was a welcome change after the sudden darkness.

"Anna, can I take one of those up so I can check on Chaz?" Ty asked.

"Sure. Let me get you a flashlight, though, they're safer." Lots of houses burned down every year due to candles being used during power outages. I hadn't heard yet of one burning down from a flashlight. I carried a pillar with me to the kitchen and pulled a couple out that had nice high power LED beams. Ned and Jed were right behind me.

"I'll get the generator hooked up," Ned offered.

"Thanks, Ned." I handed him the largest of the flashlights. "Do you need help?"

"I will assist him," Jed informed me.

"Thanks."

I carried a flashlight back to Ty. "Here. We should have the generator up and running soon. The guys went out to work on it." Carrie started to stack dishes for the trip back to the kitchen. "Rest, Carrie. I'll clean up the dishes."

"Just leave them until later. Ned can do them when he gets back in." She sounded despondent and I plopped down next to her and rubbed her arm.

"Hey, what's wrong?" I couldn't see her face very well in the candlelight, but I thought I saw tears.

"It's Fred."

"What?"

She choked back the tears but her voice quivered. "Fred. My starter."

I couldn't figure out what was going on. "What about Fred has you so upset?"

"The power's out." It was clear from her tone that this was supposed to clue me in to what was going on but I still didn't get it. I didn't want to accuse a woman of being unreasonably emotional due to pregnancy hormones, but I was starting to wonder if that was the issue. Maybe she hadn't had enough to eat and this was some sort of hypoglycemic reaction.

"Yes, but we'll get it back on soon. You don't have to worry about it."

"At home. The power is out at home." Carrie was full-on crying. "Our generator isn't hooked up. It will get too cold. Fred will die. Why didn't I remember to bring him with me?"

"Oh god, Carrie . . ." My voice drifted off because I didn't know what to say. Granted, I'd given her heck for her devotion to that bowl of fermented yeast, but it had been her great grandmother's bread starter. There was some story about how she'd immigrated to America with it, on a steamship, and kept it alive the whole time. It was a long-lived mold and irreplaceable. Another item for me to add to the list of things this week that were my fault.

I stretched out my senses to listen for anything that didn't belong. There was nothing that I could see, not even Marnie stirred in her glade. "It's okay, Carrie. We'll just go get him." If I could at least keep her mold alive, maybe it would make up, in some small way, for the shit storm of bad stuff that I'd brought into her life in the last twenty-four hours.

"Really? Can we?" She sniffled with hope. I'd never heard her sound pathetic.

"Yeah, of course we can. We'll take the tractor down, or one of the horses." It had snowed so much, I wasn't sure the horses could get through the woods, but Ned's tractor was big enough, and he'd already plowed the drive once. He had chains on the front tires and with the plowing blade on the front, well, it would be a cold drive but we could make it. I just hoped that I wouldn't have trouble convincing him that we had to go get his wife's pet mold. The power flickered back on and I geared myself up for an argument with Ned.

I found him in the barn.

"Oh shit." Ned rubbed his face and looked almost as upset as Carrie had. I'd underestimated how well he understood his wife and how important her starter was to her. "That thing practically came over on the Mayflower with her ancestors." He rubbed his face again. "She's right, it won't stay warm enough in the house. I'll go get it."

"I'm coming with you," I told him.

"No," Jed jumped in, "It is too dangerous for you."

"I thought I was the one with all the power?" I reminded Jed. "And don't think that just because I let you stick around you can tell me what to do."

He bowed in apology, but I didn't get the sense that he meant it. "Indeed, I spoke too harshly. I am but concerned for your safety and that of everyone here. I ask that you allow me to accompany you."

"All right, I know. Sorry." I relented a little bit. "So how do we do this and keep everyone safe?"

"We need more gas for the generator and the tractor anyway," Ned interjected. "I've emptied the can here and the only other we have is up at our place. The generator might only stay on for a few hours, maybe not even that long."

"Sounds like we're all going. I'll get the fireplaces going first, just in case." We shouldn't have trouble getting up there, but I wasn't going to risk lowering the house temperatures so far that Chaz was affected. He seemed to be doing better but we needed to do everything we could to keep him stable and help him recover. Getting too cold would not be helpful.

It took me about thirty minutes to get both the fireplace in the parlor and the one on the porch going strong. Jed had stocked the wood box, so I had plenty of dry logs to work with. It was a good thing because I didn't relish the thought of wading through the snow to get to the main woodpile next to the barn. You could get wet wood to burn, but it put out a lot of smoke, which wasn't pleasant. The last thing we needed was to set off the smoke detectors.

I ran up to check on Chaz again before I left. "How's the patient?"

Ty shrugged. "It's weird. I can't figure out what's going on with him."

"I know," I agreed. "The only other patient I've seen with symptoms like this was the victim of a lightning strike."

Ty raised his eyebrows. "That's not one I've run across."

"No. It's pretty rare." I talked while I looked Chaz over. "There are fewer than five hundred cases a year in the US."

"Did they make it?"

"Yeah." I nodded while I lied. This wasn't the best time to tell the truth. "He pulled through." I switched topics. "Any change in his condition that you've noticed?"

"No. He's been out for a while. I was just going to wake him up, try to get some more fluids down him. He's still pretty dry."

"I wish we had IV fluids." Ty was right. Chaz still looked dehydrated.

"Me too. We can still call for the airlift if we need to."

"Yeah. Let's give him a little longer. Those things don't have the best safety records," I said.

"Especially in snowstorms," Ty agreed.

We'd had a spate of medevac helicopter crashes in recent years, all either at night or in bad weather. It wasn't a safe occupation, nor a trip to take in a snowstorm at night if it wasn't an emergency.

"Are you ready, Anna?" Carrie hollered up the steps. She was worried about Fred and tired of waiting.

"Just a minute," I called back. Chaz didn't stir, which made me worry more. "We've got to run over to Ned's place. Carrie needs us to pick up her bread starter and we need gas for the generator."

"I think we'll be fine."

"We won't be gone long."

"I won't leave him alone."

"Never thought you would." I gave him a hug. "We'll be back in about half an hour."

"Be safe. I'm going to wake him up and get some more soup down him."

It didn't make sense for all of us to go fetch a bowl of mold, but Ned had to go in order to refuel the tractor. I was going in order to make sure Ned was safe. I didn't know if there were any lingering spooks at their house, and I wasn't ready to take any more chances with my friends' lives. Jed wouldn't hear of me being left without his invaluable protection, and Carrie didn't trust us to take good care of Fred. I tried to assure her that I wouldn't drop it. I'd delivered ninety-seven babies without dropping a single one.

Ned plowed while the rest of us jammed into the front seat of his truck. It was a good thing that Carrie and I were both small boned because Jed took up more than his fair share of the passenger seat. I sat in the middle and tried to ignore the fact that my thigh was pressed against his while we followed the Deere with caution. The truck didn't have chains on and the snow had shifted to sleet. Carrie crept down the hill behind her husband's tractor, far enough back so that if we started to slide we wouldn't run into him.

I stretched out my senses to check for ghosts and realized that something was wrong. "Someone's at your house."

"What?" Carrie's voice shrieked as her foot came down on the brakes and the truck started to skid towards the edge of the road. She released the pedal and turned gently into the slide until she had control again. I let out the breath I'd been holding. "What, or who, is it?" Carrie asked as if nothing had happened.

"I don't know." That would be a handy skill, though. I peeled my hand off of the dashboard and tried to shift away from Jed.

"I do not sense a presence, Anna," he rumbled.

"I think it's a person, not a ghost." There was a flicker of soul. "I can't tell for sure. It's like there's interference. We may still be too far away."

"You can see the living?" He sounded surprised.

"Yeah. That's just started in the last day or so." He regarded me with interest, so I guessed it wasn't an expected ability. I added it to my mental list of things that I wanted to ask him about when we had time.

Carrie started to move again. "We need to catch up with Ned." She sounded as concerned as I felt. Whoever was at her house wasn't an invited guest.

Ned stopped after Carrie flashed the headlights at him a few times. She pulled alongside him, snuggling the truck up next to the tractor with expertise. I wasn't sure I could have gotten it that close without scratching the paint.

"Anna says someone's at the house," Carrie yelled over the noise of the engines. From where we sat, we couldn't tell if the house lights were on. Then again, with the power off, it wasn't like anyone could turn the lights on anyway. Still, I looked out over the dark meadow, hoping that my eyes would provide more information.

"A spook?"

"She thinks it's a person."

He relaxed a little. "Oh. Might be someone we know, then? Came over and got stuck?"

"I can't imagine anyone would come by without calling first."

"We've been over at Anna's. Cells don't work so well over the hill," he reminded her.

"I don't have any messages on mine. I just looked."

"Jed, Anna, what do you think?"

"Given today's events, I am suspicious of uninvited guests." Jed looked across the darkness as if he could see who it was from there if he just tried hard enough.

"I don't know who it is. I can't tell," I reiterated. "Ned, I don't want anyone getting hurt. We need to be careful, but don't get trigger happy."

Ned nodded soberly. "Agreed." His shotgun was balanced in the tractor with him but he wouldn't use it lightly. "We've blown our chances to sneak up on them. The engines make too much noise, so whoever they are, they know we're coming." He revved the engine on the tractor and started forward.

We pulled into the drive right behind Ned. There weren't any other vehicles. No lights on in the house at all, and no movement, but I still sensed the flame of life inside. Whoever it was, they didn't come out. Carrie and I waited in the truck while Jed jumped out and helped Ned fill the tank on the tractor and all four of the gas cans we'd brought with us. First things first. We needed gas.

Carrie and I jumped when Jed set the full cans down hard in the bed of the truck. We shared a nervous laugh as Ned started the tractor again and pulled it around so it was facing out for an easy exit if we needed one. Carrie parked the truck the same way. It was odd that whoever was inside hadn't noticed all of this activity and come outside.

"What's he doing?" I asked as Carrie switched off the engine.

She watched her husband as he headed to the barn, shotgun at the ready. "Looks like he's decided to check the barn."

"Should we go with him?"

"Jedediah is." The big man stalked after Ned as if he was going after an errant puppy. She turned the truck lights back on so they illuminated the big metal doors. We watched Ned open the side door and then the guys disappeared through it into the darkness. My breath hitched and Carrie rubbed my arm with a reassuring touch.

"It's okay, honey. He'll be fine. Ned will take care of him."

"I'm not worried about him." It even sounded like a lie to me, but Carrie let it slide.

"He seems like a good guy, Anna."

"Yeah, for somebody who's been dead for two thousand years." They still weren't back out.

"Three," she said.

"What?"

"I thought it was three thousand years that he'd been dead."

"That's not helpful, Carrie."

"He's a fine looking man. He wants to protect you and take care of you. He's crazy about you."

"Should we go after them?" I tried to change the topic. "Why aren't they back yet?"

"He seems plenty smart, and he's polite."

"Carrie."

"Just tell me that he isn't what you've been waiting for."

"I'm not waiting," I protested.

"Is that what you tell yourself?" The words would have been cruel if they'd come from anyone else, but Carrie's tone was a kind rebuke.

"I don't believe in fate."

"I'm not sure I do either, but I do believe that God has a plan for all of us, and with your special gift, it just seems like He planned for you to have someone who understands you. Someone who can help you."

"I don't believe in God." Was she right? Had I just been waiting for someone? Jed? It was something I'd have to think about.

"I know you don't." She wasn't judgmental about it, just accepted it, as part of who I was. I loved Carrie more every minute.

"There they are." I was relieved to change the subject. Ned stepped through the door with Jed right behind him. Carrie squeezed my hand and I realized that we'd been holding onto each other the whole time.

"Okay." She breathed a calming breath, and I understood that the whole conversation had been a way to keep herself from being scared. "Are you ready?" he asked me.

I swallowed against the tight ball of tension in my throat. "Let's go get Fred."

Jed reached the truck and opened the door for me. I tried not to think about the conversation Carrie and I had just had, but no girl can help thinking 'is he the one', especially after a good friend has just told them that they should think about it. I didn't protest as he helped me down.

"How's the barn?" It was a good diversion from my train of thought.

"There's a surprise in there." Ned had helped Carrie out of the driver seat, and if I hadn't been scared out of my skin it would have looked like a pleasant double date.

"What's the surprise?" I was glad Carrie asked because I was having trouble forming more words with Jed so close to me.

"There's an SUV in there. It looks like the one your ex was driving."

"Shit," I breathed. With all of my focus on Chaz and his health problem, I'd almost forgotten about Eric.

We climbed the stairs to the house behind Ned. His shotgun was ready, but he at least had it pointed down. Carrie held the flashlight so we could find our way up the steps. Eric hadn't turned the lights on for us. Not that he could have with the power off, but he could have at least lit a candle. The fact that he hadn't made the situation feel more sinister.

"Living room," I whispered as Ned clicked the front door open. He stayed still while we all listened. All I could hear was the soft patter of sleet.

Ned stepped across the threshold and his boots scuffed against the hardwood floors. There was no way to be quiet in hard soled shoes on a floor like that. He turned around the corner into the living room with the rest of us right behind him.

"Crap," Ned muttered.

I tried to peak around Jed but he pushed me back, blocking my view.

"What is it?"

"It's him. He's out cold."

I shoved past Jed. Eric lay there on the floor, unconscious and unmoving. Was he dead? No. I couldn't tell from the flashlight beam that danced over his still form, but I could still sense him. Was it just him, or was there a bad spirit in him? Either way, something was wrong with him and I had to do whatever I could to help.

"Anna, this is not safe." Jed tried to pull me back but I pushed his hands away.

"Get out of my way, Jed. He needs help. Let me do my job."

"Is he okay?" Carrie knelt beside me.

"Eric, can you hear me?" I patted his face and his head lolled to the left. His skin was too cool. The power had been off for over an hour at my house, so it was probably the same here. It was long enough to have lowered the temperature in the farmhouse to an uncomfortable level. "We need to get him warmed up," I ordered and Carrie burst into a flurry of motion.

"I'll get the generator going." Ned followed his wife's footsteps. Jed stayed with Eric and me. He was determined to protect me, even where there was no threat. As long as he kept out of my way I could ignore it.

"Eric. How are you feeling?" I called, but he didn't respond. I loosened the button-down shirt at his throat, checking his breathing. It was steady, slow. His pallor in the LED light of the flashlight was terrible, it turned his handsome features grotesque. Everybody looked near death in that kind of light. I peeled his eyes open, one at a time, and danced the beam over them. Minimal response. There was no sign of damage to his head. If he'd fallen and hit it hard enough to knock himself out (or hit it and then fallen) there'd be some sort of swelling or blood. His heart rate was tachycardic, as rapid as Chaz's had been. There were a lot of possibilities, though, for what might be wrong with him, and most of them I could neither diagnose nor treat in the field.

"Can I assist you?" Jed squatted next to me over the inert form.

"There's a phone in the kitchen. See if it's working. We need to get him to a hospital."

"Here are some blankets." Carrie dropped a pile of handmade quilts on the floor next to me and I grimaced.

"Are you sure you want to use these?"

"We make them to use them, Anna. They aren't sacred, they're blankets."

I didn't know how many hours it took her and her mom to quilt one, but I guessed it was a lot. I grabbed the top one and tucked it over Eric's body.

"What's wrong with him?"

"I don't know."

"Is that thing still in him?"

"I can't tell. Can I have one of those pillows from the sofa?" Carrie handed me a brightly colored square and I placed it between Eric's head and the cold hardwood floor. This time, when I moved him, he groaned. "Eric?" I patted his cheek a couple of times and then rubbed my hand vigorously on his arm. "Can you hear me, Eric?" I talked to him, nonstop and all nonsense while I checked his pulse and his breathing. He'd made noise, which I counted as a good sign.

"The phone is not functional," Jed informed as he returned to his place beside me.

"Why would it be?" I muttered.

The door clicked open and I grimaced as the room flooded with light.

"Generators on," Ned announced proudly, his hand still on the light switch.

"Turn the heat up, Carrie, would you?" She sprang into action, glad to have a task to perform.

"What's wrong with him?" Ned asked as he knelt at Eric's booted feet. It was the question of the day.

"I'm not sure. He's hypotensive, but I don't know why."

I looked up and saw Ned shake his head. "We didn't all go to medical school, Anna."

"Right. Sorry. His blood pressure's probably low. I mean there could be something wrong with how his adrenaline receptors are working. It's pretty rare, but you see it in victims of lightning strikes."

"There hasn't been any lightning."

"No. But the spirit that was strong enough to possess him has some sort of internal energy source. I mean, I can't prove it, and I could be wrong, but I think that might be enough to cause similar symptoms." It was an odd theory, but it almost made sense. It had been all I'd been able to come up with to explain Chaz's symptoms. "It seems like that's what's going on with Chaz," I continued, "and we think that they were both possessed by spirits. He could have had a cardiac event, though, or any of about a thousand other things going on. We need to get him to a hospital. He needs fluids and a cardiac workup." If I was right, he was also going to need a hefty dose of steroids to help get him back on track.

"I've got some lactated ringers in the barn. The vet left them when Hattie had that infection. Would they work?"

"Really?" I perked up. "We could get him on an IV drip, at least. It would be a good start."

"I'll go get them."

"I'll need my kit from the house. We should take him back there if we can get him in the truck." I had another patient there that I needed to keep an eye on. We also didn't know when, or if, danger would return. I didn't want to leave Chaz and Ty alone without whatever protection I could offer them.

"I will take him to the truck," Jed advised. I looked him over and nodded. If any of us could carry a grown man, it would be him.

"We can all help get him up but we'll need you to do the majority of it. Let's get everything we need put together first. We'll move Eric last." I pulled my mobile out of my pocket and was relieved to see that I had two bars. I dialed 911.

I stayed with my patient for the fifteen minutes that it took them to gather the medical supplies and blankets. It took me that long to talk to the 911 dispatcher, convince her that I really was a doctor and that I did need her to send the medevac helicopter out to my coordinates. They had agreed, but we were a couple of hours away from the chopper being able to reach us. The weather had to improve before they could take off on their end, and then there was the question of landing on the driveway. If they got here and decided that they couldn't land, they'd leave without Eric.

I had a bad feeling that I was on my own, that the helicopter wouldn't be able to make it in. I'd probably have to be able to get Eric through the night, at least. Maybe tomorrow we could get through to the local medical center, but we couldn't attempt it after dark with the snow still coming down. It would be a risk to all of our lives. It did seem like his level of consciousness might be improving, as if he was coming out of deep anesthetic.

"Anna, they are ready. Shall I take him?" Jed inquired.

"Yes. Let's be careful with him. I don't want him to destabilize while we're on the way back." CPR in the backseat of a car was pretty challenging. I'd had cause to do it before and it wasn't an experience I wanted to repeat. I didn't think Eric's heart was going to stop anytime soon, but without knowing more about what was going on with him, it was hard to predict.

I got concerned when Jed knelt to pick a man up who I knew weighed around 190 pounds. "Be careful, Jed. Don't hurt yourself. Wait for Ned to come help." He gave me a scathing look and hefted Eric into his arms like a baby.

"Wow." I couldn't keep the overt admiration out of my voice. His upper body strength was impressive.

Jed flashed me a heated look and my body responded in a rush of lust. I hoped he couldn't read my reaction as well as I could read his.

"Let's get him to the car." I picked up some of the extra blankets and forced myself to stay focused on the problem in Jed's arms. I wasn't going to be able to ignore my reaction to Jed for much longer, though. Every time he got close to me I responded like a teenager. It had been way too long.

The drive back was uncomfortable. With Eric laid out in the small back seat of the dually, there wasn't any extra room for me. I crouched on the floorboard with my hips wedged between Carrie's seat back and the bench that Eric laid on. At least I could make sure that he didn't fall off.

"Anna?" Carrie hesitated as if she was afraid that she would interrupt something. I couldn't see her over the edge of the seat back, but knew from when I got in that she was driving one handed, with her free arm tucked around a crock of mold.

"I'm still here," I assured her.

"What's the thing you said that you thought Eric and Chaz have?"

"Oh. An adrenergic instability."

"And it's like when someone's been hit by lighting?"

"Yeah, a bit."

"So what do you do for them?"

"Lightning strike victims?"

"Yeah."

My thoughts filled with the memories. I had been enjoying an AA baseball game when the storm developed over us, as if out of nothing. It happens in the Midwest, a lot. The faster the storm creates itself, the more intense it will be. We didn't have any warning to get inside. In hindsight, I considered us fortunate that it had just been lightning and that only one person had died. A storm like that could have just as easily spawned a tornado and taken out everyone at the baseball diamond.

The lightning had struck the field and I'd seen the outfielder go down. I had moved before I realized I was moving, instincts honed after years of working in the emergency department. I reached him first. He was young, younger than me. He'd been awake for a minute, with this surprised expression on his face. Then his blood pressure had crashed, and he lost consciousness and stopped breathing. I'd started chest compressions and rescue breathing.

When the ambulance crew arrived, they took over for me. I was exhausted, and the player was still dead. I called it for them after they'd tried the defibrillator a few times, and after they'd had time to verify that I was a physician. They don't typically allow random spectators at sports events to declare the opposing team's players dead. His wife had been with us on the field. I'd never forget how she screamed, cried, begged for God, for anyone, to help her.

I still remembered the fine, short red hair on his head, the orange stubble, the cover of freckles on his chest, and how his ribs felt when they cracked under the pressure of my hands.

"Are you well?" Jed's hand wavered next to my cheek, as though he was afraid to interrupt the string of memories by touching me. I leaned into the comfort of his palm, pressing my face against his hand, and let it wash away the memory of that singularly bad day.

"Yeah. Sorry." You see so much awful shit in residency and throughout years of practice that you have to build a buffer against it. The doctors that can't don't make it. They either develop unhealthy relationships with alcohol or narcotics, or they commit suicide. I had a pretty good buffer, but every now and then something happened that I couldn't just put away. It impacted me too much.

Some of those things haunted me like I had PTSD. This was one of them.

Jed smelled like the woods, but sweeter and more intoxicating. It drew me back to the present.

"What do you do, Anna? For people who have been hit by lightning?" Carrie was persistent. I grabbed Jed's hand in my own, gave it a squeeze, and held on. He leaned halfway over the seat back so he could put his other hand on me and I was glad that Carrie didn't need the rearview mirror. She wouldn't be able to see out with that mountain of a man blocking the way.

"It depends. Sometimes they go into cardiac arrest right away. If they do, then your only hope is to provide cardiopulmonary resuscitation and try to get their heart started again. Sometimes the effect isn't as dramatic right away, though. You can get a lot of different symptoms. The body's adrenaline delivery mechanism can get fouled up. That's what I think may be going on with these guys."

"So what do you do for that?"

"Fluids and rest. Try to get their electrolytes back into balance. They may need sodium and glucose added in. A boost of steroids might be useful."

Eric shifted and moaned. "Eric, can you hear me?" His eyelids fluttered and he moved one hand. It was a start.

"Hang in there with me, Eric." I rubbed his arm. I wasn't still in love with him, but I didn't want anything bad to happen to him.

"I found this in the house." Carrie handed back a cell phone and a wallet. "I'm guessing they're his."

I turned the phone on and discovered that Eric didn't have it password protected. I flicked through a couple of photos and found his cute cardiologist wife holding a baby with blond hair. My gut clenched. I needed to call her, make sure she was okay. I'd have to tell her where the father of her child was, and that I wasn't sure if he was going to make it. She would ask why he had come to see me, and I didn't know how to answer that. I'd have to drive back to Ned's place to get cell service anyway. It was easy to decide to put it off. I tucked the wallet and the phone into my jacket pocket.

"We're pulling in now, Anna," Carrie announced. "I'm going to get as close to the front door as I can."

It was a little more difficult for Jed to extract Eric from the backseat than it had been to get him in, but he hauled him out and got him up the porch steps and through the front door.

"Ty, I've got another patient for you." I hollered as we came in. Ned walked past me with a box full of IV supplies. "We need those upstairs," I instructed.

Jed followed, more slowly, Eric draped in his arms like a baby. I couldn't fathom the upper body strength that it took to pick a man up like that and then carry him up a flight of stairs.

"Where the hell did you find him?" Ty growled. I ignored him. Whatever had happened in the past was long since done, and I didn't think that today had been Eric's fault.

"He was in my house. Passed out on the floor." Ned explained.

"Ned found IV fluids for us. We need to get both of these guys hooked up."

"Perfect." He was relieved to hear about the fluids. Chaz needed them too.

"Ty, my kit is in my bathroom, under the sink. Can you grab it?" He was already on the way.

We got Eric settled on a palate on the floor. I was out of beds and needed to keep our nursing efforts consolidated. He moved a bit and made some noise, but nothing coherent. It was more encouraging than when he was just unconscious, though. I still wanted him in a major medical center, but the chopper was a ways away. Chances of survival there were a lot better than on the floor of my guest room.

"It's been a while since I practiced my IV skills, Ty." He gave me a quick grin while I dug through my medical kit and thanked my lucky stars that it was well stocked. I had a handful of packages of Gelco needles. Everything we needed to get IV drips going.

"I'll make sure that you practice some when we get back to the office. I've got this one."

"Thanks. You okay sticking Chaz with a needle?"

"He'll probably enjoy it," Chaz muttered and I gave his arm a pat.

"Hard to blame him."

"I know."

I played the role of the assistant, opening the needle packages and scrubbing the backs of our patient's hands with rubbing alcohol.

Ty got both drips going and turned the flow on medium. We'd go for quick enough rehydration to see if that helped Chaz and Eric recover, but I didn't want them to get chilled. In the meantime, I hoped that the helicopter could make it through the storm in the dark.

As I came down the stairs, I heard the rumble of the tractor outside. Ned was going to clear as much space on the driveway as he could. We needed a helicopter landing pad, and the only place for it was on the other side of the bridge, right before the hill. There was a spot where the drive was quite a bit wider, and that was where Ned planned for the chopper to land.

Carrie rounded the corner from the kitchen with a wide yawn. She gave me a sheepish grin.

"You caught me. I'm tired," she admitted.

"With good reason." I was too, but I didn't have time to show it. "How are the guys?"

"Hard to say. Chaz seems a bit better. Eric's still unconscious."

"Will he make it?"

I hesitated. "I hope so. I'll feel better when he's at a hospital that can run lab work on him and figure out what's going on."

"Is it just related to the spirit that left him?"

"I don't know for sure that he was possessed, but based on the circumstances, I think we have to assume that he was. Or is." No one at the hospital would know about the possession, or be able to do anything about it. They could treat the symptoms of electrolyte and metabolic abnormalities, though.

"I think they're better off with you taking care of them," she informed me.

"I hope not," I told her. "I don't know what to do for them." I needed a way to anchor their spirit to their body, but the only thing my gift worked for was releasing the soul. Maybe Jed knew a better way.

"You'll figure it out, Anna. It's what you do. I believe in you." She leaned down and gave me a reassuring hug. "I'm going to lay down for a few. Soup's hot if you want some more."

"Thank you. I know we just ate a little while ago, but I'm still starving."

"Just doing what I can." She started up the stairs.

"Carrie?" She paused and turned back. "How's Fred?"

That got a big smile out of her. "I think he's going to be fine. I just fed him."

"Good." It was something. Her footsteps echoed down the stairwell and then the bedroom door clicked shut. I turned and went to look for Jed.

CHAPTER FOURTEEN

JEDEDIAH STOOD in the kitchen and poured me a cup of coffee. "I made this for you."

"Thank you. I need it."

"Yes," he agreed. I must look as tired as I felt. I took the mug with some chagrin and took a grateful sip. He'd made it sweeter than I liked, but at least it didn't have the grounds in it.

"I would like to speak with you, Anna."

My brow wrinkled in confusion. "Aren't we talking?"

"I would prefer that we find a place that is quiet."

With a pointed look around the empty kitchen, I arched one skeptical eyebrow.

Jed ignored me and poured himself a cup. "Will you join me in the barn?"

I sighed. I had just gotten warm again. I didn't bother to keep the irritation out of my voice. "Sure."

He held the door for me and then followed me through the darkness to the barn. The horses nickered gentle welcomes as I slid the door open and entered the musty sweet warmth. It wasn't as warm as the house was, but with three horses inside it was pretty tolerable. I found the old oil lamp and lit it for the second time that day. The flame projected flickers of shadows on the wood walls around us. It was picturesque. If we weren't waiting for a pack of evil ghosts to come kill us it would have been downright romantic.

"My brother will return."

"Should this worry me?" I was tired of being scared. Sassy was easier. I'd won the last time I'd met him, hadn't I?

"Indeed, Anna. It should concern you as it does me. It is for this moment that the Council sent me to aid you."

"I thought you didn't know what his role in this was."

"I do not. The fact that Adonijah is involved concerns me. His desire for power was always great and I fear it has not diminished."

I leaned back against the mares' stall and copped a nonchalant attitude. "I kicked his ass the first time he was here."

"He is stronger than you realize. He will not underestimate you this time."

Lacking a good comeback, I said nothing.

"I would have you away from this place before he returns."

"Sounds great. How do you suggest we manage that?"

"This helicopter that is coming. I want you to go with it."

I snorted out a burst of laughter. "Jed, it's a medevac helicopter. They don't take pleasure passengers. They'll take Eric. That's it."

"You are a doctor. Could you not travel with your patient?"

"I'm not his doctor, and no I can't."

"Will they have their own physician on the aircraft?"

"I doubt it." It had been a long time since I'd had cause to work with a helicopter team, but they used to be staffed by paramedics. My clinic was so close to the trauma center that all we ever had to do was call an ambulance. "Anyway, I can't leave everyone here. It's out of the question."

"I will protect them."

"You and I both know that you might not be able to."

"I must get you to safety, Anna."

"I don't think so, Jed." It felt like there was a storm coming, far off on the horizon. Not a weather storm, something else. I'd felt it for a little while, like a change in the barometric pressure, but different. "We can't run. Don't you feel it? They're coming back for me."

"I sense it as well. Do not try to give yourself to them again, Anna. I beg you. What you did with Adoni was foolish."

"Promise me that you won't let them take me," I countered.

Jed stilled. "What?"

"Don't let a ghost inside me, Jed, no matter what happens."

"It would be disastrous." He agreed.

"So you won't let them?"

"I won't hurt you, Anna. But you have to take care of yourself." He pleaded with me. "Let me protect you." When I didn't respond he became insistent. "They cannot have you."

"They can," I whispered. It was the only way. He had to know it.

Jed moved forward in a sudden motion and pushed me back against the rough wood of the stall. My coffee cup clattered to the floorboards and I heard the wet splash of the contents as they landed at my feet.

"I will not allow it." He enunciated the words as if he were biting them.

It was hard to talk when his body was pressed against mine, inch for inch, but I managed. "I can't allow them to keep hurting the people I love." I tried to squirm away and got nowhere. When I pushed against his chest he gathered my hands into his, and then leaned down, as if to kiss me.

I hungered for it. To explore his lips with mine, to touch his face, to see his body again. The animalistic urge was overwhelming, and for a moment, I caved. I leaned into him and grasped the hands that held mine, pulling him to join me. The gesture elicited a raw moan from him.

When his mouth met my lips, I allowed myself to linger, to taste. Then I crushed the burning desire that fed me with a willful snap. I couldn't afford to rely on him too much. It was too risky, scarier than facing Adonijah again. I sank my teeth into his lower lip in a bite that was warning without lust. I could hear the surprise in the breath he took in.

"Let go of me," I demanded, and he released me so quickly that I would have fallen, had the slats of Hattie's stall not been imprinted into my backside.

"Forgive me. I was overcome-"

"I'm not your Queen of Sheba. Don't touch me again." I walked a few steps in my righteous indignation and was relieved to find that I was able to move at all. The words had less impact when you were too affected to walk away. "Not for any reason." I blew out the oil lamp and let the barn door slam shut behind me. Fury carried me into the house, and up the stairs. It would have been gratifying to slam my bedroom door behind me, but I had other obligations.

"How are they?" I whispered at the guest room door. Ty gestured for me to stay where I was, and came to join me.

"Not much has changed, but they're stable. Everyone's asleep. Let's leave them be."

"It might be what they need most." I checked the slim watch on my wrist. "If we're lucky, we'll have medevac here within the next hour." I was tired, it was late and I wanted to go to bed, but that wasn't going to happen. The back door clicked shut downstairs. Jed had followed me back in. My cheeks flushed at the memory of that brief kiss.

"What happened to you?" Ty's voice was too knowing, his arched eyebrows said too much.

"Nothing."

"We've been friends for too many years for you to lie to me."

"It's nothing," I said it more vehemently as if that would make it true.

"Anna, do us all a favor and just take him to bed."

"Ty!" I slugged him in the shoulder as if my indignation was back. It was pretense. Whatever mock rage I'd summoned in the barn had fizzled out, and I was embarrassed. I sagged against the opposite wall.

"He's hot, honey. Why do you fight it?"

"I've already had this conversation today, Ty."

"Did you listen the first time?"

My cheeks flushed as I shook my head. "No."

"Well maybe you should. It's amazing to me how stupid you doctors can be." It's hard to argue with something that's right, so I settled on embarrassed silence. "I only say it because I love you."

"I know."

"Whatever this dream is you're carrying around of some perfect guy, he doesn't exist. You're gonna have to accept that men have flaws. All of them do." He gave me a wicked grin. "Trust me, I tried all of them before I met Chaz."

I burst out laughing. "You were not that much of a slut, Ty."

"Not for lack of trying."

"Now you're the one who's lying." Ty had only dated two guys before Chaz.

"But I made you smile." He pulled me in for a hug and I wrapped my arms around his neck. He was almost as short as I was so I could lean my head on his shoulder without using a step stool. "So give him a chance, okay?"

"I'm not promising that."

"Anna." Ty and I both jumped at the sound of Chaz's voice. I eased the door open.

"Hey there." He had himself propped up on one elbow and looked more alert than I'd seen in some time. "How are you feeling?"

"Better."

"You don't look quite like the ghost of Christmas past anymore." It was a lame joke but it earned me a fleeting smile.

"Anna, I have to tell you what I saw." I had a thousand questions for him about his experience with Jed's brother, but I didn't want to exhaust him.

"I'm not sure your nurse is going to let you talk for very long."

"She's right, Chaz. You need to rest. Your body didn't handle this very well."

"I know I'm lucky to still be here," Chaz admitted. I perched on the edge of the bed next to him and watched while Ty checked Eric's vitals. He didn't look much better. I hoped the helicopter hurried. He needed more care than we could provide. "How did you get it out of me?"

"I don't know what to call it, Chaz." It was hard to explain something that I'd never talked about before. "It's like energy."

"Our Anna can see ghosts."

"My Abuela could do that." He said it like it was a normal thing, like being able to roll your R's, or curl your tongue.

"Really?"

"That's what she said." He shrugged and lay back on the pillows. "I never could myself."

"Maybe I could talk to her." If we ever got out of this. "Is she still . . . ?"

"No, chica. She's been gone a long time." He gave me a gentle pat on the hand and closed his eyes. "Sorry."

"It's okay. I've just never met anyone else who could see them." Other than Jed.

"Don't try to talk too much. You need to rest," Ty ordered as he adjusted the flow on the IV fluids running into Chaz's right arm.

Chaz ignored his lover's warning. "I was kind of surprised when I realized I had company."

"So you knew?" Curiosity got the better of Ty and he sat down next to Chaz's head.

"It took me a while to figure it out. It was like being in a dream, only I couldn't wake up. It hurt, a lot. Like he was using a knife on the inside of me."

I nodded as if I understood what he meant, but I didn't. He'd had a singular, unique experience. From a scientific standpoint, it was fascinating, but I was mostly just terrified that ghosts could do that.

"This can wait, baby," Ty admonished him again.

"No. It's coming back. She has to hear this." Chaz reached for my hand again and I took his. It was strange to see him so vulnerable.

"I know." That pressure change, a storm that wasn't related to the weather.

"The one that was in me, he hates his brother."

"I got that impression."

"He will do anything to destroy him."

"It seemed like he didn't care much for me either."

"They don't want to kill you, Anna."

"I haven't been getting a warm and fuzzy feeling from these guys, Chaz. I think that must be what they want."

"No, they want you alive."

"Why? I can stop them."

"If they have you, then no one can stop them."

"Why would they think that I would help them?"

"You won't have a choice, Anna. Once he is in you, they will control you, just like they did me."

I shivered. "So they just plan on preventing me from being able to release them?"

"Once he has you, he thinks that he can use . . . whatever that is." Chaz's voice was thick with urgency. "You have to stay away from them, chica. If they have you, they can use that thing you have on anyone they want."

"They would turn our only defense against us." I jumped as Jed spoke from behind me in the doorway. I hadn't heard him come up the stairs.

"That seems bad," Ty said.

"It would be very bad. This is why we must get Anna out of their reach."

"Good idea." Ty looked serious. "What's your plan?"

"I had hoped to send her with this helicopter. If that is not possible then we must attempt to get out with a vehicle."

"We won't get far, Jed, not with the Interstate closed."

"They will come again tonight, Anna."

"I know. I can feel it."

"I will not risk losing you to Adoni. With your power under his control, he could destroy this world."

Chaz squeezed my hand again.

"Okay. We'll figure it out," I told them, but I didn't know how.

The front door clicked open and Ty and I both jumped. Jed was his usual unflappable self, but from his vantage point, he could see down the stairs. "There is no cause for concern. It's Ned." Footsteps tapped up the stairwell.

"I think I hear the helicopter. I've got everything ready. Can you come help?" He addressed this to Jed.

"I would be pleased to assist you."

I followed them outside and grimaced as tiny slivers of ice pelted my face. I wished I hadn't been so anti-technology at the farm, because access to cable TV and a weather report would have been useful. Lights appeared over the hill towards Ned's house as a helicopter roared into view. The rotor blades sounded out of place in the still meadow.

Ned had my Subaru on the far side of the spot he'd cleared in the drive with its lights on. His truck faced mine, thirty yards back. The high beams on both vehicles shone into the space between. There was plenty of room to land a helicopter, as long as they could see well enough to drop down onto the makeshift area. We piled into Chaz's SUV and drove the half mile to the landing site.

The chopper circled over us as the pilot assessed the ground situation. I contemplated ghosts with strange names and the fragile existence of life on earth, global warming be damned. Adonijah was the one who wanted me. If he controlled me, then he could use my gift to destroy whomever it was that he was working for. Then he'd be the ruler he'd always wanted to be. With my power under his control, he would play god. Jed and my friends would be first on his list to be destroyed. Chaz was right. Adonijah couldn't have me. I just hoped I had enough energy left when he came back to deal with him first. If not then I'd have to go with plan B. My plan B didn't have a lot of options.

When it came down to it, it wouldn't be a difficult decision to make. I had done hard things before, made sacrifices for others. This was no different. If I had to, I would give myself for my friends. I just had to figure out how to take Adonijah with me, if it came to that. The anxious knot in my chest loosened.

My breath hitched as the helicopter dropped over the two vehicles. As it neared the earth, the blades picked so much snow off the ground that it obscured the helicopter in a whirlwind of white. I wanted to look away. The effect was nauseating, but I forced myself to watch. I'd brought them out here, and while I couldn't do anything to help them land safely, it felt disrespectful to not watch. When the whirring of the blades began to slow, I decided it must be on the ground, even though I couldn't see it yet.

"I'll go meet them," Ned announced, and when he got out of the vehicle, Jed did too.

It took a couple of minutes for anything to appear out of the wall of snow, which gave me plenty of time to compose myself. Through the settling snow, I made out four forms, two carrying baggage and the ubiquitous emergency stretcher. The other two were Ned and Jed. I hopped out of the vehicle to meet them.

"Dr. Roberts? I'm Jennifer Wilson. Paramedic." She was African American, middle aged: stocky and self-confident. That was all the impression I could get under the layers of winter clothing.

"I'm sorry that I had to call you out here in this weather."

"It's getting bad. I'm not sure that you would have been able to make it in. I assume you know that the highway is closed?"

"We figured it was, but we don't get much cell service out here, and the power has been out for quite a while. We just got the generator on." I gestured to the vehicle. "We can take this up to the house, save a bit of a walk." It took some maneuvering to fit the backboard in, along with the medical personnel. Jed and Ned hopped into Ned's truck. They could bring it back and light the area again when the crew was ready to leave.

"Was it hard to find your way up here?"

"A bit." She didn't sound too concerned. "We normally just follow the highway, but with it closed there aren't any car lights to follow. The wind's strong up there, too."

"Will you guys be able to make it back all right?"

"We plan to." I liked her confidence. I wanted to borrow it.

"This is Jones." She gestured to her silent partner in the backseat. "He drew the short straw for this shift with us."

"Hi." I turned the car off in front of the house and turned to shake hands with the red headed Caucasian man that was almost the same size and shape as his partner.

"There's someone else with you?"

"Our pilot. Lieutenant Spears."

"You guys are military?" I was surprised. I didn't think they did civilian runs.

"No, we're private. The lieutenant, he's ex-military. Served in Iraq, the first time. I figure he gets to keep the title."

That made sense to me. "Come on in." They followed me through the door into the sanctuary of the warm entryway. I led the crew into the parlor.

"Tell us about your patient."

"I have two of them, actually. The most serious, though, is Dr. Eric Steinman. He's a cardiologist at St. Luke's." From their blank stares, I surmised they didn't know him. "We found him a couple of hours ago at a house up the road a ways. He was unconscious, on the floor. No sign of head injury."

"Where is he?"

"Upstairs." I led the way, rattling off his vital statistics and what I could recall from his medical history.

"Sounds like you know him pretty well."

"I haven't seen him in several years. We don't know what he was doing up this way." It wasn't quite the truth, but I'd decided that honesty wouldn't be the best policy in this situation. Better to feign ignorance.

"You guys are kind of out of the way for a casual acquaintance to drop in."

"Yeah, we are," I agreed, and let her make of it what she would.

She grappled with it and apparently decided that it wasn't her problem. "Let's take a look at him."

Ty came out of the guest room with a professional smile and an outstretched hand. "Glad you made it safe. We need your help."

"This is our resident RN. Ty, Jennifer Wilson and Jones." If Jones had a first name, or a better last name, he didn't seem inclined to divulge it.

Jennifer surveyed the room with both patients. She took in the IV drips hanging from the bed frame and raised her eyebrows. "This is quite the setup, doc."

I didn't appreciate being called 'doc,' but I wanted her cooperation so I let it slide. "Well, this far out in the country we like to be prepared for emergencies."

"What's wrong with him?" She gestured at Chaz who was waking up again.

"I'm not sure."

"But you want me to take this one?" She pointed to Eric on the floor.

"If you have room, I'd like to send them both, to be on the safe side."

"We aren't able to transport more than one patient."

"I didn't think you would be. He seems to be improving, so I'm okay with him staying. Dr. Steinman has been unresponsive for the last two hours and was unconscious for an unknown amount of time before that. If I didn't feel like his condition was critical, I wouldn't have asked you to make such a dangerous flight."

"Spinal injury?"

I hoped not, because we'd moved him a couple of times. "I don't think so but I can't rule it out."

She contemplated that, then nodded. "Jones, get his vitals. Check the stability of that drip. Where's the EKG?"

Ty and I backed into the hallway and gave them as much room as we could.

"Anna," Jed called me from downstairs, but I wasn't willing to walk away from the workup in the guest room. I hadn't seen Eric's EKG strip yet, and it could provide valuable information. I motioned for Jed to come up and join us. He walked past Ty and pulled me down the hallway to my bedroom. "Are you listening?"

"Did you say something?" I was perplexed but he gave me a little shake.

"Listen, Anna. Listen." I relaxed into my other sight and felt it. The pressure that had been building, the storm that wasn't a storm. It was close.

"What is it?" I whispered.

"An army." An army of ghosts, not the flesh and blood kind.

"But Adoni is gone."

"He is not gone. You delayed him when you drove him from your friend. You did not release him."

"That's a technicality I'm going to have to fix."

"This is quite serious."

I glared at him. "Trust me, I'm serious."

"You need to leave with that aircraft."

"I can't," I hissed, hoping that the paramedics couldn't hear us. "I will stay here, and I will protect my friends." I'd made my decision, and I was at peace with it. I didn't want to die, but I wasn't going to let anyone I loved die for me either. If I was lucky, really lucky, neither would be necessary, but I didn't know how we would get out of this.

"We cannot let them have you, Anna."

I summoned my bravado. "No. We can't. If it comes to that, you know what to do." If he'd been a warrior and a king, he ought to be able to handle one woman. I needed to have the same conversation with Ned. If it came down to it, I hoped that Ned would be the one to take me out. A well-placed bullet sounded like a better way to go than Jed's sword. I needed to make sure he had his sig out. The shotgun wouldn't be much fun. As long as neither one of them let me get taken. Everything depended on it.

"Anna, no. It does not have to be this way." He looked alarmed, and I could tell he wanted to touch me, but he didn't. I'd told him not to and he wouldn't, not without my permission. I swallowed the urge to reach out to him.

"I've got to get a helicopter off the ground, Jed." I walked past him, back into the hall. "Jennifer." I filled my voice with urgency. "It's time for you guys to go. Load up." I banged on the door to Carrie's room. "Carrie. It's time."

Jennifer leaned around the doorway. "We haven't finished our initial evaluation yet." She was annoyed and she didn't plan to let some country doctor bully her. I could respect that. I changed my tone.

"I don't mean any disrespect, Jennifer. Some very strange stuff is coming this way and if you guys don't get off the ground, I'm afraid you will be stuck here. It is not safe."

"What do you mean?" Her tone demanded an answer, no

nonsense, no bullshit. I couldn't tell her the truth though she deserved it.

"There's some very bad shit coming this way, Jennifer. Like bad weather, but worse. I need you to take my patient and get out of here before you get caught in it."

She leaned back on her heels. "I didn't see anything unexpected on radar, Dr. Roberts."

"It's not the kind of thing that shows up on radar. I wish I could tell you, but I can't. Please." I squatted beside her. "You can finish your eval in the air. Please. I don't want you to get hurt."

"Are you threatening me?"

"I just want you guys to be safe. I don't want you in danger just because you are near me."

She sighed. "Dr. Roberts, did you forget to take your medication?"

"I wish."

She considered that, and I could see her weighing the pros and cons, what the likelihood was that I was geeked up. She decided to be cautious. "Jones. Let's get him on the board." I breathed a sigh of relief. Now I just had to keep the path clear for them.

"How many more can you get on that chopper?"

"No way, doc. I'll take the unconscious one. That's it."

"I've got a pregnant woman here too."

"I'm not leaving," Carrie insisted from behind me as Jennifer responded.

"No can do." She wasn't going to budge.

I gave in. "Understood. Go." I wished there was some way to get the others out, but I didn't know how.

Though paramedics preferred to take their time with a patient – evaluate his current status, determine what they were likely to need while they were in the air, and what facility they needed to get him to – when they had to, they could pack up quick. Eric was on the board in a fast movement that made him grunt out of his stupor. He made a noise that almost made sense.

Jennifer strapped him down while Jones taped his IV lines so they wouldn't pull out. They maneuvered him down the stairs with skill and core body strength that I didn't possess. I followed them through the front door, into the cold night. The front steps were slick with sleet and I half skated down them.

The backboard fit in the SUV with the rear seats folded down. Jones scooted in and crouched next to Eric while Jennifer and I got back into the front. It took a minute to get the windshield warmed up enough to see the drive. I pulled into the place that Ned's vehicle had been and left the engine running and the lights on so that we could see the red and blue markings on the helicopter. Ned's truck pulled up behind us adding more light to the scene.

Jennifer and Jones pulled Eric out and led the way to the back end of the chopper. A wide door opened up under the tail and a man hopped out and took Jennifer's end of the backboard.

I handed Jennifer Eric's mobile phone and the wallet. "These are his. I didn't have the opportunity to contact his wife. Her name's Dr. Ashley Steinman. She's in his favorites list. Will you let her know where he is as soon as you get him to the hospital?"

She gave me a strange look but nodded. "I'll make sure she knows."

"I appreciate it. You guys fly safe. May I?" I gestured at Eric.

"Make it quick. I don't like this weather."

I lay my hand on Eric's forehead. It felt strange to touch him, as strange as it had been to see him after so long. "Goodbye, Eric. Good luck. I'm sorry you got caught up in this mess."

"I will not be leaving you, Anna." His eyes opened and fixed on me. I stepped back. It wasn't possible, medically, for a patient to go from comatose to that level of alertness that quickly. Jones and Jennifer looked as surprised as I felt.

"Eric?"

"I will make you a queen. All will worship you. Jedediah no longer has that power." He struggled against the straps and looked angry as he realized he was trapped.

"Settle down, Dr. Steinman!" Jennifer's order was ignored.

"Adonijah?"

"Beloved. I command you, untie me."

"I thought you hadn't seen him in some time, Dr. Roberts."

"I haven't," I assured Jennifer. "I don't know what he's talking about."

"Release me," Eric roared, his face distorted through his rage. Jed arrived at my side as if he could sense my dismay.

"What has happened?"

"I think Adonijah is back." Jed growled and started to advance on Eric. I grabbed his arm, as if I had the strength to stop a man his size. "Leave him."

"You will regret this, Anna." Eric's body shouted while he fought against the straps holding him to the backboard, and Jones almost dropped him.

We had an army of ghosts descending on us. We suspected Adoni was their leader, and we had the opportunity to send him away. It wasn't fair to Eric, but it might be the only chance I had to survive this. I wasn't sure Eric could take another dispossession event anyway, given how badly he'd been affected the first time.

"Jennifer, the weather isn't getting any better."

"When I come for you, you will regret this." Eric's face had turned purple. I hoped Adonijah didn't let his blood pressure get too high or he'd have a new set of problems.

"I think y'all are insane." Jennifer looked a little spooked.

"Hurry, Jennifer. He may be having a neurologic event as we speak," I reminded her.

"Jones, load the doctor." They got Eric in the back end and the backboard secured while he yelled in languages Eric had never spoken.

"We're leaving. Clear the area!" Jennifer ordered just before she closed the rear door.

"Let's go, Jed. Get back." I turned and ran, head down as the rotors started to rotate overhead. I might die soon, but I didn't care to be decapitated by a helicopter.

The blade speed increased, and the upward push threw snow out in a blizzard. I knew we should be clear but I couldn't tell where the cars were. With that ringing noise overhead, it didn't feel safe to be upright. I crouched into the ground and closed my eyes. A protective warmth enclosed me as my self-appointed guardian folded his body around mine, pulling me into his chest. He wrapped his arms around me and turned me in a half circle so that his back took the brunt of the pelting snow.

From his breath against my ear I knew that he was trying to say something, but the vibration of the helicopter made it impossible to detect words. The air around us cooled. Jed's hands clenched me tighter in what felt like caution and I braced myself. Ghosts crashed over us like a wave. I felt them sift through me, so many grains of sand finding their way to the bottom of the ocean. I felt sick and struggled to get away. Jed held me tighter and the chopper whined from overhead. It was off the ground.

"Let me go," I yelled as loud as I could so that my throat hurt from the effort, but I still couldn't hear myself. The spirits were like a pure noise river that swirled in a fog around us. I shifted in Jed's arms, so that I wouldn't blast him with my energy, and then released it.

Invisible fire exploded out of me with such force I screamed, certain that I'd torn myself apart. The air around us cleared as my power touched each soul and released it. I sagged back against the strong arms behind me, spent from the effort.

"Well done." I heard Jed and realized that the helicopter was up high enough that I could hear again. "The next are almost upon us, Anna. Are you ready?"

I wasn't.

The sudden whine of helicopter blades reversing for descent had us both scrambling towards the SUV as if it offered us safety. The lights dropped towards us, too fast.

"Oh my god!" I hadn't realized that Ned was there, but he was hunkered down, shoulder to shoulder with Jed, clutching his shotgun although he knew it wouldn't help.

Spirits dropped down around us like snow. Jed stood up and swung his sword free of his coat. I heard the squeals of the ghosts he touched as they dissolved into nothing. How the hell did he keep pulling that thing out of his jacket? Did it fold up like a Swiss Army knife when he wasn't using it?

The helicopter rushed overhead, way too close for a controlled landing. I leaped, out of instinct, to follow the disaster, as if I could save it. Ned grabbed my legs and hauled me back to the ground. Jed landed over us as the medevac unit crashed into the earth.

CHAPTER FIFTEEN

I BRACED MYSELF for an explosion, but it didn't come. I hoped that meant that the gas tank wasn't compromised. We needed to get to the helicopter in order to help any survivors. The next wave of ghosts slowed their momentum as if they too were taken aback by the crash. Or they'd just lost contact with their commander. Last I'd seen of Adonijah, he'd been on the chopper.

"Help!" Carrie's cry stretched across the meadow to us. I ignored the burning pain and stood up within the circle of Jed's arms, and out of reach of his blade. His left arm pulled me into him as if I belonged there. From that safe point, I tried to figure out where I was needed most.

The next group of ghosts hadn't stopped but they had slowed their momentum. I felt like there would be a gap, maybe a few minutes before they appeared. The spirits that hadn't been caught in the net of my power dissipated as if they were confused about what had happened to their buddies. I didn't waste my energy on releasing them. They seemed to have lost whatever malicious intent they had, and a helicopter had just made an unplanned landing in the south field.

It was a long ways away, but I could see Carrie on the front porch, illuminated by light that spilled from the open front door. She waved her arms at us, as if we weren't aware of what had just happened.

I pushed against the circle of muscle that held me. "Jed, I have to go to them."

He pulled me closer. "Anna, it's unlikely that any survived."

"I can see them." I couldn't see the helicopter with my eyes, but my other sight showed me the bright beacon of life in the field just to the south of us. They were so close together, I couldn't tell how many of them survived, but some did.

"Then they will have to wait. We must fight this battle, Anna. You must."

Jed's tone of voice demanded compliance, but my first obligation was clear. I'd spent my adult life in medical school, residency, and half a dozen years at my clinic taking care of the living.

"I will do that, Jed, I will do all that you have asked of me. After I go to that helicopter and help every single person. You can help me, or not."

There was a brief pause before he conceded. "I will assist you."

"Ned. Have Carrie call 911. I need my medical kit, everything you can find from the house. And Ty, if Chaz can spare him." A good RN was worth their weight in gold, and Ty was better than most. We weren't prepared for the kinds of traumas that would come from a helicopter crash, but I was a doctor. Caring for the sick and injured was what I did. It defined me.

"We'll need the tractor," I added. I couldn't access the field without it, and we might have to move some heavy piece of the wreckage in order to get to the survivors. I wanted to have all the tools I might need at my disposal.

The silence was frightening. If they could, they would yell for help, they would get themselves out of the wreckage. The truck started behind me as Ned went to get the tractor. I ran to the edge of the drive and stared out over the pasture. I wished there was moonlight to see by.

The next wave of spirits fell over us like a cloud. There wasn't time to count them. Were there a hundred, or just a few dozen? Jed and his sword fought their way towards me. I invited the ghosts in, opened myself to them. Gathered them so close to me that I could feel them, as they clawed their way into me. Not into my body, for some of them that was as easy to pass through as the air, but into my essence, my being. They weren't strong enough to take me, but my skin crawled as their nasty thoughts lingered. I smelled the decay of their souls. Only when I had collected them did I allow a small burst of my energy to sizzle through me. God, it hurt. I sank to my knees and fell back into the snow as they died for the last time. I hoped that each of them went straight to hell.

"Put the sword down and let me see Anna. Is she all right?" Hands touched my face, cool against my fevered skin. I smelled Ty, the hint of vanilla from his aftershave. Where had he come from? The tractor rumbled nearby and answered my question.

"Should we move her to the SUV?"

I tried to shake my head. I didn't want them to move me. The snow-covered ground beneath me was the only thing that cooled the burning pain. It felt like I was too hot, like I could explode.

"She will recover. Give her time." Jed, close enough that he must be standing over me. My guardian.

"Has this happened before?" Ty demanded.

"It has." Jed's tone was implacable. I forced my eyes open. It was important that Ty see that I was okay. We had to get to the helicopter.

"Anna. Are you all right?" Ty hovered over my upper torso, Jed straddled my feet, sword at the ready.

"Never better," I whispered.

He leaned back on his heels. "When we get out of this, you are going to have some explaining to do."

"I already told you everything." It wasn't quite true but at this point, I didn't expect to make it to the next day. I'd used so much of my power already, and there were so many more ghosts. Survival didn't feel possible. The fewer people that realized that, the better. "How's Chaz?"

"He looks a damn sight better than you do."

I hoped that meant that he was improving. I was glad that Jennifer had refused to take Chaz and Carrie, or they'd both be in the wreckage too.

"Jed, help," I grunted out the command.

He picked me up with a gentleness that was surprising from a man who carried a sword and steadied me against him with one arm while I found my feet.

"I need to get to the wreck." It was part plea, part order.

"Ty. Will you drive us?" Jed helped me to the SUV.

"Yeah. Your kit's in the back, Anna. We brought blankets and water, too."

I didn't have the energy to respond. Jed handed me into the backseat and then scooted in next to me. He leaned his sword between his knees so that he could keep an arm around me. It looked like a risky place to keep a sharp object but I didn't figure he needed me to point that out to him.

Carrie was in the front seat. She leaned over so she could see us. "Are you okay?" I didn't answer, and she continued. "I'm sorry, I should have thought to bring you some food." Since a helicopter had just crashed in the yard, I thought we could overlook that, though I was very hungry. "I called 911 and told them what happened. They can't send ambulances since the road is closed. They're calling the air ambulance folks."

I nodded. I'd known we'd be on our own for a while. The vehicle jerked and then heaved itself over the edge of the driveway and I was glad that Jed supported me. The motion caused my limbs to burn even more as if it forced the fire to work its way through them.

Ned had the plow down in front of us clearing a path down the edge of the field. There wasn't a road here, but the field was flat enough after decades of being farmed that it was possible to drive through it, as long as it wasn't too wet. It had been below freezing for months, so that wasn't a concern.

"Are there more of those things coming?" Ty guided the vehicle around an obstruction that I couldn't see from the backseat. He'd spent time on his grandparents' farm growing up, so I trusted him to be able to get us through a snowy field without getting stuck.

"The next are nearly upon us." I leaned my head against Jed's shoulder as he answered.

"Can she keep this up?"

"She is stronger than she realizes." It wasn't much of an answer but I wasn't going to call him on it. It sounded better than telling Ty that we were all going to die.

"There it is." Ty pointed.

I strained forwards and saw a flash of blue and red in the bouncing headlights. It looked as if it had landed upright and was in one piece though the tail was bent at a strange angle. As the tractor reached it, Ned turned so that the headlights lit the aircraft from the side. The blade closest to us was broken off at the shaft. It wouldn't be flying again, and I wondered for a moment how we would even get it out of my field.

First things first. Survivors. Some lived, I could feel their souls. I grasped the door handle but Jed stopped me.

"Wait." He was right, the car was still moving.

"I'm going to get as close as I can, Anna. If anyone is wounded, we don't want to be carrying them a long way to the car."

"We may need a backboard." If they were going to make it, I didn't want to exacerbate any spinal cord injuries when we moved them.

"I'm hoping there's a spare one in there," Ty commented.

"We've got plywood in the barn," Carrie offered, but it seemed like a long way from where we were. Still, it was an option.

Ty stopped so that his headlights complemented Ned's by shining on the parts of the helicopter that were still dark. It was tilted on the axis as if it might list further and fall over on its side. Jagged rips went up the side of the fuselage.

"The gas has spilled," Ned yelled out the warning, but it wasn't necessary. We could all smell it. That put the danger of rescuing the survivors up a few notches. If the gas tank exploded, we'd all be dead. The farmer in me mourned. A fuel spill would lose us our organic certification for the field. How long would it be before we could grow something that wasn't toxic?

"Can we risk it?" Ned asked as I stumbled out of the truck. My legs hadn't recovered enough strength to walk. I needed more time and I wasn't going to get it. Jed stepped out behind me and grabbed my elbow to steady me.

"You think they're still alive?" Ty asked.

"Yes. I can see them." The souls of the living were still identifiable in the wreckage.

"Then we have to try." Ty sounded like he was trying to convince himself. I felt the same way.

"They will be here soon," Jed cautioned in a growl. He hadn't let go of his sword. He was right, the ghosts were coming with renewed vigor as if they'd figured out their purpose again. I ignored him, and them.

Now that we were at the crash site, I wished I didn't have to go any farther. Like most physicians, I've seen my fair share of terrible events. None of us enjoy that part of our calling. I wanted someone else to turn to, someone who could be responsible for this. Someone whose lead I could follow. In this nightmare, though, I was the highest qualified person present. I straightened my shoulders and advanced on the side door with Ty behind me. There wasn't any other choice.

I stuck my hand into the pocket on the aircraft door and pulled on the lever. With the truck lights reflecting off the outside of the plane, I couldn't see inside the dark interior, and it was silent inside. I could tell that the seat closest to me didn't have an occupant, but that was about it. Given the angle the cockpit was tilted at, I couldn't really see anything anyway.

"I need a flashlight," I hollered, and heard crunching snow as Ned ran up behind me.

"Here." He handed me the torch and I flicked it on. It was really bright, which I was grateful for. Ten years ago all we had were the soft light batteries and I wouldn't have been able to do much with one of those. "How are they?"

"She doesn't know yet." Ty shouldered Ned out of the way and boosted me into the cockpit.

"Hello? Jones? Jennifer? Eric? I need you to talk to me," I shouted as I pulled myself in. I didn't get a response. I assumed it was the lieutenant slumped in the seat across from me, head lolled to the side. I scooted towards him, mindful of the shattered glass all over the seat. A quick flick of the flashlight to the back showed me two more bodies. Eric was still strapped onto the table, and Jones was sprawled over him. He must not have been belted in. Jennifer was in the seat behind the pilot's. It looked like she'd had the safety belts on, but I couldn't see her face. She wasn't moving. None of them were moving.

"Jennifer, are you okay?" I raised my voice, but she didn't respond. I reached the pilot and switched my attention to him. "Lieutenant? Can you talk to me?" Nothing.

I ran a hand under his nose and felt the warm rush of air as he breathed. It was a start.

"Patient number one. The lieutenant. He's unconscious." There wasn't room for Ty in there too, so he leaned in the door and took mental notes. The lieutenant was wearing a headset, and I removed it with care. My hands came away wet. "Blood. Probable head injury." I felt his scalp, grateful for the buzzed haircut, and found a gash on the left side of his head. "Probably hit the window. We've got a lot of blood here, Ty."

"Freakin' scalp wounds, they always bleed like crazy," he muttered. I heard him rustle with bandages.

"Yeah, we need to get some pressure on this right away. Get Ned over here." Applying pressure was an easy job that Ned could handle.

I held onto the lieutenant's shoulders while the pilot door popped open. Ned couldn't get in all the way, because of how the helicopter listed, but it was enough.

"Tell me what to do," he said.

"Ty." I reached back and felt a stack of gauze bandages in my outstretched hand. It was great to have someone who knew me well enough to anticipate what I was going to need in an emergency situation.

"Hold these, here." I took Ned's left hand and braced him so he was helping to hold the pilot up. I placed his right hand on the scalp wound. "Hold pressure, but don't move his head. If he's got a spinal injury we could make it a lot worse."

The man had delivered cows, gelded horses in his own pasture, and sat in on more animal surgeries than I could count, but he looked a little scared. People were different than animals. "You okay?" I asked. He nodded. "Okay. If his breathing changes at all, you let me know. Ty, can you go around the back, see if you can get that back door open?"

"I don't think we can. The tail wing is broken and looks like it could detach at any moment."

"That's okay." It was decidedly not okay. That meant that our only access was through the tiny side door. It made things a lot more challenging.

I crawled over the console and squeezed through the tight space into the back compartment, past Jennifer. There wasn't much room to move, so I braced my knee on the stretcher next to Eric's motionless head.

Ty squeezed in behind me. "Can you get to Jennifer?" I asked. I was going to have my hands full with the other two.

"She's breathing. No sign of injuries." I left her to Ty.

"Jones, Eric, can you hear me?" My hands were busy. Eric had a pulse and good respirations. He might have been in the best position for the crash since he was already tied onto a backboard and strapped down. I turned to the form that lay motionless across Eric's body. Why hadn't Jones been buckled in?

"I can't find any obvious signs of injury on Jennifer. She's not conscious, but good respirations and heart rate." Ty imparted the good news with caution.

"Let's leave her there for now." The five point harness offered pretty solid spinal support. If it was something internal, I couldn't help her anyway.

Jones didn't look good. There wasn't much light to see by but when I reached his neck I couldn't find a pulse. I could still feel his soul, but it flickered, in and out of his body. I needed him out in the open where I could work on him. Whether or not he had a spinal injury was less important if his heart wasn't beating.

"We've got to get this guy out of here, stat."

Ty was small but strong. He was with me in an instant, and we manhandled Jones' stout form out over the front seat and handed him down to Jed.

"Double check those two. Eric had respirations and a pulse, but was non-responsive." I hopped down to follow Jed. Jones was in the worst shape, so he was mine.

"Get a blanket on the ground and put him on it. Try not to let his head move too much." I shouted instructions as Jed and Carrie scrambled to comply. It was good she'd come down. I needed another set of hands. I needed a few teams of ambulance crews, or a field hospital. Those weren't options.

"Do either of you know CPR?" Jed shook his head.

"No. I mean, I took a class once, in high school . . ." Carrie trailed off and knelt next to Jones' head. As long as she had the basics, I could talk her through CPR.

"Okay, that's good. I may need your help." I ripped his jacket open and found a torso free of hair and riddled in tattoos. Ty dropped down next to me and handed me a stethoscope and an oxygen bag. I looked up and realized we were sitting next to a mobile, crashed, medical center.

Jones didn't have a heart rate to speak of, and he wasn't breathing. "Defibrillator?" I asked with hope.

"I'm sure they've got one in there somewhere." Ty disappeared again. As long as it didn't go up in flames we had access to better technology than I had in my office.

I checked his mouth for obstructions and didn't find any. CPR time. "We're going to need help," I yelled. Ty dropped back down next to me, flipped open a tan box holding a defibrillator, and turned it on.

"How are the others?" I needed Ty but wanted to make sure he could be with me.

"More stable than this one." I nodded. It wasn't a great position to be in. We were just going to have to do the best we could. Ty continued, "Ned's trying to get the radio to work on the helicopter so we can see if they are sending help. It's the best option to call something in."

"The helicopter probably has an emergency locator on it that activates if it crashes, and 911 knows. If they can make it out here, they will." I dropped into the rhythm. Thirty compressions. Three in, I hadn't cracked the ribs yet.

"You aren't deep enough Dr. Anna," Ty coached.

I nodded and put some more oomph into my effort. It was hard work. Brutal, and unlikely to be successful.

"Leave him, Anna. He is already lost. They are almost upon us. You must fight." Jed's voice was a rush of urgency.

"Kinda busy right now," I muttered through clenched teeth. I couldn't walk away from someone in need no matter what else was going on. The bones beneath my hands gave the sickening crack that said I was deep enough, and the movement grew a little easier. Ty fixed the respirator over Jones' face and gave Carrie a quick lesson when I paused.

"Like this. One, two." He pumped the bag twice, forcing air into Jones' lungs. I dropped back into the next thirty compressions.

The defibrillator spoke in a strange robotic voice. It was ready.

"Anna." Jed's voice seemed distant because I was focused on trying to save my patient's life. "They are coming, Anna. You must let that one go so that we may save the rest."

"No." It was all I could get out as Ty and I counted down to the end of my repetition. "Clear," I yelled. Ty placed the paddles on Jones' chest. His body jerked and Ty pulled the paddles back. The machine told me to keep doing CPR. I dropped back into compressions. Jed was muttering in a foreign language, or several of them. Based on his inflection, I guessed he was swearing.

He straddled Jones' legs and pulled his sword. "Do not stand up. I will protect you for as long as I can."

"Anna, I've got this. Go save everyone." Maybe the long length of sharpened steel hanging over us made Ty nervous.

I didn't bother to answer, just kept counting the compressions. My hands hurt from being clenched together and my arms ached but I knew from experience that I could do this for a long time. "Thirty." Ty and I said it together and he inserted himself into my space.

"My turn, Anna. Carrie, I'm going to need your help."

Jed pulled me back off Jones' chest while Carrie took up the oxygen mask. "Anna, the time has come."

"I know," I whispered. I didn't want to die.

A cloud of spirits swept over us, the souls a murky blur compared to the eight beacons of the living around me. They came with such force that the helicopter groaned in protest. Its position shifted several inches from the force of the impact. I remembered the flying tractor and raised my hands, hoping I could draw them away from that projectile.

"I'm right here." I heard my voice, more of a scream than a yell, over the whipping sound that the ghosts made with their gale force movement. Jed pulled me back against him as if he could shelter me. His sword stretched over us and a handful of spirits were vanquished as they ran themselves into it.

"Come to me." I didn't try to yell over the noise this time. They were listening to me now. I had to get them away from the helicopter, away from the ones I loved. "You can have me. Leave my friends." They came.

"No, Anna! There are too many." Jed's command was one that a king could have issued and his subjects would obey, but I wasn't his. I stepped out of the safety of his arms and into the cloud. They closed around me, separating me from him.

The air was so thick with ghosts I had to fight them to move forward, and every breath stank of rotting and cold. Their thoughts were a rush of anger; muted voices that swelled to a cacophony inside the eye of their storm. I forced myself to take a few steps farther away from Jed, from the helicopter. The farther away my friends were, the safer they would be.

The spirits closed in on me and I couldn't walk anymore. A thousand hands with bony clawed fingers reached out to me. Skulls with skeletal teeth tore at my clothes and flesh. I collapsed into the snow as the roiling mass consumed me. Oxygen dissipated as they took up the space where air would have been. I gasped in a last breath and held it.

There was a spark inside me, a small ball of nuclear energy. It couldn't be enough, but I pulled it forth and ignited it with as much force as I could muster. Every fiber of my being screamed with the release as it emptied out of me. The ghosts roiled as the fires caught them, each dissipated with the touch of my energy.

I rolled over and watched as they were freed from the dark memories that held them to this earth. It was beautiful to me. The satisfaction of victory set into me. Somehow, I had done it.

"Anna!" Jed yelled a warning, and I recognized the flash of one last soul as it dipped down to me. It was too late. It was inside of me.

The soul tore at me as if it would rip out my insides. I heard the hoarse scream of my own voice and couldn't make it stop. I sought one last shred of my energy to burn the interloper away, but I had used it all. There was nothing left. The scream turned to a laugh as he took final control of my body.

"Thank you, Anna. That was perfect." It was my voice, but it wasn't. I struggled against him, but Adonijah was more powerful. He laughed against my efforts. "No, little one. You are mine now. We will do great things together."

Jed approached, sword out. I could still see, could hear, but all of my senses were filtered through the cloud of Adoni's soul. Jed seemed far away. I tried to reach out but my hand didn't move. Adonijah twisted inside of me causing a visceral pain.

"Cease your efforts, beloved. I don't like to hurt you." I didn't believe him. I fought, I tried to push him out of me, but it was futile. Without my fire, I had nothing. The pain came again, intense and searing. I couldn't see through the haze of it, couldn't do anything but let it ride over me. My cries were silent ones that no one could hear.

"Adonijah, you will release her." Jed's voice drifted through to me.

"No, Jedediah. She is mine now. This Sheba is not yours to keep." It felt like Adoni was tearing off strips of my flesh inside me, piece by piece. I tried to retreat from the agony, but there was no place to go. I was captive, trapped in my own body. I couldn't even scream.

Jed's eyes burned with fury, his sword still held before him, but he didn't advance on us. I wanted to reach out to him, to go to him, but I couldn't.

"Little one, if you will stop fighting me, I will leave your friends be." Another strip of flesh ripped off the inside of my belly. I was nothing but a quivering mass as I tried to ride out the pain.

He pushed us to our feet. "Very good, little one. I am glad that you are able to be reasonable. That will make our alliance more enjoyable."

I stirred in anger against his words but he was waiting for that. One more invisible strip of tissue ripped free. I couldn't fight him through the agony. It was too much. I wasn't that strong. I curled up in the corner of my mind and lay as still as I could.

"You cannot have her." Jed's sword wavered.

Remember your promise Jed. It was a fervent whisper of a thought that he couldn't hear. *Don't let Adonijah have me. I would rather die than live with him inside of me like this.*

"Put your sword down, foolish brother, before you hurt this girl that you are so in love with." Adonijah's words overpowered my own, his were the ones that my body gave voice to.

Ty was still doing compressions on Jones' chest. I couldn't tell if his soul was there or not. Adonijah had control of my senses, my sight, and my body. He had the power to torture me and he enjoyed it. It aroused him to have me helpless. I could see too many of his thoughts, his plans. Chaz was right. Adonijah couldn't be allowed to have me.

I felt the first atom of my energy create itself, deep within my body and knew that it belonged to Adonijah now. He felt it too and threw my head back with laughter as he turned towards his brother.

Jed took a wary step back as Adonijah reached for that speck of power. It didn't take much to drive a soul from their body.

I panicked and forced myself into the center of my mind, trying to access my central nervous system. I didn't have a chance, but I fought hard enough that Adonijah paused while he crushed my rebellion with cruel blows into my psyche.

A blunt object struck us and pain seared into my back and knocked the air from our lungs. We reeled into the snow, unable to breathe. I caught a glimpse of Ned as he jumped away from us. *Shoot me, Ned!* I begged him but Adoni still controlled my voice.

Jed stood over my body and raised his sword. "I am sorry, Anna." Adonijah tried to release the spark, but he didn't have time. I felt his shock as Jed's blade flashed down and cut through the thick jackets on my chest, slicing into the flesh on my breast. It stopped when it struck bone. My body screamed.

It was a different pain, twofold. Adoni fought against the power of the blade that stuck into my pectoral. An icy flame released into my blood stream and filtered into every tissue in my body. It lapped at me, just as he did. I embraced it. I would rather die than be trapped with that evil being inside me. The pain from the blade in my skin was intense. I felt the wet heat of my blood as it trickled out of the wound. If he took the blade any deeper it would cut through my ribs and go into my lung.

There were cries other than mine, but my world dwindled to three things. Jed, Adonijah, and the sword in my chest.

Adonijah's soul wrapped around mine, his hold on my body weakened by the swords power. He entwined himself with me as if that would save him. I held him close though the evil in him violated me. I clung to that cold fire, to Jed's blade. It was all that could cleanse me.

My heart rate slowed as my soul released its hold on my body. After so many years witnessing death, it was fascinating to feel it happen. Adonijah was with me. He gambled that I would fight to live. By tying himself to me, he had already lost.

Jed pulled his blade free of my bone with a violent jerk and knelt over me. Big hands cupped my face. "Anna. Please, stay with me."

I wanted to touch him, but I was too far gone. I regretted that it was too late to tell him that I loved him. My breathing slowed and my heartbeat stuttered. It was weak enough that the tether that held me to my living form loosened. I slipped out of my body, pulling Adonijah with me. He was too frail to put up a fight. Once we were free, it was easy to let him go into the night. I could tell how the power of Jed's sword had damaged him. It had me as well, but with the pain gone I was stronger now than Adonijah. He would not be able to harm my friends again, not anytime soon, anyway.

My free soul felt the peace of the night air. Without a body, it wasn't cold. I marveled at the brilliance of the stars and realized that I could hear the hum of their energy, could feel them call to me. They wanted me to join them. I drifted higher, letting my soul take its natural path. This was what was supposed to happen. It was so peaceful. It was death, and I welcomed it.

Then another soul was with me, shining with golden beauty.

Marnie. She stretched out her hand, more solid in death than she had looked when I was alive. She pulled me to her and drew me back to the earth, away from the peace of the stars. I protested but she quieted me. She was Marnie. I trusted her.

She held me above my body. Ty knelt over it, his hands pumped up and down as he performed CPR. Jedediah stood behind him, looking to the sky. He could see me. Marnie took me to him, and he opened his arms to us. Tears wet his cheeks. I wanted to soothe him but I didn't have that power anymore. Marnie and I stayed with him. I would give him what comfort I could for as long as my soul's tenuous claim to the earth held. The stars still called me to them with their sweet song. I would go soon.

Ty had the tan box out and laid paddles on the bare chest beneath him. He needed to give up. It was too late for my body. My spirit was gone. I wished I could tell him to stop.

Then I felt it, the tether that had once held me reached out to me again. Marnie encouraged me towards it. I had to choose. I could reattach myself to the damaged body that lay in the snow or I could go to the stars.

Marnie radiated love around me. She wanted me to stay. I was what bound her to the earth now, and she liked it there. I looked at Jedediah, who had loved me enough to release me. His eyes begged me to come back to him, and I wavered. The stars were so beautiful, but they would be there forever. I turned from them, with a twinge of regret, and grasped the rope that led to my body. It pulled me in with a painful thump.

CHAPTER SIXTEEN

A **DISCORDANT MIX** of senses assaulted me. Pain was foremost. The strange rush of sound was second.

"I've got a heartbeat." The yell was too loud, too close, but the body that encased me seemed like lead after the lightness of my freed soul. Attempting to move would be futile. I didn't have the strength to force the lump of flesh I inhabited to do anything.

My chest exploded in agony as my lungs filled with air in a motion that I couldn't control. I would have cried from it, but it hurt too much.

"Her hand just moved." A woman's voice, also too loud.

"She's breathing. I've got a pulse." Relief filled words.

"Is she back? Will she be okay?" I realized that I knew the woman that the voice belonged to. Her name was Carrie.

"I don't know." This was Ty. Why did he sound so stressed?

Ah yes. My heart stopped. I died and then Ty brought me back.

It felt like something that had happened a long time ago, like I hadn't been with these people in years.

"Her soul has returned to her body. If it is not too damaged, she will survive." This was the voice that I yearned for, the man I had come back for. My eyesight seemed fuzzy, as if my real vision was hampered by the constraints of the body. Perhaps only the spirits of the dead could see. I would never forget it.

"What the hell did you stab her for?" Now that I was breathing again, Ty had time to be pissed.

"Adonijah was in her. She was lost if I did not release him."

"Couldn't she do it herself?"

"She used up all of her energy on that last wave of ghosts. It was his plan, to weaken her enough to take over her body."

"Will she make it?" The woman, Carrie again.

"They're here." I registered Ned's voice, and absently wondered why I couldn't move. Then I heard them, helicopters. More than one. It sounded like a dozen of them.

"Thank God. We've got to get her to a hospital. Carrie, keep the pressure on that wound. She can't afford to lose more blood." Ty still sounded anxious. Was I bleeding? Oh yes. Jed's sword, the jolting feel of it lodging into my bones.

"Anna, can you hear me?" I turned my eyes up to Jed. I couldn't talk but I could shift that much.

"Look, she just moved again."

"Anna, can you talk?" Ty leaned between Jed and me. Did I control my own speech again?

"It . . . hurts," I managed to mumble.

"I know it does, baby. You've got some cracked ribs. We're gonna get you outta here, though, real soon." Ty was talking to me like I was five, but it didn't bother me. I was going to think twice before I busted through someone's ribcage to do CPR again. Broken ribs made every breath hurt like hell.

"Jed," I whispered. I wanted him with me.

"I'm here." He knelt down next to me and I turned my head a little towards him. I reached a bare hand up and he grasped it in his, covering it entirely.

"Don't leave me."

His hand squeezed mine. "I will stay beside you. She's very cold," he announced.

"I've got an emergency blanket pack in the truck." Carrie, always ready to help someone. Ty took over the pressure on my shoulder and Carrie disappeared. It hurt so much to breathe, thanks to Ty's handiwork with my ribs, that I almost didn't notice the open wound in my chest wall. Two helicopters circled overhead.

"Why are they here?" My voice was hoarse, my throat dry. It took too much effort.

"The crew must have radioed in a mayday when they were going down. That's the only way they'd make it here so fast." Ty looked around. "Ned's guiding them to the driveway to land."

"Here's the blanket." Carrie ripped into a foil package and came out with a sheet that looked like it was the ground cover for a tent. It didn't look like much, but I felt a little warmer once it was tucked over me.

"Take over, Carrie. I'll go check on our other patients," Ty instructed. I wanted to ask about them, but it took too much effort to speak.

"So, is he gone, Jed?" Carrie's tone was softer now, or else my senses were adapting to my body again.

"Not forever, but he is weak. My blade stripped him of his strength, and Anna is free of him."

I liked Carrie holding pressure on my shoulder more than Ty. She was gentler and it didn't hurt as much. She pulled the blanket up over my bare chest so that her arm tucked underneath it. If I'd had the wherewithal to care, I would have appreciated it. By then, though, Jed had seen my naked soul and held my essence in the palm of his hand. Bare breasts didn't seem like such a big deal in comparison.

A car engine approached and then there were voices, commotion. I tried to look but Carrie stopped me.

"The first helicopter crew is here. Ty is talking to them," she narrated, so I wouldn't try to move again.

"There are two men going with Ty to see to the helicopter crew," Jed added.

A man popped into my vision. He wore a dark blue coverall jumpsuit and a black ski cap. "Dr. Roberts?"

I tried to nod but wasn't sure if I'd been successful or not.

"My name's Michael and I'm a paramedic. I understand you have some injuries. Can you talk?"

"A little," I gasped out and he nodded.

"That's great. I won't make you do too much." He and I both knew that was a lie. "What happened?" He asked Carrie and Jed.

"She's got an open wound to the chest. We're holding pressure." Ty darted back in. He was out of breath from running back and forth. "She went into cardiac arrest, so she's at a minimum got some broken ribs from chest compressions. When I used the defibrillator her heart started again."

"What caused the cardiac arrest? How did she get the chest wound?"

"She was too close to the medevac unit when it crashed," Ty lied with ease. No one disputed it. I hoped Jed had hidden his sword again. If anyone figured out that he'd stabbed me with it, we'd have a whole new set of problems.

"Okay, let's take a quick look." Carrie moved her hand and I felt the brush of freezing air as the blanket lifted back. "That's a really clean wound. Looks like a knife." Michael sounded suspicious. Ty shrugged.

"I think she's very lucky."

"Where'd the debris go?"

Ty shrugged again and looked into the darkness. "I threw it over there."

Michael could tell something wasn't right. "Dr. Roberts, is that what happened to you?" He asked me.

I tried to nod and thought I'd succeeded that time. Ty's story was as good as any. We'd go with it.

"All right then. Dr. Roberts, we're going to get you on a stretcher and get you out of here in just a few minutes. Hang in there for me, okay?" He disappeared again and I grasped for Ty's hand.

"You okay, baby girl?" He asked as he leaned over me.

"Jones?" I whispered. He pulled away, a look of regret on his face. He gave a tiny shake of his head and I knew. I closed my eyes against the wave of despair that accompanied that news. It hurt almost as much as breathing. His death was my fault.

It took Jed a while to convince them that he had to travel with me, but in the end, they relented because I was a doctor and because I asked them to let him. They hauled everyone out in big police helicopters, with the exception of Carrie and Ned, who saw no reason to leave home. Ty got to go because he was a nurse and had all of the clinical details on the patients. He and Chaz went with Jedediah and me. They took Jennifer and Eric away with the lieutenant in the helicopter before us, but Jones' body was still there when we left, waiting for transport.

We entered the Emergency Department of the trauma center that I'd trained at in a rush of commotion. I'd spent countless hours here, caring for patients. It was the first time I'd come in on a stretcher. Being the patient made a remarkable change in the dynamic.

There were more questions. Four different people asked me about the wound on my chest, wondering aloud how it was possible that helicopter crash debris could look so much like someone had taken a meat cleaver to my chest. At this hospital, that was an injury they were familiar with. Since I'd been found right next to a crashed helicopter, though, they couldn't say much to dispute it. The fact that so many of the staff knew me made my story more believable. I had worked beside them here for years.

Rumors flew through the hospital like wildfire. Dr. Roberts and Dr. Steinman had come in together, been injured together in a helicopter crash. We'd been dating when we were here in training, and Eric and his pretty cardiologist had gotten together while they finished their fellowships here. Everyone knew it, and wondered if we were back together again, if Eric's wife knew. Perhaps Jed was my jealous lover. I discovered that the morphine drip made me not care. I closed my eyes and slept.

"Anna. You have a visitor." Jedediah's voice was low, reassuring. I knew it meant that nothing was wrong. His presence kept me calm. The nursing staff had learned to ignore the bear of a man who sat next to my bed and didn't say much. When he did leave my side, I got very nervous. I suspected I was having a post-traumatic stress reaction to having been through a series of battles with an army of ghosts. I'd been possessed and tortured by an evil spirit, cut with a sword, died, had an out of body experience and been brought back to life.

Since I couldn't tell anyone any of that, though, I kept it to myself. The nurses thought I was a very needy girlfriend who might be in an abusive relationship. They sent social workers to talk to me that I sent away again. I refrained from telling them that we weren't dating. It would only complicate matters.

"Hey, Anna." Ty slipped through the doorway and nodded to Jed. "Hello, Jed."

"Ty," Jed acknowledged him with a nod but didn't move from my side.

"How's Chaz?" I struggled to sit up, decided it hurt way too much to try, and instead found the button that raised the bed.

"He's rehydrated and his vitals have all stabilized. The nursing staff can't figure out why you, he, and Eric all have the same symptoms."

I looked up at the saline drip that fed into my own arm. I was getting an odd mixture of sodium and glucose, and I'd had enough steroids I could plan on taking up bodybuilding when I got out. "It's bizarre, I know. I told them that I thought it must be some virus that we all caught. They don't believe that it's possible, but they can't come up with a better explanation, so that's the one that's going in our charts." I paused. "Is Eric okay?"

"Better. I ran into his wife in the corridor. She asked me why he'd come out to see you."

"We'll let him answer that one." At least we knew he wasn't possessed anymore. I hoped it was safe for him to go back home with her.

"Yeah, I didn't know what to say, other than I was certain that you and he hadn't talked in years."

"Has Jennifer awakened?" The last update I had gotten the paramedic was in a coma. The lieutenant had recovered and been discharged with a head full of stitches. I felt terrible, for involving all of them, though the crash might have been due to the weather. I suspected, though, that Adonijah had somehow managed it. Either way, it was my fault that they were all there to begin with.

"Not yet."

I tried to shift and grunted from the pain that tore through my chest wall. Ty and Jed both leaned forward, faces etched with concern.

"I'm so sorry I had to do that to you." Ty grasped my left hand.

"You saved my life, Ty. You don't ever have to apologize for that." Ty had saved my body, Jed and Marnie my soul. I didn't tell Ty about that part. He'd had his fill of the supernatural. I also didn't tell them about how I still yearned for the stars, and the peace they offered me. I should have felt lucky to be alive, but I wasn't there yet.

"I know, but it killed me to do that to you." He was distraught. I tightened my fingers around his since that was all I could do without causing more pain. "What was the final tally?" He nodded at my chest.

"Seven ribs and the sternum. You did a good job of it." It would hurt to breathe, and move, for a long time. There wasn't much you could do for cracked ribs. At least they weren't displaced. I felt strange not wearing a bra, but I doubted I'd be able to for a month.

"Sorry." Ty rubbed my arm with gentle fingers and I forced myself to not pull away. I didn't like to be touched, after what Adonijah had done to me.

"Stop it, Ty. You did what you had to. I'd do the same for you."

"Thanks, I think." His tone was wry.

"Don't mention it."

"How's the cut?"

"It was clean. I think I've got thirty-nine stitches in it. It was a two-layered closure, though. Itches like hell, and I won't be able to take a shower for weeks." I expected a joke about how bad I smelled, but he passed on the opportunity.

"I can't believe you took the sword to her, Jed." Ty was still mad.

"He had to, Ty. I made him promise."

"To kill you?"

"Yes."

He stood and walked away from the bed. "I don't understand."

I wanted to go to him. He was my best friend. I couldn't even get out of bed, though, without help. "I hope you don't have to. But I'll tell you sometime, if you want me to." He deserved to know. They all did.

Ty changed the topic. "They're letting us go home this afternoon."

"That's great. I'm supposed to get out tomorrow."

"Can you even walk?"

"It hurts to," I admitted. "Jed will help me." After what we'd been through, I knew that there wasn't anything Jed wouldn't do for me. Including stab me with a sword, if I needed him to.

It didn't mean we were in a relationship though things between us had shifted. I didn't feel the need to figure out where we stood. We had time again, a gift I hadn't expected. The whole death experience had changed my perspective. I felt like I had to rebuild my life from the ground up. Everything that I believed was in question, everything was being reshaped. I didn't know who I would be when I came out the other side. I was certain that Jed would be with me, though, as long as I allowed him to be.

"Call me when you get home." Ty gave me an awkward kiss on the cheek since he couldn't hug me.

"Take care of Chaz."

"I always do." The door clicked shut behind him.

"You didn't tell him." It was almost the first time that Jed had spoken to me all day. It occurred to me that he might be the one person who could understand how I felt about being back in my body. I wasn't ready to talk about it, though. I might not ever be able to. Did he feel that way too?

"It was easier not to." I shifted in the bed in the futile hope that I could find a less painful position. "He wouldn't understand."

"He'll know soon." Jed's voice was gentle.

"Rita said she wouldn't tell him until he got back to work."

"We must return to the farm."

"I know. The investigators." The aviation officials that investigate air accidents had been to see me in the hospital, but they wanted me to come out to the farm for an interview there. It didn't look like something that I could avoid. I'd agreed to meet them there the following afternoon, assuming I could get the hospital to release me.

"Ned will pick us up." I nodded and looked away from him. It was easier to look out the window than to risk continued conversation. I had nothing to say.

CHAPTER SEVENTEEN

IT TOOK ALL MORNING to finish the discharge paperwork. Ned waited with reasonable patience while Jed paced the small room and grumbled about the delay. When they wheeled me out to the small circle drive where the Ford Explorer waited, Ned stood there with Eric and his petite, pretty wife. She looked stressed but I was glad to see that she was okay. I didn't know who the ghost was that had been in Eric. Adonijah hadn't told me, and I hadn't seen him after he woke up.

"Help me stand, please." I didn't want to be in a wheelchair when I talked to Eric. Jed grasped me by the forearms and tugged. We were getting pretty good at getting me upright without me having to use the muscles in my chest and abdomen, all of which were attached to broken ribs.

"Anna." Eric looked me over as if he hadn't seen me in a few years. Which was accurate. It hadn't been him at the farm. I didn't know how much he remembered of the time that he had had Adonijah inside of him, but I hoped it hadn't been as terrible for him as it had been for me. Every time I slept I had nightmares, flashbacks to the tearing pain, the knowledge that I was helpless and trapped. The horrible sense of Adonijah's pleasure as he tortured me.

"Hello, Eric. How are you feeling?"

Ned kept Eric's wife engaged in conversation, but it didn't keep her from glaring at me. I ignored her. It wasn't very polite, but it was the easiest thing to do.

"Better." He wrinkled his eyebrow at me. "You look awful."

"Thank you."

He paused and looked up at Jed. Eric was tall enough he didn't have to look up at many people. It looked like he wanted me to introduce them. I didn't. "Look, I think I owe you and Ned an apology. I don't know what made me come up there. I can't remember a thing."

"It wasn't your fault," I said. He looked confused at that but I wasn't going to explain it. If he didn't remember, that was better for him in the long run.

"I guess you took care of me?"

"Yeah. We found you unconscious in Ned's house." I spoke loud enough for his wife to hear me.

"What was I doing there?" His voice was filled with confusion.

"I don't know," I answered with as much honesty as I could, under the circumstances. "You needed medical care, so I called the medevac." I shrugged. "I'm sorry it crashed."

He looked more confused. "It wasn't your fault."

I had my doubts about that but I didn't voice them.

"Then you got hurt when the helicopter went down?" He knew it didn't make sense. It was like he knew what had happened, but was still trying to understand it.

"Yeah."

"That seems strange." He paused again. "What about the virus?"

I shrugged. "I guess it's some weird bug that's going around."

"The ED guy who admitted me said my metabolic profile looked like a lightning strike case." I didn't respond and he made one more bid for information. "And you don't know why I was there?"

"Not a clue Eric. Next time you need to see me, use the phone. It's safer." I hobbled over to the car door with as much dignity as I could muster. Which I lost when I realized that I couldn't climb into the passenger seat. Jed scooped me up, set me inside, and closed the car door against further discussion.

The drive north was beautiful. Ice coated trees shimmered in the sunshine as they reflected light off each glazed branch. Deep snow covered the pastures and hillsides.

"They say it was our heaviest snowfall in a decade." Ned did small talk well.

"At least the highways are open again." I forced myself to engage in the conversation.

"Yeah, took them a few days to get out our way with the plows."

"Everything's okay, though, at the farm?"

"Will be, once they get that helicopter out of the south field."

"When will that happen?"

"Don't know yet." He tapped his fingers on the steering wheel in a thoughtful motion that I knew well. "They say they have to talk to you again first." Ned turned into the long drive that led to our houses. When he crested the hill, I saw four trucks parked along the edge of the drive, the red and blue helicopter sat sideways in the pasture.

"Let's get it over with." I wasn't looking forward to the bumpy ride through the field to the helicopter.

"They can come up to the house, Anna," Ned informed me. "I already told them that you were in no shape to stand around in the cold, or to walk out to the site."

"Thanks."

"Sure. Carrie's there already. I bet she's got some fresh coffee brewed." My stomach rumbled at the mention of her name and Ned chuckled in response. "Yeah, she's fixing you dinner too, no worries there."

"Thank god. Hospital food is the worst. I'm starving." I'd been hungry for days but nobody wanted to let me eat anything other than broth and Jello. I was tired of the bland diet.

By the time I finished my interview with the FAA team, darkness was starting to fall. It was just late afternoon, but I was exhausted, hungry, and in pain. Jed handed me a Vicodin to go with my coffee and I took it without question.

"Carrie?" I asked.

"What can I get for you?"

"Do you have time to help me?"

"Of course. Chicken's in the oven. What can I help with?"

"I need to pack."

"I can assist you," Jed offered.

"I'd prefer Carrie, if you don't mind." I wasn't ready to have Jed dig through my underwear drawer.

"Of course." He bowed but I could tell that my rejection of his offer upset him. "Perhaps I can assist Ned with the horses."

"That would be great."

"Where are you going?" Carrie interjected into Jed's departure. "Ned said you'd be away, but not where to."

"Jed's taking me to his home in Switzerland. We'll spend a few days with his family. From there I think we may go to Turkey." If Jed could convince me that I needed to visit the Council.

"Jed's family?"

"Well, Tobias's."

She nodded. "Seems strange."

"Yeah. But as far as they know, he's their son."

"I guess he is. So what do you need?"

It took a while, but Carrie packed everything I needed into two suitcases. By the time the men came back in from doing their chores she pulled the chicken out of the oven and we enjoyed a quiet supper together.

"When are you leaving?" Ned asked.

"First thing in the morning. Are you sure you don't mind keeping Luna for me?"

"Not at all. She's so sweet," Carrie answered. I noticed that Ned looked less enthused than his wife appeared to be.

"She's shy. Thank you, for taking care of her."

"Do you need us to check on your place in the city?" Ned asked.

"No, Rita will run by every now and then, make sure it's okay."

"When will you be back?" Ned held Carrie's jacket for her while she slid into it.

"I don't know." It was the honest answer. Ned heard the doubt in my voice.

"Will you be back, Anna?" He had known me long enough and knew me well enough to be able to tell that I was struggling with something.

I didn't know for sure, but it wasn't the time to tell them that. "Yeah. I will. I just need some time to heal." Switzerland sounded like as good a place as any for it. My emotional wounds were far deeper than the physical ones, and I had to figure out how to cope with them. I needed time, someplace where I could process what had happened and how my life had changed.

Jed wanted me to go talk to his Council, but I hadn't decided if I would do that. He seemed to trust them, but my interactions with them hadn't given me a reason to believe that they were any better than Adonijah.

"Will you be safe?"

I glanced at Jed, but he didn't give me any sign of how to reply, so I chose honesty. "I don't know. Adonijah is still out there."

"Will it ever be over?" Carrie asked, but she didn't sound as scared as I felt.

"I wish I knew." I forced myself to exchange gentle hugs with both of them. "I'll email you."

"You'll call," Carrie ordered and I acquiesced.

"I'll call when we get there."

"Good." Carrie pulled the door closed behind her.

Jed walked beside me up the stairs, ready to help if I needed it. I took my time, made it on my own. Small victories were sometimes the ones that mattered most.

I had my hand on my doorknob when Jed turned back to the guest room he had slept in just a few days before. "Do you require further assistance?" He asked.

"No, thank you, though."

He nodded. "I wish you a good night, then." He bowed and ducked through the doorway of the guest bedroom.

"Jed?"

He stepped back into the hallway. "Yes?"

"Would you mind staying with me?" I hated to admit that I was afraid to be alone, but I was.

"Of course. If that is your wish, I will do so." He followed me into my bedroom and stood in the middle as if he was uncertain of what came next. I was too. "There is room for me to sleep on the floor," he announced.

"There is room in the bed for you to sleep there," I informed him.

"It would not be . . . inappropriate?"

I started to laugh, then choked it back because laughter made everything hurt. "I'm not well enough to do anything but sleep, Jed."

He looked affronted. "I was not suggesting . . . I didn't mean to say . . ." He stammered over the words.

"It's okay, Jed. Just come to bed. You make me feel safe." Safer, anyway. I wasn't sure if I would ever feel safe again.

He gave me a cautious smile. Neither of us knew quite how to navigate our new relationship. We didn't know what it was. I wanted to define it, but I couldn't.

"I will always protect you, Anna."

I smiled at him. "I know." We both knew that he wouldn't be able to. I'd seen Adonijah's thoughts. No one could protect me from what was out there. I didn't want to have a conversation about it, though. I wasn't ready to. It was enough, that Jed was there with me.

"Come to bed," I told him.

THE END

ACKNOWLEDGEMENTS

THANK YOU to all of the wonderful people who helped me with *When They Come Calling*. Special thanks to Greg, who gave me time to write and encouraged my dreams. To Dr. Turner for her medical expertise, painstaking proofreading and correcting my medical terminology—Dr. Anna Roberts would not be possible without your efforts! To pilot and friend John Roguski for his guidance on how to crash a helicopter and to Julia Roguski, for being my friend through everything. To my Mom, for raising me and being one hell of a grammar queen. Dad—my only regret is that you didn't get to see this book published. To Aunt Ann and Buddy for loving me unconditionally and reading a painfully early draft of WTCC. Heathre—I'm so blessed that you have been my friend for over 30 years. Matthew Johnson—there aren't words. Mr. & Mrs. Costas—for unfailing friendship through some dark days in my life.

This book is so much better thanks to the efforts of Chris and Emily at Atthis Arts, editor Abigail Hodges, and everyone who believed in me enough to back our Kickstarter campaign.